CONTENTS

PART ONE:
THE LOST GIRL

1 PURSUIT ✛ THANIEL GETS A CRUEL SURPRISE ✛
FIRST IMPRESSIONS   1

2 THE IRREPRESSIBLE MISS BENNETT ✛
MEET DOCTOR PYKE ✛ A NAME FOR THE GIRL   12

3 A WOMAN OF ILL REPUTE ✛ TURNING TRICKS ✛
AN UNHAPPY TWIST OF FATE   28

4 ALAIZABEL'S FEVER ✛ AN UNWELCOME OBSERVER ✛
A LETTER FROM DOCTOR PYKE   35

5 A RACE AGAINST TIME ✛ MAYCRAFT ✛
THANIEL GETS A SECOND CHANCE   52

6 CATHALINE'S ATTIC ✛ A RITE IS PERFORMED ✛
PLANS ARE MADE   67

7 A DISTURBANCE IN THE NIGHT ✛
THE FRATERNITY SHOW THEIR HAND   82

PART TWO:
STITCH-FACE

8 CHARITY STREET ✛
THE GREEN TACK MURDERS   97

9 THE CROOKED LANES ✛ GRINDLE ✛
CARVER MAKES A DISCOVERY   109

10 AN AUDIENCE WITH CROTT ✢ A DEAL IS STRUCK ✢
THE RAT KING 119

11 THE STRANGE DEATH OF ALISTA WHITE ✢
A CARRIAGE AT REDFORD ACRES 125

12 THE FIEND IN THE SEWERS ✢
A TRICK TO TRAP THE WYCH-KIN 134

13 PERRIS THE BOAR ✢ ELISANDER AND SANFORTH ✢
MAYCRAFT GETS A CALL 145

14 HONOUR AMONG VAGABONDS ✢
AN UNEXPECTED ALLY 163

PART THREE:
THE FRATERNITY ASCENDANT

15 A LADY IN DISTRESS ✢ THANIEL FIGHTS ALONE ✢
DISASTER STRIKES 177

16 VIGIL FOR THE DYING ✢
DESPAIR IN THE BELL TOWER 188

17 A GATHERING ✢
CURIEN BLAKE 194

18 THE GIRL IN THE WHITE SHIFT ✢
AN ILL MEETING 201

19 THE BEGGARS READY FOR WAR ✢
THE INEVITABLE ARRIVES 218

THE
HAUNTING
OF
ALAIZABEL CRAY

CHRIS WOODING

THE
HAUNTING
OF
ALAIZABEL CRAY

SCHOLASTIC
PRESS

Scholastic Children's Books,
Commonwealth House, 1–19 New Oxford Street,
London, WC1A 1NU, UK
a division of Scholastic Ltd
London ~New York ~Toronto ~Sydney ~Auckland
Mexico City ~New Delhi ~Hong Kong

First published in the UK by Scholastic Ltd, 2001

ISBN 0 439 99896 4 (hardback)
ISBN 0 439 97918 8 (paperback)

Typeset by M Rules
Printed by WS Bookwell, Finland

1 3 5 7 9 10 8 6 4 2

The right of Chris Wooding to be identified as the author
of this work has been asserted by him in accordance with
the Copyright, Designs and Patents Act, 1988.

PART FOUR:
THE DARKENING

20 PORTENTS ✢ THE NIGHT MARE ✢
THE FIRST DARK DAY   227

21 AT STITCH-FACE'S MERCY ✢
THE SIEGE OF THE CROOKED LANES ✢ REUNION   238

22 THE WYCH IN ALAIZABEL CRAY ✢
THE HALLOW GHOUL ✢ THE PUPPETS SEE THE STRINGS 252

23 CALEDONIAN ROAD ✢ BENEATH THE CITY ✢
AN OLD ENEMY RETURNS   265

24 GENERAL MONTPELIER ✢ LONDON BY AIRSHIP ✢
THE HEART OF EVIL   281

25 THE CATHEDRAL ✢
GUARDIANS   294

26 THE WYCH-DOGS ✢ PROPHECIES FULFILLED ✢
THE AMERICAN WAY   302

27 THE GALLERY ✢ GREGOR GAINS HIS FREEDOM ✢
THE TIDE COMES IN   314

28 PYKE HOLDS THE ANSWERS ✢
THE WYCH-KIN REVEALED ✢ ALL IS ENDED   325

29 AFTERMATH   335

PART ONE:
THE LOST GIRL

The airship lumbered low overhead, its long, lined belly a dull smear of silvery light in the fog as it reflected the gas lamps of the city beneath. The heavy, ponderous thrum of its engines reverberated through the streets of the Old Quarter, making the grimy windows of the tall, close-packed terraces murmur in complaint. Like some vast, half-seen beast, it passed over the maze of alleys and cobbled walks, too huge to consider the insignificant beings that travelled them – and finally it moved on, its engines fading to a dull hum, and then gradually to silence.

There was a chill in the air tonight, a cold nip that had crept in from the Thames and settled into the bones of London. And of course there was the fog, which laid itself over everything like a gossamer blanket and softened the glow of the black lamp-posts to a haze. The fog came almost every night in autumn, as much a part of London as the hansom cabs that rattled around Piccadilly Circus or the stout Peelers that walked their beats north of the great river. Not to the south, though; not in the Old Quarter. That was the domain of the mad and the crooked and the things best left unthought of. The good people of the capital knew better than to remain there after the sun had dipped beneath the skyline; not if they valued their necks, anyway.

Thaniel Fox listened to the quiet left in the wake of the airship. Somewhere distant, a rusty steamer sounded its horn as it made its way up the Thames. Beyond that, there was nothing but the soft hiss of a nearby gaslight. No footsteps, no voices, and only the dim whiteness at either end of the road, swallowing the cobbles and the weathered stone shops with stern placards above their doorways.

"You mean to hide from me, then," he muttered to his unseen quarry, before drawing a shallow golden bowl from his coat pocket, about the size of a biscuit. He crouched down to the cool stone of the pavement and, placing the bowl before him, he filled it with a dark red liquid from a small phial that he produced from another pocket.

It would have been an odd sight for a passer-by to come across: a pale and stern-looking seventeen-year-old boy, hunched intently in the middle of the pavement on a foggy night. A wise man would not stay to inquire, for there were dangers in the Old Quarter that came in many guises, even with the Thames scarcely a kilometre to the north. But if he *should* stay, he would see the boy replace the first phial and bring out another one, this one full of clear liquid. Had he been close enough, he would smell the acrid stink of sulphur as the boy unscrewed the top, in which was set a small pipette full of the liquid. He would watch as the boy squeezed out a single drop into the bowl, and see the drop begin to fizz and glow bright white, a tiny ball of fury that slowly travelled to the edge of the bowl and remained there, nudging against the gold as if seeking to jump over it. And he would see it fade and die in a matter of seconds, before the boy turned to look in the direction that the fizzing drop had travelled.

"There you are," Thaniel said quietly. He picked up the bowl, dashed its contents across the road and replaced it in the pocket of his long coat.

He headed off through the streets, walking warily along the cobbles, eyes and ears alert. Absently, he slid his pistol from his belt and held it ready as he walked. This close to the Thames, chances were good that he would run into nothing other than what he searched for; but it was dead men who took chances, so his father said. And he should know. He cheated death so many times that people used to say Old Boney had given up on him.

It was his father who'd taught him the trick with the bowl, too. Put a single drop of sulphur mixture in pig's blood and watch in which direction it travels. That's where your target is. Crude, but it worked fine, if you knew what to mix the sulphur with.

A sound rose out of the murk then – a high gibbering howl, rising to a crescendo and then fading – a cry not human, nor bird or animal. Thaniel tried to pinpoint its source, but the mist baffled his attempts. But it was close, no doubt about that.

He picked up his pace, accelerating to a jog. Down a narrow alley, where the houses leaned inward and no lights burned. He stepped over the slumped body of a vagrant, who lay unconscious in the shadow of a set of stone steps, reeking of rotgut and mumbling to himself as he stirred restlessly, plagued by nightmares. The man was taking his life in his hands, sleeping on the streets in the Old Quarter, but by the smell and look of him he didn't have much life left anyway. Thaniel ignored him. This was London, and you either held on, or fell by the wayside like that fellow had.

Something moved at the end of the alley, where it met a narrow thoroughfare. Despite himself, Thaniel breathed in sharply, his knuckles whitening on the grip of his pistol as he halted. A wolf was poised there, watching him, frozen in the process of crossing the alley entrance. It held his gaze for a moment, amber eyes studying him in the murk; then it slunk away, dismissing him. Evidently, it had recently fed, and was not yet interested in another meal.

Thaniel let out his breath softly, relaxing. Wolves were a hazard throughout London, even north of the water. They were rarer up there, of course, and usually ended up being shot, but while they kept breeding in the Old Quarter, they'd keep crossing the river at night. Not a few vagrant orphans and painted ladies had fallen victim to the hungry wolves of the city.

He gave it a few moments to be on its way, then he hurried down the alley and onward. Again, the gibbering, insane cry of his quarry sounded through the fog, very close now. It was going to ground, heading back to its lair.

He'd surprised it out near Chadwick Street. It wasn't the first time it had strayed out of its home territory. Two babies gone missing from their cribs, both the work of the thing he hunted. It was his job to make sure it didn't happen again. Bad enough that a large portion of the city was deadly by night, bad enough that the honest shopkeepers had to hurry back to their homes on the other side of the river before the sun went down; but when the creatures that stalked the streets started roaming beyond the Old Quarter, it was time to take action.

The noise of his boots was swallowed up by the gently drifting murk as he headed towards the source of the cry. The shops had given way to dereliction by now, and ramshackle stone houses leered at him with broken teeth and jagged eyes. He ran over what he knew of his quarry, preparing for confrontation the way his father had taught him.

It was a Cradlejack, of that he was sure. As if the missing babies weren't enough, he'd already seen it when he chased it off back at Chadwick Street. They made their lairs in quiet areas, dark and sheltered from the daylight. Usually high up, because they climbed so well and it was safer – lots of escape routes. They never cornered themselves. The area around the lair tended to be scattered with rat bodies, which were their staple diet when they couldn't get the flesh of a human. They were scavengers, back-stabbers, cowards; like weasels to birds' eggs, they preyed on the defenceless young. They'd run if they could, but they'd fight if they had to, and Thaniel knew better than to underestimate wych-kin of any type.

Thaniel slowed his pace, looking up at the tumbledown buildings that faded to black and then grey as they rose into the fog. A sign to his right read: E. CHELMTON, *Broker and Purveyor of finest Tobacco*. Over there, a grim accountant's building frowned at him. The Cradlejack had fallen silent now. Thaniel had no doubt that it was close by, but *where?* He took out his shallow gold bowl once more and repeated the procedure he had executed earlier. His bearings renewed, he struck out in a direct line, across a courtyard flagged with cracked and chipped slabs; and on the other side he halted.

"So this is where you've been hiding," he muttered. He had a habit of talking to himself — or to his quarry — when he was on a wych-hunt alone. It quelled his unease. He was seventeen, and a wych-hunter. He'd been earning his keep since he was fourteen, and apprenticed for six years prior to that. He was *good*. But the things he hunted were more dangerous than any animal prey, and only a fool would think of them without fear.

Before him was a tall picture-house, a triangular construction with a blunted nose that nestled in the V between two converging roads. Dark and brooding, it loomed over him like the prow of a ship, for he stood at the tip of the V, and it rose three storeys high. Its lower levels were boarded up entirely and most of its upper windows had been smashed. Once, it had held a cinematograph, a wonder of science that made moving pictures appear, and people from all over Europe had flocked to see it. Now it was just another casualty of the losing battle that the folk of London fought to keep hold of their city.

It had to be here. It had all the hallmarks of a classic Cradlejack lair. And besides, his intuition crowed at him, you *know* it's in there. Wych-hunting's in your blood; isn't that what father always said? You've got the wych-sense just like he had. You just *know*.

Thaniel scouted round the exterior of the building, but he could see no obvious way in. Not that it would make much difference to a Cradlejack; they were gifted burglars, with their long, spindly fingers and narrow, skeletal bodies, and a window was as good as a door to them. He tugged at the boards over the entrance, but they held fast. Undeterred, he headed over to the narrow house that nestled in behind the cinema, rubbing shoulders with the grand old building. The lock on the door had long since been broken. He pushed it open cautiously, the muzzle of his pistol poking carefully into the darkness that lay beyond.

Nothing stirred.

The room smelled musty, with a faintly sickly-sweet edge to it. Thaniel waited a moment for his eyes to adjust to the gloom and then stepped inside without a sound. The Cradlejack would run if it knew he was coming; his only hope of catching it lay in stealth. Quietly, he shut the door, and the chill darkness consumed him.

He chewed his lower lip, senses straining to pick up a noise, a glimpse, anything that might warn him of the wych-kin's presence.

The interior of the room was a mess, he saw. Faint light struggled in through a single filth-streaked window – which miraculously had managed to remain whole – and by it he could spot the half-chewed and mangled corpses of rats and a few small dogs, strewn about the room. The smell that hung in the still air was of old blood and dust.

Satisfying himself that the Cradlejack was not in the immediate vicinity, he pushed quietly onwards. The house had only a single downstairs room, with steps leading to the next floor. It had been a humble dwelling even before the dereliction of the Old Quarter overtook it; now it was crumbling inside and out.

He ascended the steps into the waiting darkness

above. Here, ragged cloth curtains had been left hanging over the pair of windows that allowed the muted gaslight glow inside. It was even darker than the last, and smelled of animal – a musky scent that made him gag as he crept up. This one was scattered with boxes and old crates, a hundred hiding-places, any one of which might conceal the wych-kin he sought. Quietly, quietly, he stepped into the room. The night air seemed to exude menace, a cold deeper than the night chill that slipped through his nostrils and down his throat to cool his heart.

A thump on the ceiling made him lurch in alarm, and he instinctively brought up his pistol.

Upstairs. It was on the top floor.

He crossed the room soundlessly, his pistol trained on the hatch at the top of a rickety ladder. It seemed a little lighter up there. For a moment, he fancied he saw something flit across the hatchway, but then it was gone, and he was unsure if it had ever been there at all.

He pushed down the trepidation in his gut and put one hand to the ladder rung, the wood rough beneath his palms. His pistol aimed up the ladder, he crept slowly, silently, praying that the aged wood would not creak and give him away. Miraculously, it held his weight with ease, making not a sound. Up, up – each step seeming like a mile.

He poked his head out of the hatch, gun peeping out with him. There were a few nauseating moments when he expected to be hit from any direction – he was sure to check *up*, as well – but nothing came. Cautiously, he ascended until his head and shoulders were in the room.

It was a bedroom, the same size as the other two

floors. A single bed stood aslant against one wall, its bedcovers long disintegrated into a cobweb of frail strands. More pieces of rat and other, less identifiable animals were strewn here and there, but the room was largely empty. Where the window should have been, a great hole gaped in the wall, allowing in soft wisps of fog and the glow from the lamp-posts. Thaniel clutched his coat tighter to his chest with one hand and climbed into the room. The Cradlejack was not here.

Then what had made the noise?

He stepped over the corpse of something pale and lightly furred, drawing closer to the hole in the wall and ceiling. What could have caused this, he had no idea. Shoddy workmanship, perhaps, causing the wall to collapse under its own weight? A stray bomb from an airship? Who could say?

Peering out, he saw a wide, ornamental stone ledge that ran along the terraces just below their upper windows and across the flank of the picture house. There, by squinting through the drifting translucency of the fog, he could spy another hole, similar to this one, leading into the upper floor of that building.

"Ah, so *that* is how you get in," he said.

He looked down. The fog prevented a clear view of the cobbles beneath him, a dozen metres below, but he did not think it would slow his fall very much if he should slip from the ledge.

There was really no question of turning back, however. Not this close. He meant to rid London of one more wych-kin tonight.

Treading with care, he stepped out on to the ledge, testing its stability by steadily applying his weight until he was certain it would not crumble. His pistol in his right hand, his left trailing along the wall for comfort, he moved slowly away from the safety of the hole and began to shuffle along the ledge. To his right, an ocean of fog waited, stirring hungrily. Beneath his feet there was scarcely twenty centimetres of granite and mortar holding him aloft.

It came for him when he was halfway there. So deeply intent was he on keeping from toppling that he was a moment too slow in raising his pistol. A dark, scrawny shape, a flash of insane amber eyes and short, needle-point teeth, and then the roar of his pistol and the terrifying sensation of weightlessness as he knew his balance had failed him. For a moment that stretched into eternity, he hung above the fatal plunge to the street below; and then he fell.

His hand snapped out, instinct driving him faster than thought, and before his rational mind had caught up, he had already grabbed the ledge with one hand. The jolt as his shoulder took his weight almost tore the muscles there, but it was enough to make him swing round so that his other hand could grab the ledge too. Before he knew what had happened, he was holding on for his life above the fog-shrouded cobbles.

The Cradlejack sounded its mad gibber as it disappeared into the house once more, knocking something over as it scuttled down the stairs, intent only on escape. Thaniel barely had time to feel the shock of his brush with death; he was already pulling himself up, cursing, his wiry but strong muscles lifting his light frame with ease. One knee, then another, and he got to his feet, shuffling hurriedly back along the ledge. He drew a second pistol from his belt as he reached the hole that admitted him back to the upper floor of the ramshackle house; his first weapon had gone spinning into the murk as he fell. Had he hit the thing? Probably not. But he would not let it run, either.

His caution forgotten in his haste, he ran across the room and slid down the ladder, blundering through the darkness in pursuit of his target. Down the stairs, towards the door that had been left open in the Cradlejack's wake, he—

A shrieking, and something cannoned into him from the side – some howling, whirling thing that scratched and flailed and spat. He yelled in surprise as it bore him to the floor, struggling beneath its grasp; but it attacked in frenzy, and was too wild to be effective. Scrambling out, even before he knew what was really upon him, he had its arms pinioned behind it. His cheek blazed from a deep scratch, and he ached from numerous other bruises that had been inflicted upon him.

Not the Cradlejack, though.

"What manner of thing are you?" he asked, though he didn't really expect a reply. The creature that had attacked him had gone limp in his grasp, breathing shallowly, eyes glazed and half-lidded.

It appeared to be a girl, but Thaniel knew well enough that appearances were deceptive in the Old Quarter.

She moaned softly and collapsed.

Wych-hunters came in all shapes and sizes. It took a certain something to make a person feel the need to pit themselves against a near-unmatchable foe. For some it was the challenge they craved, the need to excel; for others it was because they believed they were doing a service to the world. Some were motivated by religion, some by vengeance. Some were born into it, some carved their own niche. Some were attracted by the money, some by the danger. Almost all of them had their reasons, and even those who seemed normal on the outside nursed secrets within, secrets that made them crave the job that nobody else wanted.

The only reason Cathaline Bennett needed was that she was odd.

The streets were awakening as she walked along Crofter's Gate at dawn. Market stalls were beginning to open; beggars were shuffling to their favourite spots. Smells of roasted chestnuts and jacket potatoes were beginning to rise from the street vendors' dark iron oven-carts. Cabs rattled this way and that, scarcely heeding pedestrians as they clopped and clattered over the cobblestones.

The house that she lived in with Thaniel Fox stood under the foreboding gaze of St Luke's

Cathedral. It was a grandiose, terraced affair, with a door and a bay window on its ground floor, and two more windows above it. The top floor had several tall studio windows, intended to maximize the light. A black iron railing guarded its precious few square metres of flagged front yard. Dull green in colour, with beige stone sills and steps, number 273 Crofter's Gate was not a pretty place, merely a functional one. The cathedral loomed high and stout over the surrounding buildings, a Teutonic mass of curves, arches and spires, dark and frowning in the dawn light. Gargoyles leered from the corners of the towers, pawing towards the dwellings below, scratching at the streets that surrounded the cathedral.

Cathaline reached the front door and let herself in. The warmth that greeted her as the door opened told her that Thaniel was home; the soft sobbing was something else altogether.

She stepped inside, shutting the door behind her.

"Thaniel?" she called.

"In here," came the reply from the living room.

She followed his voice to its source. A fire was burning and the gas lamps were still lit, despite the approaching morning, creating little focus-points of light that faded to ruddy darkness at the edges. The room was full of deep greens and browns, wood-panelled, with a thick rug before the hearth and several hard, uncomfortable armchairs arranged round it. A dining table of heavy teak sat on one side of the room. The sturdy curtains were drawn against the outside.

Kneeling on the hearth rug was a girl, probably Thaniel's age if she was any judge, even though

Cathaline could only see her from behind at the moment. She had long, blonde hair, muddied and clumped, and she wore a thin white dress that was torn and dirty and smudged with blood in places. She was drinking from a brown ceramic bowl of what smelled like beef soup. Thaniel knelt next to her, looking up as his friend came in.

"I need your help," he said.

Cathaline Bennett had been Thaniel's mentor during the latter years of his apprenticeship as a wych-hunter, and a friend ever since. Thaniel suspected she was nearing the end of her twenties, but it was extremely difficult to tell, as she acted with such youth and immaturity that she might have been ten years younger than that. She was tall, a little *too* tall in proportion to her body, giving her the slightly graceless quality of a newborn foal. Her face, neither pretty nor ugly, was nevertheless infused with an inner radiance that lit her features from within and made them mesmerizing to watch. Her hair was cropped to a nape-length bob, an impossibly daring and eccentric cut in a time when women were supposed to be feminine and demure, but it was made even more shocking by the two dark red streaks that ran through the black, from scalp to tip.

She was wearing an odd assemblage of clothing; a dark crimson pigskin jacket over a black blouse, and black trousers of heavy-stitch cotton with red edging. A smile curled the edges of Thaniel's mouth. Trousers, on a woman! Cathaline was beholden to nobody's rules, and that appealed to him. He looked up to her, maybe even more than he had done to his late father, Jedriah Fox – London's greatest wych-hunter.

"I found her in the Old Quarter," he said, calmly.

"She will not tell me her name. She will not speak at all."

"How did you get those scratches, Thaniel?" Cathaline asked, walking over to them.

"I was hunting a Cradlejack, and—" Thaniel paused at his friend's sudden look of alarm. "It was not *that* that scratched me. It was her. She is mad, I think."

Cathaline knelt down on one knee next to the girl, the glow from the fire warming one side of her face. Now that she could see the waif, she could see the glazed, distant look in her eyes as she stared into the fire. The girl looked terrified, as if she was watching something just beyond the snapping flames that they could not see. Occasionally, she took a mechanical sip of soup from the bowl clenched in her hands. Cathaline gently brushed a strand of hair back from the girl's muddy face, to better see the cuts and grazes there. There was no response to her touch.

"Thaniel, where *do* you find these girls?" she sighed.

Thaniel smiled at her. "You do not approve?"

"I think you could do better," she replied. "You'll never find yourself a suitable young lady running with the wych-kin in the Old Quarter." She stood up and looked down at the girl. "What about her? Is she hurt?"

"I did not see anything that looks like it might be an animal- or wych-scratch," Thaniel said. "I think these are from falling over several times."

"Has she been like this the whole time?" Cathaline asked. "So quiet?"

"She was quite manic when I met her. I scared her, maybe."

Cathaline rubbed the back of her neck with her hand. "Well, you have that effect," she said. "Anyway, here I am, though I'd rather be in bed. You had better tell me what happened."

Thaniel explained the events of the night, how he'd been on a regular patrol when he'd come across the Cradlejack that had been plaguing the area round Chadwick Street, how he'd chased it back over into the Old Quarter and how he'd tracked it to its lair, where he'd found this girl.

"And you're sure the Cradlejack didn't scratch her?" Cathaline prompted, after Thaniel had finished. Cradlejacks were one of the rare types of wych-kin that could pass on their condition by scratching or biting another person. And if it had scratched the girl, and she had scratched *Thaniel*. . .

"I have dealt with Cradlejacks before, remember? I have been bitten before, and I fought it off. I am immune."

"I was thinking about me," Cathaline said, pacing the room. Whatever it was that turned a person into a Cradlejack was like an ague or a fever; you either fought it off and were for ever immune, or it got you. Cathaline had never been caught by a Cradlejack.

"I'm sure she has not been scratched," said Thaniel, running a hand through his fine blond hair and returning his eyes to the girl.

After the soup, the girl became suddenly drowsy, and her eyelids and head became ponderous and heavy. Thaniel led her upstairs, where he put her in his bed, and she was instantly asleep. He checked the windows were secure and fastened, and then locked the door behind him. Better to be safe, until they knew what they were dealing with.

When he returned to the living room, Cathaline was sitting in a chair, warming herself before the fire while she ate soup with hunks of black bread.

"Do help yourself to my soup," Thaniel said. Cathaline raised a hand in thanks.

"You think the girl is mad?" she asked.

Thaniel nodded, chewing his lower lip absently. "Mad she may be, or possessed; or maybe only scared out of her wits. I'll go and see Doctor Pyke at the asylum, and ask if he is missing any patients." A wrinkling of his nose indicated how distasteful he found that idea. "I did not want to leave her alone. Will you stay with her for a while?"

"Do I get more soup?" Cathaline asked.

Redford Acres Asylum stood on the outskirts of London, brooding alone on the side of a low hill, surrounded by a stretch of fields through which a single road led. It was a wide, squat building, devoid of ornamentation – a solid rectangle of stone with tiny square windows evenly dotted across its face. Everything about it radiated dour strength, like a craggy cliff or a thunderhead in the sky.

Where the road curved through the fields, there were tall gates of wrought iron set into a great wall; the metal in the centre of each had been twisted into the initials RA. A surly-looking gentleman in a flat cap and brown jacket asked Thaniel his business and let him in, pulling the gates apart with a screech. As the cab moved on, Thaniel saw him return to the gatekeeper's hut and pick up the earpiece of the telephone.

The driver of the hansom cab scowled at the building and hurried his horses on, obviously eager to be gone. They crunched to a halt on the gravel of the driveway, before the great stone portal that was the main entrance. Doors of dark mahogany glared at them. The driver looked about nervously, and his face fell when Thaniel told him to wait; he had been hoping for a quick exit. Somewhere above, a thin scream cut through the day, sounding alien in the grey light and making the driver jump.

The doors were opened just as Thaniel was climbing down from the cab, and there was Doctor Pyke. He was a pinch-faced man, with a narrow, pointed nose on which was perched a pair of small, round spectacles. His hair was greying to white, and had been receding back from his forehead at a steady pace. His frame was as lean and scrawny as his features, but his blue eyes were bright and sharp behind their round windows and heavy lids.

"Ah, Master Thaniel Fox!" he said, his face creasing into a grin. "Your company is always welcome. My gatekeeper informed me of your arrival."

Thaniel clasped his hand and shook it. "Good to see you again, Doctor," he said, though he could not make his tone convincing.

"Well," Pyke said, clapping his hands together and rubbing them. "Let us not stand out here, dismal day that it is. Do come inside."

He ushered Thaniel into the foyer of Redford Acres. It was a high-ceilinged chamber, with a curving staircase running up one wall to a balcony, a black and white tiled floor and a carved desk behind which sat a pert-looking receptionist with black hair in a bun. Thaniel had always been struck by how misleading the foyer was; it was clean, efficient, pleasant. The majority of the building was none of these things.

Pyke chatted with Thaniel as he led the way upstairs to his office. It was a small study, the walls lined with folio edition books, and a green leather chair behind a desk which was covered in neat stacks of files and dominated by a book of phrenology and a model of a human skull, with different sections neatly marked off and named.

He invited Thaniel to sit and then took his position on the other side of the desk, in front of a tall, rectangular window that let in the steely daylight. Thaniel never liked Pyke; the man always made him uneasy. He supposed it was partly the job Pyke did. A person couldn't work in an insane asylum five days a week without it affecting them just a little. It affected Thaniel, certainly.

Pyke was one of his father's old acquaintances, for his job had meant that he had been forced to visit Redford Acres many times. Not all wych-kin were like the Cradlejack; there were some that trailed insanity in their wake, and only the strong-minded could resist them. Some of the people now languishing in the dingy cells of Redford Acres had been put there by Jedriah and Thaniel themselves. Just being within the walls of this place made him edgy.

"So, young man, I understand you wanted to see me about something?" Pyke said, steepling his fingers on the desk before him and gazing at Thaniel with his piercing blue eyes.

A haunting wail sounded through the room, quiet but anguished, reverberating eerily. Pyke didn't blink.

"One of our more troubled souls. There never seems to be a way to shut the sound out, you know. You get quite used to it after a while."

19

"Doctor Pyke, I came to see you to ask you a question. In confidence, of course."

"In confidence?" said the elder man, his eyes sparkling with amusement. "Oho! I see I am in some trouble!"

"Not at all, sir. But your reply could be perceived as damaging to your reputation, if it should reach the wrong ears."

Pyke became a little more serious, leaning back in his chair and opening his arms, palms up. "Out with it, then."

Thaniel drew a breath, hiding his unease behind a long-practised shield of efficiency. He hated this place. He could almost feel the prisoners, languishing in their torment, locked in cells, tortured by their own private demons.

"Doctor Pyke, how is the security in Redford Acres?"

A fleeting expression of irritation crossed Pyke's face, as if to say: *you came here to ask me* that?

"I only ask," Thaniel continued, before Pyke could reply, "because last night I came across a girl who was in a considerable state of madness. My first suspicion was that she may have been touched by a wych-kin, but it is not an easy process to determine if insanity is natural or wych-borne. Then I thought that she may have escaped from this facility, and—"

"Well, I can assure you, she has *not!*" Pyke snapped, faster than his namesake. "Our security here is top-notch, and not one patient has left these grounds without first being cured by us."

"I apologize, sir," said Thaniel, bowing his head. "I had to check before I attempted the Rite to determine the source of her madness. But sir, let me assure you, if someone *had* escaped and you *were* to tell me, I could bring her back to you safely and none would be the wiser."

Pyke looked like he was about to bark something at the boy again, but he calmed suddenly. "Ah, forgive me. I did not mean to be short with you. I slept little last night. No, my friend, let me assure *you*, no patient has gone missing from Redwood Acres, now or ever. However, I can check with some of the other asylums further afield, if you wish. Do you have the girl?"

"Yes," Thaniel replied.

"Do you think it might be a good idea to bring her to me, so that I can hold her for you? It may be dangerous for the untrained to look after her."

Thaniel thought of the dank corridors, the rusty cell bars, the screams and howls and tears and cackles that lay beneath the respectable façade of Redwood Acres. "She seems content with my care," he replied diplomatically. "Best not to upset her."

"Very well. Does she have a name, perhaps?"

"She does not speak."

"Ah well," Pyke said, giving him an apologetic smile. "Most likely some crazed waif. You say you found her in the Old Quarter? What does she look like, so I can inform my fellow doctors?"

Thaniel paused for a moment.

"She is about twenty-five years old, with black hair and dark brown eyes," he lied.

Pyke wrote it down on a notepad. "I will ask about for you. Now, Master Fox, it is always a pleasure, but I must be getting back to work. I will see you out."

"Thank you, sir," said Thaniel.

Thaniel and Pyke exchanged pleasantries as they

descended the stairs, and Pyke watched him from the doorway as he climbed into his cab. He closed the door with a final wave as the cab driver shook the reins and the horses jerked into life.

They rattled and bumped down the driveway towards the gate, but Thaniel paid no attention. He was deep in thought.

He had never said that he found the girl in the Old Quarter. So how did Pyke know that? It was a natural assumption, he supposed; after all, he had said he was out hunting when he found her, and most wych-hunting was done in the Old Quarter, for that was where the wych-kin were. But still, it did not quite sit right with him.

He dismissed it for now. More urgent was the question of the girl's identity.

When he returned to Crofter's Gate, it was late afternoon. He looked in on the girl, and found her still asleep, though her turning and thrashing in his bed had muddied and tangled the sheets around her. Cathaline had fallen asleep on a chair in the living room. She had put Wards all around Thaniel's bedroom. Thaniel smiled. Cathaline may have seemed flighty, but she was one of the best in London. There was no sense taking chances with the girl.

Thaniel was dog-tired, having not slept since the previous evening, so he stoked the fire and curled up on the rug. That night, he decided, they would see if the girl was any better and determine what to do with her if she was not. But for now, he dreamed.

Thaniel had no need for a timepiece. He had the enviable ability to decide what time he would awaken, and he would wake up exactly three minutes before that. It was one oddity among many. He supposed he was abnormal in several ways, he thought, as he washed his face in the bathroom and looked at himself in the mirror. How many people could claim to be a wych-hunter at seventeen? How many could afford to live in their own home, even if it *was* bought by his father?

And he certainly did not *look* abnormal. He had clear skin and pleasingly placed features, and no smallpox or trench fever had ravaged his face like so many he had seen. He was a little pale, perhaps, and he would never have the build that his father had, for his shoulders were narrower and he was naturally leaner. But he had fine eyes of pale blue and smooth blond hair, gifts from his mother, whom he resembled greatly. His father had often commented that he could see his mother in him; sometimes it was affectionate, sometimes in disappointment when Thaniel had failed to match the expectations laid out for him. Those latter moments crushed Thaniel inside, and he died a little each time.

But his father was gone now, like his mother before him. Thaniel was alone.

His childhood had not been an easy one. He was born the only son of a man who was already a legend by that time. Jedriah Fox, the foremost wych-hunter in London, possibly the world. He knew more about wych-lore than any man or woman who lived. He had been a tall, heavy-set man, with a thick black beard; strong as a bull, and quick-minded with it. A veteran of a hundred scrapes with death, he had attained the status of an icon among the wych-hunters of London. In the early days, when nobody knew anything about the wych-kin and wych-hunting was akin to suicide, it was tales of his exploits that drew new hunters in, and essays that he published that spread the knowledge of how to defeat different wych-kin. Thaniel had been in awe of his father.

But then his mother had gone. Chiana Roseleaf Fox, a senseless and brutal murder in a graveyard in Whitechapel. She was beautiful, artistic, sweet; his father had worshipped her, and Thaniel had loved her dearly. But she died anyway.

After that, Jedriah had changed.

"She was too good for a world such as this; she was meant for the next life, for the angels." He had said that once, when Thaniel was six. His voice had a terrible melancholy to it as he looked out of the window. "There is no place for people like your mother in this world. Her sweet nature, her compassion, her creative fancies . . . where once these were strengths, they are weaknesses now. We are in an age of industry, Thaniel. The Age of Reason. Men toil in factories, scientists create wonders; we are unravelling the mysteries of the universe, and they are cold and hard. Science is the new way, and science has not time for poetry or stories or careless folk. I fear for you, son. I fear that those traits that were your mother's will mean your undoing one day."

"What of the wych-kin, father? Where do they fit into this new age of science and reason and logical thought?"

Jedriah's head had sunk a little. "They do not fit," he said. "That is why we kill them."

When Thaniel was eleven years old, his father's

fabled skill had failed him. They never discovered what he had been hunting, but there was little left of him when he was found.

It was Jedriah's friend Cathaline that took up the education of the boy. Jedriah had left him a house and a healthy income, for wych-hunting was an extremely lucrative profession by virtue of its danger, and Parliament offered salaries and bounties that would make a lawyer gnash his teeth in jealousy. She moved into his house and continued Thaniel's apprenticeship as a wych-hunter; for it was all he had been schooled in since age eight, and he knew no other way. In time, the teacher and the apprentice became friends and finally, hunting partners.

Thaniel twisted the brass taps to turn off the water in the sink and went to look in on the girl again. She was an interesting development, at least. He had not thought about what he was doing when he first brought her back, only that she was in distress and that she should not be allowed to roam the Old Quarter on her own. Truthfully, he had not even considered what might happen after she was better. They would find her parents and return her to wherever she came from.

And if she does not get better?

Thaniel debated the question as he walked down the corridor to his bedroom, where the girl was locked in. He argued with himself all the time. He had few friends, and none that he would call close. It was the lot of a wych-hunter. Working at night, most often alone; all his schooling done at home. But he had Cathaline, didn't he? And he knew some other wych-hunters as acquaintances. He was happy. He could have been in a workhouse right now, instead of earning many times what most people in London made.

It could have been worse.

He unlocked his bedroom and stepped inside, still intent on his own private thoughts.

"A gentleman would knock," said the girl, quietly.

Thaniel was surprised out of his introspection. "Ah . . . I beg your pardon, I . . . didn't expect you to be awake."

She was lying on her side in his bed with the covers drawn tight up to her neck. Her skin shone with sweat and her blonde hair hung lank across her cheeks, but her eyes were open and she was watching him.

"Do you have a fever?"

"I'm cold," she said. Her eyes darted to the open door and then back to him. "Who are you?"

"Thaniel Fox, miss. At your service."

"May I have something to eat?" she croaked.

"Of course. Some stew, perhaps?"

She nodded feebly and licked her lips, finishing with a faint smile that made her look like a satisfied cat.

"I'll be back shortly," he said, and turned for the door.

"How did I get here?" the girl said from behind him.

"Don't you know?" Thaniel asked.

"I cannot remember," she said. Her eyes widened in distress and she drew the covers of the bed closer to her. "I cannot remember *anything!*"

Thaniel went over to her. She had the expression of fear and mania that he had seen when he first met her. "Calm yourself, miss. It will all come to you in time. Do you know your name? Begin with your name."

She seemed to relax a little. "I remember my name," she said, apparently relieved by the notion. "Alaizabel Cray."

"Then allow me to fetch you some stew, Miss Alaizabel, and then perhaps we can talk more?"

She nodded again, shivering and sweating. Thaniel got up slowly and left her, closing the door behind him. As an afterthought, he quietly turned the key in the lock.

Marey Woolbury had been born under a bad star. It was the only possible explanation. How else had a girl from a well-to-do family ended up standing on Hangman's Row on a freezing November night with her face painted up like a doll's, making kiss-faces at the cabs and carriages that rattled by?

She was heartily depressed, and even the tots of warm gin that she slugged from a flask did little to stave it off. She'd had two clients so far that night, both of whom had pawed and mauled her in a particularly uncomfortable fashion in her room before putting their suits and mantles back on and walking out of the building like they were the most proper of gents.

At least the fog wasn't so bad tonight, she thought, looking over her shoulder at the Waterside Inn and wishing she was in there instead of out here. It'd even be worth having one of those two maulers back if it'd get her into the warmth of the room she hired on the top floor. As she watched, two portly, rubicund old soaks burst out of the door, followed by a wave of heat and light and laughter. Then the door swung to, and the merriness was muffled again.

"Some womanly companionship, sirs?" she asked, flashing them a wink and a sight of her brown teeth.

"Ah, my good lady," said the most sober of the two. "Our purses have been emptied by the demon in that inn."

"Aye, the demon Whisky," added the other, slurring abominably. "He's a right old thief, a thief he is. Whisky, whisky. Yet he pleases me so."

"Be on your way, sirs," Marey said, losing interest in their babble. She had no patience tonight. They stumbled away, laughing, leaving her alone again in the chill.

Marey arranged herself with a curse. Any sane lady would be trussed up in two layers of long johns and undershirts if she were out tonight, not freezing her bones in a single, frilled dress, a hat and shawl and nothing but lacy underwear on beneath. Her breath steamed the air as she looked first one way, then the other, up Hangman's Row. Nobody was about. The Thames, which ran right alongside, made its torpid way past her towards the sea. She took her flask from a pocket of her dress, took another swig of warm gin, and waited for the next potential client to pass.

A bad star, surely. After all, she had been dogged with ill fortune ever since she had been brought into the world. She had been a breech birth, and her mother, always a frail one, had died in labour. Her father, perhaps guilty that he had been the instrument of his wife's death as much as Marey, turned to drink and gambling. He would beat her savagely when in these stupors, especially when he'd had a bad night at cards, which was often. Then he would make her sleep in the coal basket. Often he had a lady with him, who would laugh a lot and make bawdy comments. It was a different one every time.

When she was eight, she remembered cowering on the hard, shifting bed of dirty rocks after a particularly vicious beating, tears streaking her face, and hurting in more places than she could count. And she remembered the towering shadow of her father storming out of the door, no doubt in search of a drink or a whore, or both. He never came back. He left her alone. Alone, that is, except for the enormous debts he had accrued through his gambling.

For two days she awaited his return. She was used to cooking and housework, so she took good care of herself. When there was a knock at the door, she opened it, expecting to see him back again. Instead, it was a moneylender named Scrimp, with two hard-faced bailiffs. That was when she discovered that she was a debt, too. Her father had bet her on a hand of brag. And lost.

It was illegal, of course, but there was nothing she could do. Now an orphan, she had nobody to fight for her. She was sold to a workhouse for two shillings.

Seven long years, it was. Day in, day out, stitching till her fingers cramped and then stitching some more. Dozens of them, all crammed in a small warehouse, making shirts in return for meagre food and lodging. She must have stitched a hundred thousand hems. A life of endless toil, of sweat and heat and pain. But they were the best years of her life, she had to decide. Because of one thing only. A boy called Kairan.

He was from Ireland, and he was two years her senior. She remembered his always eager face, his lean body – stripped to the waist in the sweltering heat of the summer – and his roguish eyes. But best of all, his voice. That accent, promising things far away, adventure and excitement. He was a roof-runner, one of the boys who worked the pulleys up in the rafters, a nimble climber with a breathtaking disregard for heights.

She fell in love with him, and he with her. For the first time she was wanted and needed by another human being.

Then one day, he got influenza. The work master made him work anyway. He was running along the rafters, and he was dizzy, and he fell. And the greatest chapter of Marey Woolbury's life was over.

She ran then. She escaped the workhouse, not knowing where she could go, prepared to starve rather than stay there. It was a kind-hearted prostitute called Elsbey who spotted her wandering the streets and took her in. As chance would have it, there was a man there who was in the business of looking after the ladies of the night, a man named Ratchet. He saw in her a prospect, and within a week she was on the street, turning tricks for him. That was five years ago now. She had been there ever since.

The echoing sound of footsteps brought her back to the present, and she realized she had been drifting. The alcohol was fuzzing her brain quite nicely now, and she was even beginning to forget about the cold a little. She squinted to see who was coming, and groaned to herself when she saw who it was. Mr Wardle: one of her regulars, and one whom she particularly detested. He was a vile creature, unhygienic even by her standards. She steeled herself and put on a smile.

"Mr Wardle, sir!" she called. "Marey is cold, and wishes you would come and warm her up!"

Mr Wardle huffed up to her, fat and sweating. He wiped a handkerchief across his brow and over his bald pate. "Sorry, Miss Marey. I'm otherwise engaged tonight. Merely passing by."

"You have something more important than your Marey? Shame on you!" she teased.

He bowed to her and hurried away, clearly uncomfortable at being seen with her. How odd, she thought. Oh well, she would have liked the money, but it was a relief not to have to make sweetness with that odious man tonight.

She had been standing there perhaps five minutes after Mr Wardle had left, and not another soul had passed. Her mood was bleak, and she was cold and bored and feared the touch of pneumonia. It was then that the sound of a carriage came to her ears. She looked: a black carriage with a carven wooden step leading to the door, pulled by a black stallion and a white mare. The driver was hunched over in his seat, his coat pulled up tight around him, wisps of breath coming from beneath the brim of his top hat. She prepared herself to strut and call as it approached, but decided after a moment that it was not worth the effort.

To her faint surprise, however, the carriage slowed as it neared her, finally rattling to a halt. The horses snorted and stepped from hoof to hoof eagerly, steam rising from their flanks. Marey looked up at the driver, a little fearful of his shadowed face.

"Good evening to you, sir," she said, her voice small.

The driver took off his hat and folded his collar

down, smiling at her. She felt a strange sense of relief. He had a pleasant countenance, a small brown moustache, and gentle eyes. "Good evening, madam. Are you waiting for a cab, by any chance?"

She smiled at his flattery. It was quite obvious what she was doing. "Perhaps I was waiting for a cab *driver?*"

"Ah, but you see that I am a *carriage* driver, madam. A shame, I think."

"And would this handsome carriage driver like the company of a woman tonight, sir?" she asked, crooking her hips seductively.

"I am afraid this humble carriage driver is on duty, madam," he said, smiling apologetically. "However, I seem to have an empty carriage, and you must be cold. Perhaps you would like a ride home?"

"I could not afford to travel in such a fine vehicle," she said.

"There is no charge, madam."

"That's very kind, sir, but I have to—" she began, and then caught herself. What was the point of staying here anyway? It was clear that tonight was going to be a bad one. Only one of her regulars had turned up, and that was the detestable Mr Wardle, who had spurned her anyway. She was freezing to death for no good end, and besides, she thought she might be catching a cold. Ratchet would never know.

"Well, sir, your offer is much appreciated," she said. "I accept."

"Capital!" he said. "For what's a carriage without a passenger, and a beautiful lady like yourself? Where are we going?"

"To Archerwood," she said, and the driver put his hat back on and picked up the reins.

She climbed inside, feeling a little giddy from the gin she had drunk. The interior was plush and comfortable, although not much warmer than the night outside. Settling back, she took another tot from her flask and relaxed. This was a kind turn of fortune, for sure. Perhaps her bad star was shining only weakly tonight.

The ride was surprisingly smooth, and the gentle motion combined with the gin began to make her drowse a little. It was a short journey to her home – she didn't live at the Inn, no, that was for business only – but there had been tales of wolves and things worse, and it was always chancy this close to the Thames. She'd had some run-ins before, and a carriage was safer than being on foot in London at night.

She woke up as the carriage pulled to a halt, not realizing until then that she'd fallen asleep. Blinking, she sat up and stretched, listening to the crunch of boots on gravel as the driver slid to the ground to let her out. She felt like a proper lady, she did. Yes, a truly kind turn of fortune.

Her rouged cheeks paled as the door was opened. No handsome driver any more, but a mask of grey sacking, a patchwork of pieces crudely sewn together, with holes cut into the eyes and mouth, and a lady's wig of fine, fringed brown hair. The mouth of the mask seemed to be gaping, as if in a gasp of death; in conjunction with the beautiful hair, it looked horrific.

"Stitch-face!" she breathed, and she knew then, as her eyes travelled to the long knife in his hand, that her bad star had finally got the best of her; and she wished more than anything that Mr Wardle had not been otherwise engaged that night.

A laizabel sat up in bed, the blanket wrapped tight around her shoulders and knees so that only her arms and head showed out of the cocoon. It seemed a curiously childish thing, but it pleased Thaniel, who remembered doing it himself when he was little.

She had awoken with an appetite bordering on ravenous, and was on her third bowl of stew by the time Cathaline returned from the apothecary across the road with a tincture for her fever. The apothecary had been closed, of course – distantly, Big Ben had just struck the hour of one o'clock in the morning – but Cathaline knew the family who owned it, and they were accommodating to her needs when she knocked on their door at such a late hour. Alaizabel spoke little while she ate, her attention entirely on the food that Thaniel provided. She swallowed the tincture without question or complaint, wincing as it seared down her throat; and finally, she handed her empty bowl to Thaniel, and was sated.

"How do you feel?" Thaniel asked.

"Better," she said, with a little smile. "Not so cold. Not so tired."

"Would you like to come by the fire? It's warmer than my bedroom."

She nodded, her bright eyes fixed on him. Thaniel helped her into the living room, where Cathaline was already building up the hearth. She was still wrapped in her blanket as she nestled cross-legged into one of the chairs, the glow of the gathering flames dancing on the moist sheen of her fevered skin. The room warmed quickly, dim and cosy. Thaniel brought her a brandy, and one each for him and Cathaline; then he took a chair beside her.

"I'd better get to hunting," Cathaline said. "There's a pair of roofcreepers spotted in Kensington; some solicitor put a bounty on them. I should get there before everyone else hears."

"Good luck," Thaniel said. "And watch out for their tails."

"Didn't *I* teach *you* that?" Cathaline grinned as she left.

"You are hunters? In London?" Alaizabel asked, her interest piqued as she sipped her brandy.

"We're wych-hunters, Miss," Thaniel replied.

"Oh," she said, a strange tone in her voice. She looked across at him, the firelight picking out her small, babyish features even under the straggle of hair, the grime and the sallow complexion that the fever had given her. "You have been very kind to me," she said, fiddling with the small silver chain on her wrist.

Thaniel blushed, turning to gaze into the fire to disguise the heat on his cheeks and taking a small mouthful of his drink. "No gentleman could have done any less," he replied.

There was a moment of silence, counted in heartbeats.

"Why can't I remember?" she asked quietly.

"Perhaps the fever is muddling your brain," said Thaniel. "As the fever passes, so will the confusion."

"I hope so," she replied. She frowned suddenly, as if struggling to recall something that remained just out of reach. "I remember . . . scattered things. I remember my parents' faces. But not where I live. I know this city, I know the streets and alleys . . . so why can I not remember where I live?"

"It will come, miss," said Thaniel. "In the meantime, I have left buckets of hot water, should you wish to bathe."

Alaizabel lifted a strand of her straggly blonde hair and looked at it closely. She looked at the back of her hands, turning them before her face. An expression of dawning realization rose on her face. Until that moment, she had not been aware that she was dirty; more than that, she was *filthy*.

"Tell me," she said, distantly. "Tell me how you found me."

So Thaniel told her, and as he did so he found himself assessing the girl who sat before him, hunched and fevered and shivering slightly. She was a strange one, for sure. He wondered about her, where she came from, who her parents were, how she grew up. Was she like him, lonely and driven? Or had she a happy home, with many friends, filled with laughter?

He found himself observing her as he explained what had happened, noting details about her. Her dress, for one. Tattered and torn and muddied, but no doubt it was at least moderately expensive. The thin silver chains on her wrist and around her throat; unornamented and simple, but still beyond the means of a scullery maid or a workhouse girl.

Despite her sickly appearance, she had not wanted for food, and she showed no signs of lice in her hair. Her voice, too; her vowels were cut-glass, her words perfectly pronounced, the product of good breeding or elocution lessons.

When he was finished, she was silent for a time. "I must bathe," she said at length.

She found the water in the bathroom, as Thaniel had promised, three buckets of a temperature just shy of boiling and one of ice cold. The cool air was full of steam, and the single small window was misted over, the dark-green tiles of the walls dripping with condensation. A deep tub lay against one wall, and there was a full-length mirror fastened to another, its silver surface running with rivulets of warm dew. There was also a dressing table with ointments and oils, and she was surprised to see a set of clothes laid out on it, neatly folded. Lifting them up, she saw that they consisted of a blue- and pearl-coloured dress, some hair grips, stockings and shoes. Thaniel's mother's, she guessed, and briefly wondered when she would meet the lady of the house to thank her.

She walked over to the mirror and wiped it; when that did little good, she found a cake of soap, dipped it in the cold water and rubbed it over her hands. When she wiped the mirror this time, the condensation receded. She found a towel and, using the soap and water, she scrubbed her face clean. Yes, she knew this face. At least she had that; she was not a stranger to herself. She took off her filthy and tattered dress and looked at herself; her body she knew as well, familiar with every curve and mole and freckle. There were bruises on her ribs, and her lower back ached abominably. She turned around and looked over her shoulder at her reflection, and her heart jumped in her chest.

There was something there that she did not know. Its presence seemed alien to her, unfamiliar and sinister. A tattoo, a circular tattoo at the base of her back. She stared at it for a long while. It was difficult to tell what it was supposed to be depicting. A stylized image of a many-tentacled thing, seen in three-quarter profile, etched in simple blue-black ink. The sight of it disturbed her. She did not like having it on her; the skin surrounding it seemed to want to crawl away from it. It spoke darkly to her subconscious, and brought up feelings of dread.

She shuddered and looked away from it. Its very presence on her body was shaming to her. It was not proper or decent to have *any* kind of tattoo *there* on her body. She could not remember the circumstances that had attended its creation, but she was not sure that she wanted to.

She poured the bath, making it a little too hot in her haste to get clean. As she lowered herself in, the blood rushed to her head and she felt giddiness swarm up towards her.

Careful, Alaizabel. You are still weak.

But weak from *what?* Was her illness somehow connected with her madness and amnesia? And with the horrific nightmares that she half-recalled from her sleep?

Softly, she began to cry. What was happening to her? Who *was* she? Who was Alaizabel Cray?

Without craning, she could not see the single window in the room, above and to the right of her.

There was nothing out there but darkness, anyway, set as it was on the upper storey of the house; and the steam from the hot bath had turned it opaque. Therefore, she did not see an imprint slowly resolve itself in the window, a spread hand, as if it were laid against the glass from the outside, dissipating the interior condensation where it touched. And though there was nothing outside that was visible to human eyes, another imprint slowly cleared next to the hand; the shape of a jawbone and an eyebrow, such as might be made if a face was pressed to the window, looking down at the girl in the tub.

When Alaizabel came downstairs, washed and dressed, her hair combed and neat, Thaniel was lost for words; this scarcely seemed the same girl that he had brought home two nights ago. That one had been haggard and drawn, wasted and mad-eyed. The girl who stood before him was almost doll-like, with smooth, unflawed features like a child's; her pale green eyes showing no tint of illness. Her blonde hair, once tangled, had been combed straight and tamed with clips, so that it fell about her shoulders in corn-coloured waves. She wore the blue and pearl dress that he had left for her in the bathroom, and it fitted her perfectly.

He got to his feet, raking his hair back, and bowed deeply.

"My lady," he intoned. "I had no idea there was a princess under all that dirt."

She laughed lightly and blushed. "And I had no idea there was a scoundrel underneath that gentleman."

"You do me too much honour," he said. "How do you feel?"

"I feel better now," she said. "I think the fever is going."

Her voice was still weak, but it did little to mar the transfiguration. Thaniel found his eyes drawn to her more frequently than was proper.

"Would you like to sit?" he asked. But she shook her head.

"I am tired. I must rest, I think. I just came . . . to thank you. For looking after me."

"I am only glad I found you before you were hurt," he said.

"This dress . . . is it your mother's?"

"It was," he replied. "But she is gone, like my father. Like all things precious."

She was saddened a little by his tone. "Some precious things last for ever," she said.

The fire snapped.

Thaniel looked over his shoulder at her, his expression strange. "You are my guest here, Miss Alaizabel, until you are well. I want you to think of this house as your home."

She smiled.

"We will find your parents," he said. But Alaizabel, oddly, felt nothing about that.

"Goodnight," she said, and left.

She woke with a small cry, to darkness – her pulse racing and her brow and back soaked in sweat. She looked around wildly, not knowing where she was, only that she was pursued by some vast, dark, unseen thing that yowled and moaned and *wanted* her. Then sanity returned, gripping and steadying her, racing to assemble the jigsaw of her thoughts.

She was in Thaniel's bedroom. It was night. She

had been asleep, dreaming. A nightmare, a terrifying nightmare, but that was all that it was. Taking a deep breath, she tried to calm herself.

The room was chilly and full of darkness, as she lay listening to her heartbeat decelerate. The black iron lamp-posts outside shone through the window, casting dim yellow shapes across the bare wooden floor. At night, the room seemed larger somehow, as if the walls were breathing in. One of the talismans that hung from the roof chimed softly as it stirred.

I forgot to ask about them, she thought wearily, as the final tatters of the nightmare fluttered away from her and tiredness began to return.

She had noted the talismans for the first time when she had retired after her bath. They had the temporary look of things that were not ordinarily there. The rest of the room was neatly arranged; a chest of drawers, a dressing table with a comb and an old book on it, the bed itself, a polished wood floor with a single rug. There was little decoration in Thaniel's room; it showed nothing of his character. It was merely a room.

But the talismans . . . now they were interesting. There, a fox's brush hung above the window, a tiny phial of something tied around it and wrapped in a long string of odd-smelling wooden beads. She'd found a coil of rope beneath her bed, but the intertwining strands were dyed red, white and amber, and tiny bells were tied at various points along its length. Just beneath her door, little symbols had been carefully drawn in some kind of black, ashy paste across the doorway. Another small mobile of tiny bells made of various metals hung above her bed.

She shucked the blankets and stirred, her nightgown

cool on her skin. It was a soft purple silk, elegant and luxurious, and fitted her perfectly. She had found it laid by her bed when she had retired last night. Thaniel's mother's, she thought, and felt a little sad.

It was then that she realized her fever had gone. She sat up, testing to see whether the giddiness would return. It didn't. The bedclothes still smelled of illness, an acrid scent of unhealthy sweat, but she felt fine.

There is that to be thankful for, at least, she thought, and lay back again.

She listened to the creaks of the house, the settling boards and pipes, and became suddenly aware of being terribly, horribly alone. Not just now, not just because the house was empty; instead, it was something that swamped her and promised to stay. She was entirely adrift, with no port to call home. She felt a deep sinking in her stomach, and she wanted to cry.

Perhaps she slept, perhaps not. It was difficult to tell. Skimming like a stone over the surface of awareness, she could not tell whether she had truly dreamed or whether she had only drowsed until her eyes opened again with a jolt of alarm.

Something was up there, on the ceiling.

Her chest froze in panic. The room had darkened, she was sure of it, the shadows thickening until they choked out the light, and the temperature had fallen to the point where her breath panted out in rapid clouds. But even in the blackness, she could see the deeper shadow, the vast thing that stood at the foot of her bed and bent over her, pressing against the ceiling, a clot of congealed dark that oozed malevolence. It was impossibly tall, an undefined, faceless, looming presence, motionless, paralysing her with fear.

It is not there! something inside her screamed, her rational mind beating frantically at her whirling panic, fighting to cage it again. *It is but a shadow, just a shadow!*

But it *was* there, and it radiated evil so thick that she felt she might gag on it; a thing with no shape and no form, yet she could feel its eyes, staring at her unflinchingly, regarding her with a dread gaze.

She was hardly even aware of her hand scrambling for the matchbox that lay on a table next to the bed, kept there for lighting the oil lamp nearby. She did not dare look away from the swarming blackness above her, fearing that the moment she did so, it would descend on her like a shroud, and she—

The crack and hiss of the match broke the spell, and a small glow of light drove back the dark. She took the glass from the oil lamp and shakily touched the flame to the wick, then held it up without even replacing the glass, thrusting its light to the ceiling.

There was nothing there.

She sat up in the bed, panting. Was it gone? Had it ever been there at all?

She'd been so *sure.* . .

Fearfully, she slid out of bed. The cold raised goosepimples along her flesh, beneath her nightgown. She placed the glass on the oil lamp to diffuse the glow and spread it wider, then turned it up to full brightness and checked the room. She looked behind the chest of drawers, under the bed, and finally turned the key in the door to lock it.

Night chills, she told herself. *That is all it could be. Perhaps I am not as fully recovered as I thought.* She slipped back into bed, replacing the lamp next to her on the table. For a time, she lay awake, staring at the ceiling where the thing had been.

Something happened to me, she thought. *Something happened, and that is why I cannot remember, and that is why I was ill, and that is why I was mad. But I am getting better. I am!*

Suddenly feeling idiotic, she tipped the glass of the oil lamp and blew it out. The darkness slunk back into the room, and settled. She watched the ceiling for a time, but all she saw was blank white plaster. Steadily, she began to feel herself descend towards sleep once more.

The stairs creaked – a long, low moan.

She was instantly awake again, her eyes wide open, alert. That was no natural night sound, no clank of cooling pipes or sigh of flexing boards.

The next stair creaked, quite deliberately.

Someone was coming up.

It took several seconds for the realization to sink into her, during which time the slow, heavy tread ascended up two more stairs. There was a terrible purpose in those footsteps, something unnatural that she could barely place, and an awful feeling of foreboding clutched at her, accompanied by a terrible sense of vulnerability.

It is Thaniel, Thaniel or Cathaline. It must be. There is no reason to panic so.

But somewhere inside her, deep and instinctive, she knew that whoever or *whatever* made those footsteps was coming for her.

The room had cooled further, and the darkness had deepened again. She pulled the blanket tight to her collarbone and shuffled backwards so that she was sitting against the headboard, and searched about the room with her eyes for something that might serve as a weapon.

The dressing table!

There were drawers there; there had to be a letter knife in one of them. But she was frozen. She did not dare leave the imagined safety of the bed to cross the room.

The intruder had reached the landing now, and she knew suddenly why it was that she had thought the footsteps unnatural. They were *wet*. This was not the clump of boots, but the soft slap of something like fins or webbed feet. And accompanying it was a laboured wheezing, like the phlegmy breath of an old, old man.

Somehow, it was that sound that got her moving, made her slide the blanket aside and put her feet down on to the rug. She did not dare light the lamp in case it alerted the intruder, hoping against hope that whatever it was outside did not know she was there. Silently, her body so tense that it was painful, she padded across the room. Her shadowy reflection crept towards her from the other direction, approaching from the far side of the dressing-table mirror. She was surprised at how normal she looked, when her insides were seized with utter and complete terror.

The slapping feet came closer, approaching slowly, and there came also the long dragging sound of something heavy. Alaizabel cast a fearful glance at the door, fancying that the thing outside was already opening it, and then tugged one of the dressing-table drawers as quietly as she could manage.

Locked. She tried another drawer, trembling, and

in her haste she let it grind along the inside of the dresser, making a scrape that was deafening in the glowering darkness.

The feet ceased their advance. Somehow, the silence was worse that when she could hear them. She could smell salt, even taste it on her lips and tongue. The room was freezing now, so cold that she began to shiver violently, and every breath was like a plume of white fog.

Like the cold, dark depths of the sea, she thought, and she realized that dew was clinging to her, moistening her nightgown and making her fine blonde hair stick to her face in lank, chill tentacles. Juddering uncontrollably now, she looked down into the drawer. There was a knife there, not a letter knife but a curious thing with a wavy blade.

The door thundered at her, shaking violently, deafeningly. She screamed, grabbing the knife and scrambling back to the bed, where she knelt facing the door. It rattled against its frame as if something was pounding it from without, clattering and thumping until Alaizabel screamed again to shut out the noise.

How was it that Thaniel had not heard such a din? How was it that he was not awoken and alerted?

Unless it was Thaniel that was outside her door.

Then came silence. Alaizabel watched, panting, shivering and wide-eyed, the knife held before her in a futile threat against anything that might try to come through the door. Her skin was clammy, her hair a straggle like kelp.

The key began to slowly turn in the lock.

Terror-stricken, Alaizabel stared at the circle of the key's grip as it rotated, millimetre by millimetre, each one bringing her closer to the moment when there would be nothing between her and whatever waited outside. She could not move.

The click of the lock as it was disengaged sounded like a pistol report.

The door swung inward gently, opening a gap of perhaps ten centimetres of pure, utter darkness.

Silence, and stillness.

When Cathaline returned from hunting that morning, she was scratched and scuffed but otherwise unharmed. The night had been unsuccessful. The roofcreepers were gone when she got there, and the rest of the night had been a pursuit in which she had never quite caught up with them.

She found Thaniel sitting in an armchair with a brandy in his hand.

"Good morning," she announced cheerily. Thaniel didn't reply.

She walked over to him and sat in a chair next to him. He picked up another brandy and offered it to her.

"For me? Thaniel, you *are* sweet," she said.

"There has been a development," he told her.

Cathaline settled into the chair. "Sounds bad."

"I heard Alaizabel screaming this morning. When I found her, she was half-insane with fright and babbling. It took me an hour to calm her and for her to tell me what had occurred."

"And what was that?" Cathaline asked.

He told her then about Alaizabel's night and the intruder on the landing.

"I gave her a sedative afterward. She sleeps now, and will not wake for a while."

"And you heard nothing of the intruder?" she prompted.

"Nothing," he replied. "What do you think about what she said?"

Cathaline took a long time to reply, swirling the brandy around the bottom of the glass to warm it in her hand. "I am inclined to think she is mad," she replied slowly.

Thaniel did not speak for a while, the shifting play of cold morning light and warm fire rendering his still features animate.

"You believe her," Cathaline stated, her voice echoing in his glass as he took a sip of brandy.

"It was the way she described it. . ." he said thoughtfully. "How could she have made that up? It was a Draug, I'm sure of it."

"It was a textbook description of a Draug," Cathaline replied. "And that's why I doubt her. She could have read it somewhere; we know nothing of her past, remember. And besides, in all recorded lore, there have only been two confirmed encounters with the Drowned Folk."

"I examined the scene," Thaniel said, getting up and pacing about the room, which was brightening fast as the sun gathered strength. "It was damp. And the Wards you drew around the door frame had been tampered with. They were twisted and incoherent. Something had sorely tested the barrier you put up."

"Or someone had erased them and scribbled new ones," Cathaline said. "It's not inconceivable. Listen, Thaniel, she is just a lost girl. Who would send a Draug after her, for pity's sake? Do you know how hard it is to summon one of those things?"

Thaniel sat against the window sill, the cool, flat

light from outside turning the back of his head and shoulders into a blazing smudge of white and throwing his face into shadow. Cathaline sighed and stood, rolling her arms in their sockets before walking over to face her former apprentice.

"I know you want her to be sane," she said. "God knows, you meet few enough people in this line of work, living at night, always on the hunt. You can only be solitary for so long, Thaniel. You're seventeen. People need friends."

"I have you," Thaniel replied.

"I don't count," she said, ruffling his hair. "I was your teacher first and foremost, and besides, I'm too old for you." She shrugged. "I'm just saying, Thaniel. Make sure of her before you start hoping. I know you too well. You're thinking of keeping her."

Thaniel laughed suddenly. "*Keep* her? Where would I put her? I would want my bed back eventually." For a moment, it seemed that he would continue, but then he seemed to sag a little, and he drew a letter out of his pocket. "This came an hour ago," he said, and put it into Cathaline's hand. Then he left the room, closing the door quietly behind him.

Cathaline turned the open envelope over in her hand, reading the return address. It came from Doctor Pyke, up at Redford Acres. Withdrawing the letter inside, she read it.

My dear sir,

I hope this letter finds you well. Further to your visit in regard to the girl that you encountered in the Old Quarter, I have made enquiries to the owners of two other asylums in the London area.

It seems that Doctor Hart of Crockerly Grange has recently had a fire in a wing of his establishment, resulting in the deaths of several inmates. During the course of the fire, the upper floor of the wing collapsed, destroying the outer wall and allowing the surviving inmates to escape the blaze. Three inmates are still unaccounted for; two males and a female. This girl, whose name is Alaizabel Cray, is of approximately seventeen or eighteen years of age and does not, alas, match the description of your own stray, having rather blonde hair and green eyes, but I am sorry to say this was the only evidence I could find of a possible escaped patient in London. I regret that I cannot be of further help. Please let me know how your enquiries conclude.

Yours,

Doctor Mammon Pyke

Cathaline reread the letter twice before folding it neatly and replacing it in the envelope. Something was sinking in her chest.

"Oh, Thaniel," she said sorrowfully.

Out in the hallway, the telephone rang.

"In here!" cried a voice, and Cathaline and Thaniel rushed past the distressed housemaid and headed up the stairs towards its source. It was a spacious Kensington property, set back from the tree-lined avenue, with three wide steps flanked by black iron railings climbing to its stout, green front door. The young woman had who opened the door to them followed them up, her black and white pinafore flapping about her ankles.

"To the right!" she called after them. "The master's study!"

Cathaline threw open the door and she and Thaniel burst into the room. It was softly lit by gaslights on the wall, and a fire burned in a small grate to ward off the November cold. Fine, carven oak chairs had been overturned, and several books had fallen from the shelves that occupied one wall, their pages bent and crumpled as they lay face down and open. At the foot of the bookshelves, a man and a woman were crouched over a supine figure; the woman had an infant in her arms, who was crying at the top of his lungs.

"Get *away* from him!" Cathaline cried as she entered the room, causing man and woman both to jump out of their skins and the baby to redouble the force of its howling.

"Bennett! What the bloody hell do you think you're about?" the man snapped as he turned around. Thaniel recognized him immediately. Regillen Maycraft, Chief Inspector of the Cheapside Peelers. He was a tall, stocky fellow with a stiff salt-and-pepper moustache and thinning hair of the same colour, running to baldness on the top of his pate. He wore a stout and battered greatcoat of faded creamy beige.

The lady looked similarly shocked. "He's my *husband*," she protested weakly, meaning the man on the floor.

"He won't be for long, madam," said Cathaline, pushing them aside and crouching where they had been, "and if he takes it upon himself to bite or scratch either of you, then you'll be following him."

Thaniel squatted next to her as Maycraft and the lady retreated a few paces to the other side of the study, where the maid waited anxiously. The man before them had been young and strong, with a fine head of blond hair and a firm jaw. Now he lay on his side, his fingers spasming into claws, his face and clothes soaked in acrid-smelling sweat. His pallor was already a ghastly porridge colour, the arteries on either side of his neck standing out sharply. He was breathing fast and shallow, like a wounded hare or a mouse in a cat's jaws.

"His eyes have turned," Thaniel observed quietly, and Cathaline nodded. The man's eyes were indeed the colour of dark honey, and his pupils had become hourglass-shaped and horizontal. Cathaline roughly pushed back the man's upper lip, revealing needle-point teeth set in greying gums. The eyes followed her, but their owner seemed too weak to move.

Cathaline looked over her shoulder at the lady. "You are the one who called us?"

"Hettie called," she replied, stroking the bawling baby's head and indicating the maid. "But I found Johnaten. He said . . . he had heard a noise in the nursery and gone in to investigate. There was someone . . . *something* in there. He fought it off, he cut it, I think, with a knife, but it went through the window and escaped. When I found him, he was bleeding from a bite wound on his hand. We called the police, but by the time Inspector Maycraft got here, he was like this."

Thaniel glanced at the lady; she was Mrs Turner, obviously, for they had been told when they were called by Hettie that the address they were required at was the Turner residence. She seemed unusually calm considering what had happened: her husband stricken, her child nearly abducted. Not even that was enough to break through her aristocratic conditioning and cause her to appear more than a little distressed.

"He has been bitten by a Cradlejack," said Thaniel. "I encountered the selfsame creature two nights ago, I'd guess. Take the baby downstairs, and have someone watch over it until daybreak. How long has it been since it happened?"

"An hour, perhaps a little longer," she said, handing the squalling child to the maid. "Do as he says, Hettie," she instructed. Hettie looked momentarily surprised that her mistress was taking orders from a seventeen-year-old boy, but she obeyed and took the wailing thing from the study.

Cathaline cursed under her breath, hurriedly opening a bag she had brought along.

"What's going on, Bennett?" Maycraft demanded, feeling a little embarrassed at being sidelined.

Cathaline waved irritably at him over her shoulder, as if dismissing a fly. Thaniel stood up and looked the Chief Inspector square in the eye.

"He was bitten by a Cradlejack over an hour ago. That means, unless we perform a Rite *immediately*, he is going to *become* one. It may already be too late."

Mrs Turner's hands covered her mouth in horror.

"And what then?" Maycraft said. "What if it *is* too late?"

Thaniel didn't reply, but his iron gaze said it all.

Mrs Turner made a little "oh!" noise behind the cage of her fingers.

"Thaniel!" Cathaline called, passing him a brass instrument similar to a pair of tongs. "Prise his jaws."

Thaniel moved to comply without hesitation. He was a different person when he was dealing with wych-kin. No doubts clouded his head, no hesitation. People respected a wych-hunter, even one as young as himself, and he was strong, confident, self-assured. He was the son of a legend, after all. He had a lot to live up to.

Before the weakened husk that was Johnaten Turner knew what was happening, Thaniel had shoved the tongs into one side of his mouth and roughly pulled his jaw open, as if he was dealing with an animal and not a man. He jerked and tried to pull back, but Thaniel had inserted them in such a way that it was more painful to resist. Quick as mercury, Cathaline had unstoppered a phial of thick, clear liquid, and now she poured it between the prone man's open lips, directly down his throat. Johnaten gagged and swallowed automatically.

"You two! Pin his arms!" she ordered, without taking her eyes off the thing that was now writhing and spasming beneath her, trapped by Thaniel's tongs like a fish on a hook. Maycraft grabbed one wrist and knelt on it; then, seeing that the lady of the house had no intention of trying to hold down her husband, he deftly snatched the other one and held that, too.

Cathaline reached over Maycraft – who was necessarily getting in her way – and brought to bear a new item that she had taken from her bag. This was a thin band of gold-plated steel, hinged in the middle, with a tiny padlock at the other end. With Thaniel driving Johnaten's head down to the floor of the study by the teeth, she snapped the band around the victim's throat and clicked the padlock home.

"It's too tight," Thaniel said, noticing how deeply it bit into his skin. Johnaten had something of a bull neck, although it was wasting slowly away as they watched.

"No time," Cathaline replied brusquely. "Maycraft, let Thaniel take one of the wrists. Spread him out."

Thaniel released the tongs and withdrew them, and almost instantly Johnaten snapped at his fingers, like a rabid dog. He had expected it, and was well clear, but Maycraft jerked back in surprise, releasing his hold on one of the wrists. Thaniel grabbed it fast, slamming it down to the floor and kneeling on it so that Johnaten was held in a crucifix position, with his arms wide and with Cathaline sitting on his upper knees. He thrashed and twisted, but he could not move, and he could not stretch to bite any of them. Mrs Turner whimpered in the background.

"If you don't want to end up like this, Maycraft, try and be more careful," Cathaline said. Maycraft seethed visibly, but he held his tongue.

His hands now free, Thaniel passed to Cathaline a pot of thick, viscous pig blood from his bag, and a deeply stained brush with thick bristles. She tore open the shirt of the thing that was rapidly becoming less and less like Johnaten Turner, exposing a chest that was thin and emaciated where it had previously been strong and muscled. The skin was yellowed, like parchment.

Thaniel shook his head. It could well be too late for this man. He watched as Cathaline set about painting a Ward on the creature's chest. The stripes of blood that she drew in the wake of the brush began to form a symbol, a curling, odd shape interspersed with short, urgent lines. Like most Wards, it had a curious *wrongness* about it, as if its form defied the laws of trigonometry; it hurt the eyes to look at it for too long, and a headache would shortly follow for those who were not used to their effects. As Cathaline drew near to completion, those in the room felt a disturbing, tugging sensation, as if they were leaning forward towards the Ward, tipping over on to it, unbalancing. And then the final stroke was complete, and the sensation disappeared, snapping them back to normality.

Johnaten had fallen suddenly still, only his horizontal hourglass eyes roving desperately in their orbits.

"You can let him go now," Thaniel said to Maycraft. The Chief Inspector released his captive arm slowly, and stepped away. Thaniel did likewise. Cathaline was already busying herself in her bag.

"What did you do to him?" Mrs Turner asked, her voice small.

"He is Warded," Thaniel replied. "He cannot move. Now we can perform the Rite, to drive the Cradlejack out of him."

"I'll handle it, Thaniel," Cathaline said, taking a lump of red wax and drawing an octagon on the floor around the still form of Johnaten. "The lady there said that Johnaten wounded the thing; that means there will be blood in the nursery. You and Maycraft go out there and find it. I'll not have it trying this again with another baby."

Thaniel drew a pistol, opened it, spun the chamber to check he had a full load of bullets, and snapped it shut.

"My pleasure," he said.

Maycraft had to admit, he was impressed. The boy knew what he was about, that was for certain. In fact, if anything, he was a little chilling in his efficiency. Wych-hunters made him nervous, though he would rather be eaten alive than admit it out loud.

It had taken a matter of moments for Thaniel to locate the blood of the wych-kin on the floor of the nursery. The cot had been overturned, and the window hung open, flapping in the cold night wind, allowing in thin wisps of fog. There were several splashes drying on the floor, dark-red stains soaking into the grain of the wood. Thaniel picked one, dabbed his finger into it and tasted it, spat and then went on to the next one. This one, though he spat it out also, he appeared satisfied with.

"Wych-kin blood tastes different," he said in response to Maycraft's quizzical gaze. "More watery. Tinny."

He had swiftly scraped some into a small container that he had in the pocket of his long coat, the same container that now monopolized his attention as Maycraft's carriage took them south through the streets of London, towards the Thames. Maycraft watched him closely as he unscrewed it, keeping it steady against the rough jolting of the carriage. It was a globe of glass, surrounded by a webwork of gold fibres that served to strengthen and contain it while still allowing its contents to be seen. It hung on a triple chain attached to a single sphere the size of a musket ball; these chains were attached to the top half of the globe. The bottom half Thaniel now held in his palm, detached from the rest of the container; it was stained with a swirl of Cradlejack blood, that pooled at the bottom.

"What was all that about before?" Maycraft asked.

Thaniel's reply was conducted as he drew out the small phial of sulphur solution that he had used the last time he faced the Cradlejack. "A Cradlejack is not the creature you see on the outside. That is what is left of the poor wretch it inhabits. I have no idea what a Cradlejack looks like before it takes over a victim; nobody has ever seen one, to my knowledge." He glanced at Maycraft, to check the elder man was still following him. "They have a particular relationship with sulphur. It is attracted to them, but they hate it. That is what Cathaline poured down Turner's throat."

Maycraft's eyes widened. "Sulphur? But that's—"

"Poisonous," Thaniel finished, putting a few drops

of the stuff into the Cradlejack blood and replacing the phial. "Not in those quantities. People take sulphur tablets to drive out illness, do they not?"

"And what about the gold collar?"

"Cradlejacks despise the touch of gold. It slows down the progress of the transformation."

"Why?" Maycraft demanded, seeming almost angry that he was forced to admit such ignorance.

Thaniel screwed the globe back together and hung it from its chain. "Who knows?" he said.

"You don't *know?*" blurted the other.

Thaniel looked at him, brushing back his floppy blond hair with one hand. "Wych-kin do not follow the rules of science, sir. The laws that apply to earthly things do not apply to them."

"That's ridiculous!" Maycraft declared.

"Unfortunately not," Thaniel said. He was gently swinging the globe on the end of its chain, letting it describe small circles in the air before him. "Wychcraft is not a science; rather, it is ninety per cent guesswork and ten per cent superstition. You wonder why the wych-kin are driving us out of our city? It is because it has taken us this long to even begin to learn how to beat them. Trial and error, sir. And every error means another wych-hunter has an appointment with Old Boney. Ah," he said, suddenly pausing in his explanation, "here is a case in point, Inspector Maycraft."

The globe had begun to glow from within, a dim yellow-white light that shone out through the gold webwork that cradled it.

"That is a simple scientific trick," Maycraft said. "Many chemicals react together in that way."

"True enough," said Thaniel. "But the *third*

element is the Cradlejack itself. The closer we are to the creature, the brighter this orb will glow."

They stepped out of the carriage somewhere in Chelsea, just north of the river. Neither of them were especially familiar with this part of London, and the fog had closed down on them again, making it difficult to spot landmarks or even street signs unless they were very close.

"I will wait here for you, Inspector," the driver declared, loading a long-barrelled rifle atop the carriage and eyeing his mares protectively. They were a little too close to the Old Quarter for comfort, and wolves loved horsemeat.

Thaniel held the globe out before him, allowing it to swing on its chain. It had been getting steadily brighter as they headed south.

"What makes you think it will be here, in all of London?" Maycraft asked, more out of a wish to stump the young boy rather than any need to know. Thaniel confounded him with an instant response.

"Cradlejacks are territorial. I found this one's lair down near Lambeth. It will have abandoned that one, but it will not have moved far. The most direct route from Kensington is through Chelsea, and fast as they are, they have to move in secret and stay hidden. I believe we are a little ahead of it now. It will be coming through this way soon. All we have to do is intercept it."

"You're sure it's the same one you found?"

"Cradlejacks are thankfully rare," he said. "I am sure."

Maycraft drew his pistol as Thaniel watched the globe swing on its chain, noting that it swung further to the west, as if drawn there by a magnet.

"Well, as long as a bullet in the heart can stop them, I'm game," he declared brashly.

"That'll stop them quite effectively, sir," Thaniel said. "This way."

They hastened through the streets of Chelsea. The public houses and inns had closed for the night, but there were still drunkards and revellers staggering over the cobbles with half-drained bottles of rotgut or whisky. They lurched out of the fog with alcohol-reddened noses, attracted to the bright light that Thaniel held like inebriated moths. One sight of the pistols that the two hurrying figures carried turned the drunkards away, however. A few ladies of the night were prowling the alleys, looking for customers, but they recognized Maycraft and stayed silent as he passed.

Every so often, Thaniel stopped and consulted the globe, but it usually swung in the direction that he was going anyway. He seemed to have an instinct for it, that was for sure. This thin, fine-featured boy with his washed-out blue eyes and floppy centre-parting of blond was far more proficient than his appearance suggested. Maycraft's work had brought him into contact with wych-kin often, and wych-hunters with them. They were notoriously of odd character. It took a special type of person to devote themselves to exterminating wych-kin, even with the astronomical wages that Parliament offered them for doing such a dangerous job. But this boy had a steely calm about him that was unusual. Maycraft had met Jedriah Fox many a time; there were few in the city who had not heard of London's greatest wych-hunter. This boy was a chip off the old block.

They headed along the banks of the Thames,

hurrying past the alley where Stitch-face had ended the life of Marey Woolbury two nights ago. A zeppelin droned somewhere distant, a vast sentinel of the city, too far away to be seen in the omnipresent murk.

There it was, suddenly; the high-pitched, maniacal laughter of the Cradlejack, sounding as if it was coming from all around them. Thaniel froze; Maycraft, too.

"It is closer than I thought. I must not have put enough reagent in," Thaniel muttered, almost under his breath, as he held up the globe. "It should have been brighter than this."

Ah, so you do *make mistakes,* thought Maycraft, with a small twinge of satisfaction.

The globe swung to their left, towards the Thames.

"It's in the water?" Maycraft queried.

"Maybe," Thaniel said. "That is probably how it gets across from the Old Quarter. If we hurry, we may catch it."

They ran along the street until the railing at their left gave way to a set of stone steps, descending along the wall that lifted the road above the muddy banks of the river. The tide was low, and the shadows of grounded ships hulked in the gloom beneath them, waiting for the water to rise and lift them once more. They went down, the tapping of their boots swallowed by the mist, their hands clammy and their breath visible before them.

Maycraft made a faint sound of disgust as his boots squelched into the wet, freezing mud, much deeper than he had expected, and vile ooze dribbled in around the laces and through the eyeholes. Thaniel had made a similarly unpleasant discovery, but he had at least expected it and was not perturbed.

"I hear no splashing," Maycraft said quietly, as they waded through the muck and filth. "Perhaps it has already crossed."

"Perhaps it knows we are chasing it, and it lies in wait," Thaniel suggested as an alternative.

Now the bulk of the ships loomed over them like dark leviathans, tall and imposing at this level even though they were only small fishing boats and trawlers. A faint line of lights marked the top of the embankment, the street from which they had come. Down here, the world was a shifting white nether-world of shadows. Maycraft wished he had thought to bring a lantern, then imagined it would have been no good anyway. The moon was full, at least. They had that small mercy.

The mud banks were eerily silent, the suck and plunge of their boots unforgivably rude in the softly stirring air. Thaniel glanced occasionally at the bright orb that hung from the chain in his hand.

"It is here," he said. "It is too close to have made it over to the other side."

Maycraft looked around as they trudged into the shadow of a tall deep-sea trawler, leaning wearily over them.

"You think it might have—" Maycraft began to say, but his question was cut off by a shrill cry from above, and the thing plummeted from the deck of the ship on to Thaniel. The boy's pistol fired wild, the globe fell from his hands and smashed, and he was driven into the choking dirt by the weight of the crazed wych-kin atop him. Unable to react fast enough to repel his attacker, he felt the sweep of a claw towards his cheek, but he pulled his head aside and the Cradlejack missed by millimetres. Maycraft shouted then and the creature looked up in sudden alarm.

Maycraft had his pistol levelled at the thing, but the sight of it caused him to hesitate momentarily. Once, it had been a man. Now it was a scrawny, parchment-skinned creature, thin and lank, wearing tattered rags and with its hands and bare feet tipped with long, savage fingernails. Its eyes had the same horizontal hour-glass shape that he had seen in Johnaten Turner, and its teeth – as its dry, cracked lips skinned back in a snarl – were tiny and viciously pointed.

A gun roared, but it was not Maycraft's. Thaniel had brought his pistol to bear under the creature's atrophied belly, and squeezed the trigger. The creature leaped off him, howling and hissing, thrashing in the mud, scrabbling away. Maycraft ran to Thaniel, reaching down an arm to pull him out of the sucking bog that he had been crushed into.

"Shoot it!" Thaniel cried as he came free. "Make sure it is dead!"

And, indeed, though it bled from a gut wound and it still suffered from the point of Johnaten Turner's blade across its forearm, it was running away across the mud flats towards where the edge of the Thames lapped.

"Shoot it!" Thaniel urged again, struggling to his feet. "If it gets to the water, it'll be gone!"

Maycraft levelled his pistol, his arm held straight and one eye closed, sighting down the barrel. The Cradlejack was already only a faint silhouette in the mist, and he could hear the splashing of its feet as it reached the shallows.

"Damn the thing, it's too far away." Maycraft said, knowing that he would only be wasting a bullet.

Thaniel raised his own pistol and fired, feeling the recoil jolt all along his arm. He caught it dead in the back, between its knife-like shoulder blades. It squawked, a faintly pathetic sound of surprise, and then there was the noise of its body falling forward into the water. It lay still for a moment, face down and spreadeagled, until the current buoyed it up and carried it along the river towards the sea, leaving a slowly dissipating trail of dark red behind it.

Thaniel flexed his arm. "Not far enough," he said.

"So I see," Maycraft replied, gauging the distance that Thaniel had fired and thinking what a truly remarkable shot he had just witnessed.

CATHALINE'S ATTIC
A RITE IS PERFORMED
PLANS ARE MADE
6

The first light of dawn was creeping across London as Thaniel and Cathaline returned from the Turner house, their cab forging through thinning tendrils of fog. The hours before the sun came to warm the streets were bitter with cold and eerily flat and dead, yet they were more familiar to the wych-hunters than the bright light of midday.

"Something's troubling you, Thaniel," said Cathaline, as they rode the jolts and bumps inside the cab.

Thaniel turned to look at her, then back out of the side at the patient streets, waiting for the day to arrive. "I will not take her to Pyke," he said after a moment. "Mad or not, he will not have her."

"My, Thaniel, you *are* getting protective," she said with a secret smile.

"Do not mock me," he said, and his voice was sharp.

Cathaline laughed, her black-and-red hair shaking as she tipped her head back. "You always did take yourself too seriously."

Thaniel gave her a poisonous glance and then ignored her.

"Listen, Thaniel," she said. "I know you want to save her somehow. You couldn't save your mother, and you couldn't save Jedriah, and you feel you—"

"Cathaline," he snapped. "Don't."

She splayed her hand before her and examined the tips of her fingernails. "I don't want you hurt, Thaniel. She may be mad. You have to accept that."

"I have talked with her, and so have you. She is sane, but there is something. . ." he trailed off. "If I thought she was mad, I would not have left her alone."

"She took enough sedative to keep her under until this time tomorrow," Cathaline pointed out. "You need not worry on that count."

And yet Alaizabel *was* there when they arrived, with her back to them, her long, corn-coloured hair just visible from behind the high backrest of the chair she sat in. A fire burned low before her. She did not acknowledge their arrival, not even when they greeted her from the doorway. Cathaline gave Thaniel a quizzical frown.

Thaniel, puzzled, walked around to where he could see Alaizabel's face, and his heart jumped when she suddenly turned to look at him with a sharp movement of her head.

"Who are you?" the girl snapped, and Cathaline looked up suddenly from where she had been busying herself at the back of the room.

Thaniel was stricken with horror. Alaizabel looked *old*. No, no, that was not right. Her skin was as smooth as ever, her features as small and childish, her hands pale and slender, but it was the manner of her body that had changed. She hunched forward towards the fire like a bent-backed crone. Her head protruded, tortoise-like, from her shoulders, bobbing on the end of a stiff neck. Her face seemed to have sagged, her features pulled downward in a severe expression, and her hands were bunched into arthritic claws. She was wearing only the soft purple nightgown that Thaniel had provided for her.

"Who are you? Who are you, I said!"

It was her *voice*, too. Alaizabel's voice, undoubtedly, but the vowels and pronunciation were completely different. He could not place the accent, but it was harsh and archaic.

"You know who I am, Miss Alaizabel," he said, as Cathaline came over, sensing that something was most definitely wrong.

"Know who you are? I've never seen you before! I'm no Miss Alaizabel."

"Then who are you?"

"Thatch, I am. That's all they've known me as for nigh on sixty years now, wife and widow. Who are you? Where am I? Eh? Where am I? Speak up!"

"Thatch?" Thaniel repeated, still shaken by this sudden turn of events.

"Thatch, aye. You must be a simple boy, so slow of wit. Yes, so slow."

Thaniel let the insult pass him by. He sat down on one of the hearthside chairs. Cathaline sat down on another one. The fire snapped quietly, forgotten.

"See, now they sit at my fire without so much as a by-your-leave or even names to call 'em by!" Alaizabel crowed. "What'd you bring me here for, eh? What about my purpose, eh? Eh? Wasting my time. I have powers, you know! Powers!"

"What is your purpose?" said Cathaline carefully.

"Show me your mark, eh! Show me your mark! You're not of the Fraternity, are you? Where'd this girl get to? Where, I say? Oh, my head! Why must I suffer so? Why must I battle? Who are you?"

Thaniel and Cathaline exchanged a glance, each one gauging what the other was thinking, each one hoping that they had not heard what they had just heard.

The Fraternity.

They were about to say something when Alaizabel spoke again, addressing Thaniel, her voice grating and loud.

"She wasn't supposed to still be here! See! See the mark! Oh, don't you understand, you slow-witted boy?"

At that, Alaizabel suddenly lurched out of her chair and reached behind herself, tearing open the buttons that ran up the back of the nightgown she was wearing with a short, savage tug. It came open to the base of her spine, exposing her shoulder blades and a narrow expanse of soft flesh. Thaniel had been too surprised to avert his eyes as he would normally have done; and by the time he had recovered himself enough, he had already seen the tattoo, the dark circle just above Alaizabel's coccyx, and he was unable to look away. The many-tentacled thing, etched in ink on her skin. There was something terrible about it, and it disturbed the eye the way that Wards did, though it was not any kind of Ward that he had ever come across.

"See?" she said. "The mark! Where'd this girl get to, eh? Why am I not about my purpose? Why does my head throb so?"

A moment later, she slumped back down into the chair, screwing her eyes up tight.

"Ohhh, my head," she moaned, clutching at the sides of her skull and leaning forward, her flaxen hair seeping between her fingers. She trailed off into

70

silence, her breathing suddenly slowing . . . and then with a deep inhalation of air, she sat heavily back in her chair and her eyes flew open, and it was Alaizabel again.

The change was almost physical, and immediate. No longer did she bend or stoop; her movements were smoother, not hampered by the tautness of joints and old muscles. She was young again, supple, and her voice when she spoke was back to the crisp elocution that Thaniel had come to recognize and enjoy.

For a moment, a fearful confusion swam in her gaze as it locked with Thaniel's. Then she glanced around the room, taking into account the fire and her two companions, then her own semi-dressed state. To be in a nightgown was bad enough; to have the back hanging open was both mortifying and terribly distressing. She shrank back into the chair, hugging herself.

"I was asleep," she said, unable to think of anything less obvious to say.

"No," said Thaniel. "You weren't."

Cathaline's attic was a long, spacious room, formerly an artist's studio for Thaniel's mother. It occupied the upper storey of 273 Crofter's Gate, and unlike Thaniel's room, it reflected its owner perfectly. It was wide and expansive in aspect, with space to spare and no walls or barriers to fence a person in. Everything was open and visible from everywhere else, from the miniature table to the rickety four-poster bed under the skylight. The mid-morning sun pummelled its way into the attic now, having marshalled itself into a dazzling brightness, and the tall windows on the north and south of the building captured it all and drank it greedily, filling the room with illumination.

Like its owner, the room was chaos. Nothing matched; everything was thrown together and left to find its own level. A stuffed falcon's tail protruded from the mouth of a stuffed alligator which was hanging from the ceiling, spinning back and forth when a breeze stirred it. An untidy heap of books was strewn haphazardly next to a bookcase, which was nearly empty, as if it had been too much effort to slot these books – many of which were as valuable as a month's rent on a London townhouse – back into their niches. Dark, sinister steel pentagrams and black tallow candles sat on shelves next to dolls and teddy bears. The four-poster bed possessed a strangely pathetic grandeur, bedraggled and moth-eaten and belonging in a place much more elegant than this.

"This is it!" Cathaline declared triumphantly, pulling out a grey, hidebound tome with a seemingly unintelligible scrawl embossed in gold on its spine. She scampered over to where Thaniel waited on a low wicker settee and sat cross-legged before him, laying the book open between them.

"What kind of language is that?" he asked, eyeing the strange, flowing script that swam across the page.

"Sanskrit," she said absently, already deep in perusal. "I know I saw something like that in here. . ."

She had gone for the book in a frenzy of activity almost the moment that Thaniel had put Alaizabel back to bed with a fresh sleeping draught. It was late for both of them – being mid-morning, they were usually thinking about sleep soon — but like a grey-hound set after a hare, she had pursued her new purpose with characteristic vigour until she had found it.

"I would say it was sort of like an octopus," she said.

"More tentacles," he replied, leaning over the book, which was upside-down to him. "It was set at a curious angle, too; almost like it was trying to peel itself off her skin."

Cathaline rocked back from the book and drummed a rhythm on her knees as she spoke. "You heard what she said, didn't you?"

Thaniel nodded grimly. "The Fraternity."

"The Fraternity," Cathaline agreed. She stood up suddenly, leaning backwards, further and further until she glided into an expert handstand, and then slowly brought her feet over to complete the manoeuvre. "We may be into something a lot more dangerous than we know," she said, cocking her head elfishly. "Are you sure you want to follow this through?"

Thaniel leaned back in the wicker settee, the book forgotten for a moment. "Have you ever felt. . ." he began, stopped, and then carried on. "Have you ever felt that suddenly your choice of direction is not your own? I mean, that you should be going in some way other than the road you are travelling? It feels like I am being *called*, somehow. Do you understand? And it is as if I have no power over myself, you see? Suddenly, something I have not ever seriously thought of before has become irresistible."

Cathaline linked her hands behind her back and raised an eyebrow theatrically at him. "Thaniel, you are being vague as only a man can be. Spit it out."

"I. . ." he said, and halted again. "She needs me."

"*She* needs *you?*" Cathaline asked with a grin.

Thaniel obstinately refused to take her meaning. "She is alone, and scared, and there is more to her than what we know. She has no-one else."

There was silence. A gauzy curtain stirred in a faint breeze from somewhere.

"I want to be friends with her," he said. "I want . . . something *other* than what I know. She is so strange to me, you see? I think that her life must have been very different from mine." He looked up at Cathaline. "I want to know what that is like. I want to help her."

Cathaline smiled in understanding. She always understood. She and Thaniel were kindred spirits.

"Page 127," she said, indicating the book at his feet.

Thaniel looked down at the book and then up at her. "You knew where it was all along."

"I wanted to talk to you," she said, then turned suddenly grave, "before you saw it."

"You know what it is?" he asked. "The mark? You know what it means?"

"Oh, yes," said Cathaline, and her tone told him that he would not like what he found. "It is known as a *chackh'morg*. It is a symbol used by followers of the Glau Meska – the Deep Ones. Thirteen years ago was the last time one was recorded; a conclave of occultists was unearthed in Cheapside, and this symbol was found to figure in many of their ceremonies." She paused. "These people worship the more powerful wych-kin. They treat with them, offer them sacrifice, work on their behalf to gather more power for themselves."

"Why didn't I know about this?" Thaniel asked, a little annoyed at his ignorance.

"Cults like this were all over London, but they're almost impossible to dig out nowadays. They've either learned to hide better or they've been swallowed by bigger cults. Besides, it's a job for the Peelers; wych-hunters deal with wych-kin, not with hopeful little groups of people that think they can summon a demon with a ouija board and a few backward prayers. And the Peelers have enough on their plate."

"You are saying she was part of a cult? Part of the Fraternity?"

"Possibly," she replied. "But the Fraternity aren't stupid enough to tattoo themselves so that the authorities can identify all of them when one is caught. No, the *chackh'morg* is something else. Usually it's burned on the skin when someone is to be sacrificed."

Cathaline sat down on the wicker chair next to Thaniel, leaned back and stretched.

"The lore books that I have only came up with one instance when they would go to the trouble of tattooing a victim. It was when the victim was not intended for a simple death, but for *possession.*"

"How do they do it?"

"It's all theory, you understand," Cathaline said. "There's no evidence of it ever actually working. When a spirit needs a body, the body has to be vacated by the existing spirit. A poison is administered, one that slowly kills the victim while the spirit takes residence. A spirit can't take a dead body, but it can take *over* a dying one. Then the poison is neutralized before death, and the strong spirit destroys the weak one."

"Except this time it did not happen," said Thaniel, realization dawning on him. "The spirit did not overcome the victim, and now she is in there with Alaizabel." He turned slowly on the settee and fixed Cathaline with a look of determination. "She is not mad. She is possessed. Someone *put* that thing inside her."

Cathaline nodded. "Looks that way."

"And what has the mark to do with this?"

"The mark is an invitation," said Cathaline, standing up suddenly and smoothing down her dark velvet trousers. "A beacon. The spirit must know where it is going after it has been called. They fed her poison, but it didn't work, by my guess and yours. Somehow she resisted, maybe more than they expected. And when Thatch arrived, she found the sacrifice still fighting."

"The Fraternity!" Thaniel said, getting up and pacing the room. "Remember what she said, a moment ago? The Fraternity summoned her."

"And now the spirit is inside Alaizabel," Cathaline said. "And it's my guess that they want it back." She spun suddenly, an idea striking her. "Come with me to the sanctum. I need to try something."

Every wych-hunter had at least one sanctum somewhere. It was a place where they could carry out their rituals, procedures and experiments in safety, usually a simple room – a basement or attic. A sanctum could be created anywhere, but no matter how sparse and unfurnished they were to begin with, it was never long before the accumulation of artefacts necessary to carry out the Rites gave them a mystery and a fascination, a feeling of gravity, which inspired respect.

Thaniel and Cathaline's sanctum was in the basement of 273 Crofter's Gate, a large, low, square room that was reached by a door at the end of the hallway, leading to a short set of stone steps. The room was lit by the gas lamps that hid in sconces on the wall, and their glow spread over the wood panelling and bare floor of smooth black stone. The room exuded a stolid air, a sense of heaviness, seeming to frown upon them as they entered. A spiky, two-metre tree of petrified wood stood in one corner, its branches like spears as they crooked and jaunted about its stiff, thin trunk. Beneath the tiny, high-set and blacked-out window that looked up to Crofter's Gate at the feet of passers-by, there was a hideous carving that drew the eye. Two figures were depicted, carved from a single, large block of wood. One was thickset – fat and muscular at the same time – with a horribly distended gargoyle-face that sneered and showed pointed teeth of brass behind its leathery lip; it was squatting on its haunches like a toad, leaning forward with its hands splayed to support it. The other, crouching behind it and at a slight angle, was the size of a man, with a flat, wide face and brutal features buried under a shaggy mane of hair. It wore a sleeveless shirt, and its immense, hairy arms hung down like an ape's. Beneath them, on a plaque, was the inscription *Rawhead and Bloodybones*. Thaniel hated that carving, which had been his father's, but Cathaline loved it.

The room was presided over by an altar of black marble and polished metal at the far end. This was neatly arranged with bowls, incense burners and sticks of wax. Next to it was a glass cabinet, carved of stout oak, inside which could be seen the paraphernalia of a wych-hunter's trade; talismans, powdered blood, crucibles, tallow-catchers, soul cages, wych-posts, kris knives and many more. Artefacts of superstition and folklore, yet many of them proved to be effective against certain breeds of wych-kin. It was a well accepted fact that most legends were born from a seed of truth; many a wych-hunter had been forced to stake their life on a legend before.

It was to the summoning-circle in the centre of the black stone floor that Cathaline led him to first. It was made of beaten gold, a simple ring set into the stone with a smaller concentric band just inside it. Sigils and Wards ran along the space between the two bands, also picked out in gold, and they seemed to creep if the eyes lingered on them too long, following each other around the edge of the circle.

A sanctum took months to create. It took a vast amount of Wards to ensure that no outside spiritual force would be able to enter and interfere with the complex Rites performed within, and also to ensure that if anything should go wrong with those Rites, then nothing could get out. Thaniel knew of several sanctums on the fringes of the Old Quarter which were derelict now, their owners killed by their carelessness or inexperience, and whatever they had summoned trapped, raging within the house or the room that the sanctum owner had brought them to. Such places quickly became known as haunted, and were avoided.

But nowhere in the sanctum was more heavily Warded than the summoning-circle. It was here that many of the Rites were performed, a spot where the laws of physics did not apply quite so strictly, where whatever stuff the wych-kin came from leaked through ever so slightly. And where things might happen that would normally be considered impossible.

It was a simple Rite that Cathaline set up; one of the most basic taught to apprentices. She drew a small stone from the pocket of her trousers, a chip of volcanic rock shaped like a pinecone. A Ward had been etched into it in deep, interconnecting grooves. Drawing a small phial of pig's blood, she poured a tiny amount delicately over the Ward, which absorbed it greedily.

Thaniel frowned as he crouched at the edge of the circle. "This is Strachlea's Divination. What is this intended to prove? I could do this when I was ten."

"I'm sure you could," said Cathaline, withdrawing a rattle that looked like something a witch doctor would carry; it was made of crow bones, amber beads, cats' teeth and dove feathers stained with pig blood. She began to describe small circles in the air above the stone, shaking the rattle alternately hard and softly. The noise it made set the teeth on edge; when it was quiet, it sounded like it was skulking, and when it was loud it hurt the ears. As she did this, she kept talking: "So tell me, then, what does Strachlea's Divination do?"

"It is for detecting wych-kin activity; where they gather thickest," said Thaniel. "But it is very crude and inaccurate; and if you perform it in London, the presence of the Old Quarter ruins it like a magnet will ruin a compass reading."

"Textbook answer, my young Thaniel," said Cathaline, in a stern, schoolmistress voice. The stone in the summoning circle was beginning to shake and twitch. "The Old Quarter is south from here, am I right? Which wall is south?"

"Towards the altar," he said, thumbing over his shoulder. It was directly behind where he crouched.

"Now watch," she said, and the vigorous rattling stopped dead. The stone seemed to pause, suddenly freezing where it was; then it spun on its axis and darted upward, leaping off the ground and burying itself in the ceiling.

There was silence for a moment, as Cathaline looked meaningfully at Thaniel.

"Guess whose room is two floors directly above us?"

Thaniel cursed under his breath. "What does it mean?"

Cathaline settled back on her haunches. "It means anything even faintly wych-like in the entire city knows exactly where she is," she said. "She's like a lighthouse to them. Or rather, that spirit inside her is. You can wager that if she stays here, there'll be something looking for her tomorrow night, and the night after, until they get her."

Thaniel stood up and raked his hair back. "Can you fashion something to stop it?"

"I know a Rite to create a charm for Alaizabel; that will mask her presence to wych-kin, at least enough so that she will not be detectable from miles away." Cathaline got up and studied the carving of Rawhead and Bloodybones, deep in thought. "But that doesn't solve the immediate problem. They'll know she's here, even if they can't see her. If the wych-kin don't get us, the Fraternity will."

"How long?"

"For the Rite? Six, seven hours."

"That'll take us till nightfall," he said. "I'll set Wards all over the house. We'll weather the night, and we'll go at dawn tomorrow."

"Go where, exactly?" Cathaline said, placing her hand on her hip. "The Fraternity have eyes and ears everywhere."

"Not in the Crooked Lanes," Thaniel replied.

For the better part of two hours, Thaniel checked the perimeter of the house, placing Wards on every doorway and window. He renewed the carefully inked shapes on the floor beneath the door of his bedroom, where Alaizabel slept. He locked it again from the outside, taking the key with him. This time it was for her own protection. When he was satisfied that the fortress of their home was as impregnable as he could make it, he sat in a chair in the living room and allowed himself to drift slowly into sleep.

laizabel woke to a feeling that she was not alone.

Night had claimed the sun only a moment ago. She didn't understand how, but she *knew* that, as surely as if she'd stood and watched the last of the day bleed out of the sky, the long mound of light that stretched across the horizon shrinking slowly to a thin line and then into velvety blue. She had snapped awake at almost exactly that moment, her eyes flicking open to the soft grey moonlight that seeped under the curtains of Thaniel's room, draining down the cracks in the floorboards and throwing the hanging talismans that drifted gently about on their tassels and strings into flat relief.

But yet she was *not* awake, not in the sense of being alert, anyway. It was a disturbing feeling: on the one hand, she seemed clear and bright, her senses keen and her body ready for action, but on the other, her mind was fogged by a stupefying haze, desiring only to shut down and sleep again but prevented by the more alert portion of herself. It was hard to separate one feeling from another, for her slower side — undoubtedly befuddled by the sedative she had taken — was mixing up her thoughts and making them errant and slippery.

Then she got up, and that was when she realized with a terrified inner shudder that something was seriously wrong. For she had not willed herself to move, not intended to shuck off the blanket and stand. Her body was acting under someone else's will, and it was the most deep and intense violation she could imagine. She wanted to scream, or cry for help; but her thoughts, that for her entire life had translated into movement in her muscles, provoked no response. Suddenly it was if she was merely a brain, being transported inside the skull of some hideous fleshly machine, a piece of living cargo in someone else's hold. In that single moment, more than any other, she truly touched madness.

But the very sedative that was dulling her brain cushioned the blow, stopped her mind breaking by simply refusing to accept what was happening. Without that, perhaps she would not have dealt with the trauma with her intelligence intact. As it was, she had no time to take it all in. She was walking over to the door, her body seeming heedless of her panic, turning the doorknob.

It was locked.

Something inside her blazed, made her cringe. It was the clear part of her mind, pacing around like a caged tiger, sharp-clawed and quick. She seemed to have no access to this part; she was aware only that it was there, and what it was doing, and that it did not belong to her.

Who are you?

!!Sit down, little girl!! came the harsh reply, lashing her like a whip. She retreated inside her own head.

I am dreaming, she thought, and suddenly it made sense that way. That was something for her to cling to, a way to deal with the impossible situation she found herself in. *The sedative has made me dream, most vividly—*

!!Be silent!! Be silent, I say!!

She complied. The crochety old voice sounded very unpleasant. Best to do what it said, and wait for the dream to be over.

Her body tried the door again, a hand that seemed not to be hers turning the doorknob harder this time. Her fingers hurt a little, and her back and hips ached. She realized she was stooping, but she had no power to straighten up. Inside, she had become very calm, as the shock of what seemed to be impossible settled into her brain and cooled her panic. Raw denial replaced fear. The best explanation was that it just was not happening.

She watched as her hands began to trace a shape slowly in the air before the door. At first, it seemed as if they were merely waving about without purpose or direction (and didn't her hands seem *gnarled* somehow?), but she soon saw there was repetition in the pattern. The elaborate dance of the fingertips was being enacted again and again, identical each time.

And now she could see something odd. Where the fingers had drawn invisible lines in the air, the darkness seemed to be lighter, *thinner* somehow, as if a piece of cloth had been worn down by chafing, exposing the fibres beneath. With each successive trace, the lines grew more defined, growing stronger, the fabric of the night wearing thinner and thinner. She felt a heat in her breast, welling up from her gut, a feeling like fire accompanied by the sound of blood crashing around her ears as her body became hypersensitized.

Then, the final trace, and as the fingers that were

not hers passed over the two-dimensional shape that hung inexplicably in front of the door, a burning red light followed them, a deep arterial red that glowed like sullen coals as the lines she had drawn split open along their length like an unzipped gut, as if her fingertip was the knife. And there, for a moment, was the Ward in its entirety, hanging in the air, a horizontal double-slash overlaying three curving lines and a variety of small circles and dots, a complexity that stunned the mind briefly before fading away in a matter of seconds, seeming to sink into the darkness from which it had come.

There was a heavy click as the door unlocked itself.

How curious, she thought, before remembering that she was supposed to be quiet. Everything was a little fuzzy to her, and her memory was not so good at the moment. She seemed to surface into lucidity for a few seconds at a time, and then be submerged again, as if she was a rock on a beach and the tide was surging in and out over her. During one of these moments of clarity, she was struck by a thought that surprised even herself.

If not for that sedative, you would have no power over me.

At that, the old woman seemed to shrink in her mind, as if afraid of being struck, but a moment later, she had rallied and all was as it had been before. Alaizabel's voice had been strong then; now it was dull again, her edge blunted by the sedative.

She is in fear of me, Alaizabel thought blankly. *I am stronger than her.*

Then she was walking along the dark landing, the chill house raising goosepimples beneath her purple nightgown. She could sense that the old woman — Thatch, that was her name — was trying to be stealthy, but her aged bones robbed her of such fine control and she creaked along the wooden boards. It was yet only just past sunset; the boy and Cathaline would be asleep.

!!Oh, I'll deal with them, I'll deal with them!! shrilled the voice of Thatch inside Alaizabel's skull. *!!Their time will come, soon and shortly!!*

The stairs dipped down before her, set at right-angles to the landing, tight and steep. A faint illumination crept guiltily up the steps from below, where windows were letting in the glow of the gaslights outside. Shakily, she set foot on to them, and began to descend.

Thaniel's eyes opened, and he was instantly awake.

Sleeping in a chair was not a comfortable way to spend a day. His neck ached abominably on one side where it had been pulled taut by the weight of his head as it lolled on his shoulder, and he was embarrassed to find that a drool of saliva had run out from the corner of his mouth and wet his cheek. Wiping his face with his sleeve, he looked about the living room. The fire had long since died to ash, and darkness had returned to London once more. He stood, flexing his back, and reflected what a burden it was to be a gentleman, having to allow their guest to occupy his bed.

Alaizabel. The thought made his expression grave. There was much they all had to discuss tonight. She was in more trouble than they had first believed.

A creak on the stairs made him halt midway through tousling his hair back into shape. He looked warily at the closed doorway that led out into the hall where the stairs were. A sudden sense of déjà vu assaulted him; he had dreamed that sound, he remembered. That was what had awoken him. He had been dreaming of his father – saw him walking up a long stairway away from him. Thaniel had been unable to climb the first step to follow him. Though it looked only small, when he tried to get up it he found it was taller than a mountain. Then his father had stepped on a rotted plank, and the loud creak had jolted him awake.

His sleeping mind had incorporated the sound he heard into his dream. There really *was* someone on the stairs.

He had stepped to the door, and had his hand on the doorknob when he noticed something else. There were voices coming from beyond it.

Pausing, he listened. They were frustratingly hard to hear, and impossible to make out. It was a low murmuring that came to his ears, as of someone muttering to themselves; two or three voices, difficult to distinguish. Occasionally he caught half a word, which his imagination completed for him, and sometimes there was laughter, a hiccuping sound that began low and rose to a high pitch before cutting off. It sounded as if there were people in the hallway, talking and plotting in hushed tones. Underpinning them were susurrant hisses, loud stage-whispers that were nevertheless just too quiet to be made out.

Thaniel stepped away from the door. His coat was draped across a nearby chair, with his pistol laid atop it. Swiftly, he crossed the darkened room, his feet soundless on the stone floor, and retrieved the weapon. Glad now that he had slept fully clothed, he returned to the doorway and pressed himself to it. The muttering continued, rising and falling, and the laughter came again, bursting out of the quiet with such maniacal volume that he shied away from the wood in surprise. The sound could have been coming from directly next to his ear. It possessed a distressing quality, an edge of something not sane. The murmuring was unabated by the sudden mirth. He fancied he could hear his name spoken here and there, along with dark promises and half-heard suggestions of what they would do to him in his sleep.

The stairs creaked again, nearer the hallway now. Whoever was out there was coming down from upstairs.

Alaizabel, he thought, fearing suddenly that someone or some*thing* had been up there with her, and it spurred him to place his hand back on the doorknob and pull the door open, his pistol held straight-armed and ready to face what was beyond.

The hallway gaped, an aching empty twilight, only the fog-hazed gaslights that sifted through the windows providing him with sight. The muttering was louder now, though still unclear, and that terrible shrieking laugh came again. To his left was the front door, heavy and oaken. To his right were the stairs; he could only see the bottom three from where he stood. He stepped out, unwilling to give in to the fear that had seized him, and angled the muzzle of his weapon up the stairs.

Alaizabel was there, frozen, like a cat discovered by the glow of a lamp. Her eyes reflected the faint light strangely, two burning pinpricks of white in the centre of her shadowed face. She watched him as she might watch a predator, coiled as if to run. The muttering filled the hallway, but it was coming loudest from behind him, outside the front door.

He lowered his pistol. "Alaizabel?" It did not even occur to him to think how she had escaped her room.

Alaizabel seemed to hesitate, then she descended the rest of the stairs. She was making an attempt to walk upright, but he could see that she had adopted the same bent-backed and infirm posture of before. The hairs of his neck were raised, and icy spiders scampered down his back.

The mark, he thought, and he raised the pistol again. "Thatch?" he challenged.

Alaizabel hissed at him suddenly, her face turning into an ugly snarl of malice, and she sprang past him with an agility that took him off-guard, knocking his gun-hand aside as she did so. She was a blur of shadow as she passed him, grabbing for the handle of the front door, twisting the key in the lock and wrenching it open.

"*No!*" Thaniel cried, throwing his weight against the oak at the same moment as she tugged it open. For a fraction of a second, his eyes skated over the vision of the muttering thing that lurked beyond, and a screaming howl of unearthly malevolence blasted through the hallway like a hurricane, blowing his hair back from his face and overturning the vase and the telephone on a small table by the banister. Something vast and shapeless lunged at him, but the door slammed shut, torn out of Alaizabel's hands, and the maelstrom died as abruptly as it had begun, leaving only a thin, keening wail of thwarted hunger which faded into the distance, until all was silence once more.

Thaniel slumped against the door, his eyes screwed shut as if to deny the vision that he had seen, sparkling blotches crashing and blooming on the inside of his lids. His pistol was raised blindly towards where he guessed Alaizabel was, warding her away in case she should try to get past him. He could feel tears running in halting trails down his face, and the front of his brain burned, bludgeoned with the shock of the horror he had witnessed.

"Thaniel?" came her voice, and it was that of Alaizabel, not Thatch. It trembled, fragile and lost.

He opened his eyes, and she was kneeling before him, a metre or so to the left of where his pistol pointed, her face a picture of mingled fright and concern for him. He heard her gasp, and her fingers flew to her mouth.

"Your eyes. . ." she said.

He let his arm fall limply, his pistol hanging from his wrist. His eyes burned like the rest of his face.

"Thaniel, your eyes!" she repeated, suddenly grabbing him and pulling him to his feet.

"Do . . . do you remember? Do you remember anything?" he said weakly as she propelled him up the stairs towards the bathroom.

"Look!" she urged, with an edge of desperation to her voice, and he looked into the mirror she had steered him to. He could only gaze numbly at what he saw.

His eyes had almost no white left in them. They were so thickly veined with red that there was no space for it. Practically every capillary had burst.

From the inner corner of each eye ran channels of watery red, tears shot through with streaks of blood.

A doctor was called, on Cathaline's insistence, even though Thaniel declared that he was fine. He peered into Thaniel's eyes and advised them that they should wait until the morning to see if it improved. The capillaries had ruptured most severely, but they would heal fast; it was no more dangerous than a savage poke in the eye, which was cause for concern but not for panic. He should stay away from too-bright light and alcohol for a time.

"Wait till morning!" Thaniel repeated in disgust, after the doctor had gone. "By the morning, we shall be gone from here."

"Gone?" Alaizabel asked. "Gone where?"

"To the Crooked Lanes," said Cathaline. "We have a. . ." she hesitated, "*friend* there who may be able to help us."

Alaizabel was fiddling with the charm around her neck. It was once Thaniel's mother's, a beautiful flat spiral of gold filigree, spinning inward, with tiny jade stones set in the gaps between the filigree and a sapphire at its centre. She gasped when Cathaline gave it to her, protesting that she could not accept a gift like that, but Thaniel replied: "You will wear it, Miss Alaizabel, or we shall all end up dead."

"I want to know," she said suddenly. "You must tell me what is happening. I cannot abide being pushed around like a pawn without knowing why I am treated so."

Thaniel turned to Alaizabel, wondering if she could take any more shocks tonight. Her face, however, was a picture of determination. She wanted answers, any answers, for she could not bear the anchorless limbo that she had been in ever since she could remember.

"Very well," he said, and told her everything. About the mark and its purpose, about the spirit inside her, and about what she had said about the

Fraternity when Thatch had been speaking through her mouth.

"The Fraternity," she whispered. "I know that name, somehow."

"Nobody knows how much of what we hear is truth, how much rumour," Thaniel said. "Most people have never heard of them at all. The Fraternity is a league of men and women dedicated to helping their own. Lawyers, politicians, bankers, aristocrats, doctors, newspaper editors . . . it is said that they number in the thousands. The rich, the powerful. Men and women with influence."

"It's also known to just about every wych-hunter that there is a coven at their core," said Cathaline. "The heart of the Fraternity is a cult. Anyone who's tried to prove that has generally wound up in the Thames, however; but we know. It's our business to know."

"Why . . . but how is it that they are not stopped?" Alaizabel asked.

"Who would stop them?" Thaniel replied, rubbing his eyes. "Their doings are kept out of the press. They own judges, police commissioners, solicitors. They *are* the power in London, but most of London doesn't even believe they exist."

"And now they want me?" Alaizabel asked.

"They want what's inside you," said Thaniel, touching her arm gently.

Alaizabel's head dipped, and when she spoke next, it was soft and frail. "I do not understand any of this. What did I do, to find myself this way?"

"That is what we have to find out," said Thaniel.

"Then I put myself in your hands, Thaniel Fox," she said, "for I have no-one else to turn to."

The darkness sank into London, the night deepening and clotting, and the three of them felt the weight of their unseen enemy outside their door. They slept in shifts and waited for the dawn.

PART TWO:
STITCH-FACE

CHARITY STREET
THE GREEN TACK MURDERS   8

Priscena Weston was a God-fearing woman; but there was one thing she feared more than the Almighty at this moment, and he was somewhere in the alleys behind her.

The fog was back, filling up the streets as if it had never left, laying its clammy touch upon the stones. The moon, somewhere above, was hidden behind its own layer of cloud, and invisible. London was still tonight, waiting for the dawn, praying that the things that crept under cover of the mist would be gone by then. It was bitterly cold, for the temperature had dropped further towards the heart of winter; frost cracked its way inward from the edges of windows, and there was ice as clear as water where the moisture from the fog had gathered and frozen. The pubs and inns were empty now, and only the distant grind of a factory slit through the quiet.

Pris was used to the calm of silence. She had been almost entirely deaf since she was four, when her drunken father clapped his hands around her ears and perforated her eardrums. But there was no calm now for her. Though the streets were like a grave, there was noise inside her skull. Her blood roared at her from within her head; the hissy, muted rasp of her breath passing in and out was deep and savage;

her heart thumped a rapid, thunderous rhythm in her chest.

Somewhere behind her, Stitch-face was following.

For fifteen years he had stalked the people of London, prowling the areas on the northern banks of the Thames. For fifteen years he had been a threat that mothers used to make their children behave – "To bed now, or Stitch-face will get you!" Few of those threatened were wise enough to know that it was only women that Stitch-face killed, never men and never children. Some said he was half-wych, the offspring of Black Annis, who one night took a man in his bed as she was sucking his breath from his lips and left him lifeless, but herself heavy with seed. Certainly, if Stitch-face was only a man, then he had been diabolically clever at avoiding the attentions of the Peelers. A reign of terror that had lasted for a decade and a half, and still there was no clue to who he was except the few sightings from those who had survived his attentions, which had gained him his nickname.

And now she herself had seen that dread mask, the gaping mouth in the patchwork of grey sackcloth, a death-gasp beneath a beautiful head of lady's hair, fine and brown with a straight fringe. He had been standing in the fog-choked alleyway between Charity Street and Shrew Lane. Arms crossed, a long coat buttoned around him, it was as if he had been waiting for her all night. And she had run, and though she could not hear his footsteps, she knew that he had followed. Of all the people in London, Stitch-face had chosen her tonight, and she was fleeing for her life.

The area around Charity Street was a lunacy of

tumbledown alleys, switchbacks and dead ends. A stray bomb from the Vernichtung had collapsed most of the structure, and the industrious residents had set about rebuilding it with no thought to what went where and how. The houses leaned in on each other, nudging the sky – when it could be seen at all – into a narrow strip between their roof gutters. Lights burned in a few of the windows, blurred smudges of warmth in the chill cloud that had settled over London.

She ran, her panic making her careless as she flurried through the fog. Every few dozen metres, she glanced over her shoulder at the blank face of the misted street. Once, she fancied that she saw a darting silhouette in the haze behind her, but then the greyness swallowed it up. Lamp-posts flashed past her, uncaring, heedless of her plight.

In her head, silence, but for the pounding of her internal workings. She was sealed off from the world outside, the fog dulling her eyes and her hearing long dead.

Something ran into the road in front of her, froze, and ran back to the shelter of the steps where it had come from. A cat, alarmed by this newcomer. She had barely time to notice it before she was suddenly falling, her right leg shooting uncontrollably out at an angle.

Ice, she thought, and then she smacked into the cobbles of the road and her vision exploded with white fireworks.

The pain was not enough to stop her. Whimpering, she pulled herself up, feeling her lip and jaw already beginning to swell. She'd been running down the road rather than the pavement because the cobbles provided better grip for her boots; but even that had not been good enough, this treacherous night.

Looking frantically over her shoulder, she saw Stitch-face standing there, his dark shadow just visible in the fog. He was waiting for her to keep running.

With a cry, she threw herself at the door of the nearest house, one with lights in its windows. "Help me!" she called, hammering on the door. "Help me, for the love of God! Stitch-face is here!" But though the words made sense to her, she had not heard her own voice since she was four, and the sounds she made were almost indecipherable. She shouted again, the sound muffled in her head, but she could not force the meaning of what she said past the clumsiness of her tongue.

Stitch-face began to walk towards her, approaching slowly, gaining definition with every step he took out of the mist. With a slurred noise of frustration, she ran to another house, pounding on that door too. Perhaps these people thought they were being pestered by a lunatic; perhaps they just did not want to involve themselves. Either way, they pulled the curtains and left the door securely bolted.

She shrieked in fear and looked back at Stitch-face, who was calmly walking towards her with the assurance of a cat toying with a mouse. Now she could see that ghastly death-mask again, framed in that beautiful long wig; and she could see the long, wide-bladed knife in his left hand, polished to a gleam.

She ran again, panicked prayers reciting themselves silently on her lips. Hadn't she been devout these past years? Hadn't she always been a good churchgoer? Why her? Why did he choose *her?* Even after she had been cursed with a chronic drunkard of a father, the man who took her hearing before finding his death at the bottom of a gin bottle; even after her mother had been taken by consumption; even then, her faith had never wavered. She'd had nobody to teach her – her parents were both atheists, worshipping the twin gods of alcohol and laudanum respectively – and yet despite everything, despite the fact she had more reason than most to rage against the hand that God had dealt her, she was an exemplary parishioner, a devout Catholic, and – she liked to think – a good-hearted woman.

Why was this happening to her?

For the next few minutes, she was focused only on escape, seeing nothing, hearing nothing, feeling nothing but that single desire. Twice more she fell, but she felt only numbness where bruises and scrapes should be. Her whimpering threw a rabid syncopation over the pounding pulse of her heart and the torrent of blood around her skull. She ran until her chest ached and her muscles seemed leaden, once stopping to hammer on a door and again receiving no answer. The city did not involve itself in the affairs of the doomed. The folk of the Charity Street area sat by their fires and stoves, their doors and windows a barrier to what was going on outside, and listened with hardened hearts to Pris's barely coherent screams. To open their doors was to invite trouble, they said to themselves. And besides, who knew what kind of wych-kin made such awful sounds?

Finally, exhausted, she slowed her run to a stagger, and leaned against a lamp-post while she fought for breath, her stomach cramping. Tears streaking her face, she looked behind her into the foggy maw of the alleyway, and with a soft moan she saw that *he* was there, Stitch-face, still walking as if he had never even had to run to catch her.

You can't escape me, his stride said. *Come and meet my knife.*

"Help me," she whispered, and this time it was addressed to no-one, for she knew she was beyond help now.

But at those words, a surge of new energy seemed to flow into her, enough for her to get up and stumble away again, not knowing where she was going or why, only that she could not give up.

She turned the corner into a narrow alley, one that ran into the back yard of a shop. A trellis gate hung open there, separating the end of the alley from the yard. So tired was she that she failed to see the pair of shadows that slunk after her, detaching themselves from the darkness of a hole in the wall and following. Deaf, she did not hear the low growl that they made. In fact, the first she knew of the wolves was when she felt herself shoved from behind by a great weight, and she toppled forward with a cry, cracking her head on the metal jamb of the gate and finding nothing but blackness thereafter.

A new morning, and Detective Ezrael Carver found himself adding another pin to the great map of London that hung on the wall of the office he shared with Inspector Maycraft at the Cheapside Police Headquarters. A small paper flag with the number seventy-six carefully inked on it was speared by the same pin, which he plunged into a spot just southeast of Charity Street in Holborn.

He sat down at his teak desk and rested his cheek on his fist, looking at the map. The slatted windows let in the bright sunlight, turning drifting motes of dust into miniature suns as they meandered through the air. The office was neither tidy nor cluttered but a point in-between. Made predominantly of wood panelling, it had the feel of a University professor's study or a librarian's hideaway rather than a place for police work. A stout door separated Carver from the rest of the building, where the endless in-and-out of criminals, bereaved citizens, alarms and reports and emergencies went on. Here, in his office, it was peaceful, and he got up and walked over to the window, where he peered out of the slats at the crowded skyline of London, basking lazily in the brightness – if not the heat – of the day. His eye roamed over the spires and domes of the tall churches, the grim brows of the factories and the tumbledown workhouses, the narrow chimneys that thrust up towards the sky, and he was struck by a sudden feeling of affection for this city and its people. It was a warm glow, a strange love for the place that had cradled him his whole life. Standing there, looking out, he felt that he was on the verge of something profound, a new inner revelation that might change his character, make him a wiser man.

The moment, if ever it would have come, was destroyed by Maycraft as he twisted the doorknob noisily and strode in, his eyes on a sheaf of reports in his hand.

"Morning, Carver," he said, without looking up.

"Inspector Maycraft," he replied politely, smothering his annoyance at being interrupted before this moment of insight.

Maycraft put down the papers and looked over at him. Carver was nearing the end of his twenties, neither tall nor short, with broader shoulders than was average. His black hair was slicked back, and a thick black moustache covered his upper lip. He wore a double-breasted black waistcoat over a brown shirt, and his neatly pressed trousers were a darker brown still. As always, he was turned out well. He was a stickler for tidiness. The mess of their shared office was almost entirely Maycraft's fault, but Carver was too well-mannered to reproach him about it.

"Number seventy-six," Maycraft said. "It's about time we did something about this Stitch-face fellow."

Carver smiled, as he was expected to do. It was a long-running joke between them; as if they hadn't spent the last two years *trying* to do something about it. The joke had long worn stale, but Maycraft still cranked it out for the sake of tradition on the appropriate occasions.

"How is she?" he asked.

"She's damned lucky to be alive," Maycraft replied, slumping down in his chair. "She keeps on blathering about how God saved her."

"God saved her by having her savaged by wolves?" Carver asked, raising an eyebrow as he himself sat down.

Maycraft had drawn a fat cigar from his pocket and was clipping the end off with a silver cutter. The conversation paused while he lit it and breathed out a cloud of aromatic smoke. "She's still alive, though. You can see her point. She's only the fifth woman to get away from him in fifteen years, as far as we know."

"I'd hardly call being mauled by wild animals an acceptable mode of escape," Carver said dryly.

Maycraft tipped the nub of his cigar at the younger man. "The Lord moves in mysterious ways," he replied.

"Yes, well, evidently not as mysterious as our good Mister Stitch-face," Carver said, tapping his knuckle on the desk.

"She's going to be well soon enough," Maycraft said. "A few scratches, a good scar here and there. I've questioned the man who scared off the wolves. He's a trapper, you know; travels out to the Yukon to shoot bears for their pelts. Runs that furriers' shop when he's back in London. His family look after it the rest of the time." There was a pause, during which time Maycraft sucked on his cigar and looked at Carver with narrow, suspicious eyes. "Odd that of all the people she should stumble into, it happened to be a man who is an expert in shooting wild animals."

Carver put his hands behind his head and leaned back. "You sound as if you're beginning to believe that she was saved by the divine," he said, with a wry twist to his voice.

"Hmmph," Maycraft rumbled, not committing himself either way.

"Well, metaphysics aside, we do at least have one advantage now, thanks to Miss Weston," Carver continued, getting up and walking to the map on the wall. "Stitch-face always attacks in the same area again, if he fails the first time. Or, at least he has on the previous four occasions that he's missed a kill." He pointed at where a few odd pins nuzzled together in pairs. "If he follows the pattern he has set, his next attack should be soon, and within half a mile or so of the original site."

Carver studied the map, his eyes intent. In amid the little pins and their flags were seven green tacks, each one bearing a number like the others. These were scattered all over London, instead of staying clustered around one area like the pins.

"Detective?" Maycraft prompted. "You're not still trying to work it out, are you?"

Carver wrinkled his nose. "I can't help it. There's a pattern there, I know it. Especially those damnable Green Tack murders."

The Green Tack murders were the biggest and most recent development in the hunt for Stitch-face. Carver himself had come up with the name, after he had started marking them on the map with green tacks to show that they were different from the others. It was a curiously innocuous name for something so grave, but then a little gallows humour was necessary these days if you wanted to keep your sanity.

They had begun a year ago now. Murders being committed far outside Stitch-face's territory – and he was *very* territorial in his killings – as far west as Hammersmith and as far east as Poplar, even one in the Old Quarter. They seemed to be Stitch-face's handiwork, all right; and he had something of a monopoly on serial killing in London at the moment, since the execution of Catfoot Joe. The bodies of the victims were found with their eyes, tongues and hearts removed, cut out with the precision of a surgeon; and they were arranged with their arms crossed over their bloodied chests and facing downwards, their eyeless faces staring into the road. But they were *not right*, because Stitch-face *never* killed outside his territory. Carver was convinced of that.

There was the popular theory that Stitch-face was a member of one of London's many underground cults, lent weight by the ceremonial manner in which he killed and laid out his victims. Carver didn't believe that. What passed for your average "cult" in London was just a few rich hee-haws getting their jollies with some black candles and a thrupenny book of wychcraft. Unless you believed all that rot about the Fraternity, of course. Well, he was sure no faceless organization pulled *his* strings.

He had spent hours staring at the green tacks on the map, trying to draw a shape from them. They seemed so deliberate, so even. The distance between the Kensington and Battersea murders was almost exactly half the distance between Kensington and Poplar, where another Green Tack murder had taken place. The four other murders were similarly mathematically planned. A shape was there, he could *sense* it; but it was no shape he'd ever seen, with no apparent symmetry, and so it was impossible to predict where the next murder might occur.

Maycraft stoutly insisted that the Green Tack murders were the work of Stitch-face. Though they were outside his usual pattern, Maycraft refused to believe that someone else was doing them. It was simply inconceivable that someone could get away with seven murders in less than twelve months without leaving a trace of evidence; even Stitch-face had been seen on several occasions, and that was in the early days when he averaged only three or four murders a year. Maycraft would not accept the possibility of another serial killer in London, and one more clever than Stitch-face.

Carver knew Maycraft was wrong. It was plain and

obvious to him that the Green Tack murders were not the work of Stitch-face. Which left two questions: why was Maycraft so eager to deny the evidence in front of him, and who *was* perpetrating the Green Tack murders?

THE CROOKED LANES
GRINDLE
CARVER MAKES A DISCOVERY
9

T he city of London has a secret heart. It is a clotted thing of crumbling stone and dripping gutters, and it appears on no map or guide. Through its diseased alleys the vermin run, knowing that in this one place they are no better or worse than the people they live alongside. Here, no law exists, no Peelers walk, no cabs come. Even the airships that plough back and forth from the Finsbury Park airstrip seem to avoid flying too close. And it was here, to the Crooked Lanes, that Thaniel, Cathaline and Alaizabel went; for whatever the dangers it held within itself, once you were inside the Crooked Lanes, you had as good as vanished off the face of the planet.

It was midday as they approached Camden, the streets twining under the harsh, dazzling November sun, whose light relentlessly revealed every imperfection in the skin of this part of the city, until it was almost too ugly to look at. They were still at the edges of the Crooked Lanes here; there was evidence of recent bill posters stuck to ragged stone walls by an intrepid urchin, advertising a great Russian circus's arrival in London or a new play opened on Piccadilly. Brown paper grocery bags shuffled around in the faint breeze, bumping against rat corpses that had floated into the storm gutters and jammed there, stiff and lifeless. Smoke-blackened windows gazed grimily down at them, a mute reminder of the factories not far away that choked out soot and carbon all day long. It was possible to see the dark pollution drifting up from the chimneys in the near distance, feathering into the clear sky; when the wind was right, it was possible to breathe it too.

A change had come over Alaizabel since the events of last night. Somehow, the realization that there was something inside her, sharing her mind, had renewed her natural strength of will. She came to see that it was the *not knowing* that was the true reason for her distress. The presence of Thatch in her mind, curiously, was not half so threatening now that she had identified her enemy. She remembered that Thatch had been afraid of her during that trance-like sleep-walk. Given time to think, she had worked out what had happened last night, and explained it to Thaniel as they made ready to leave Crofter's Gate at dawn.

"Things are becoming clearer now, Thaniel," she said, as they sat cross-legged on the floor together in amid the debris of his efforts to take only the barest essentials. "I think I am starting to understand."

"Do you remember anything yet?" Thaniel had prompted, and the genuine concern on his face had sent a warm runnel of happiness through her chest.

"Just . . . odd images," she said. "But I *know* things . . . if you see what I mean. I do not know how; I mean, I do not remember *why* I know them. But . . . I think I am *realizing*, not remembering. You understand?"

"I think so," said Thaniel, his pale eyes searching hers. "Then what do you think is happening?"

"The night before last," she said. "Cathaline put those things . . . those Wards on my room." She put her hand on his arm with a guilty smile. "On *your* room, I mean."

Thaniel was aware of little else but the contact between them; however, he managed to reply with something gentlemanly which he could not later remember. She removed her hand, breaking the touch, and continued.

"Anyway, that night, the thing that came after me—"

"The Draug," Thaniel interrupted automatically.

"Is that what it was?" she shivered. "I think I should rather not know anything else about it. But it was turned away by Cathaline's Wards. I often wondered why Thatch did not just make me get up and walk out to the corridor, where that thing was. After all, she did it the next night. Then it struck me."

"You were not sedated the first time," Thaniel said, catching on.

"Yes," she replied, clapping her hands. "And that was why Thatch could do what she did. You see, what you said about the ceremony . . . well, if the spirit and the host are battling, one has to be stronger."

"And you believe you are stronger? She could only exert her power when you were sedated?"

"Yes!" she said again.

"I wonder if the presence of Thatch accounts for your . . . for the state you were in when I met you in the Old Quarter," Thaniel mused. "It seems to make sense." He looked up at Alaizabel. "But I should be interested to know how you deduced all that."

"So would I," Alaizabel admitted.

There was a pause for a time. "We *will* find your parents, you know," Thaniel said finally. "We will get to the bottom of this."

Alaizabel had not replied.

Now they had passed further into the Crooked Lanes, and Alaizabel began to see why the name had stuck to them. The houses crowded in closer, and the alleys began to jink left and right in an apparently random fashion. Tiny jetties ran between empty warehouses. Occasionally, a heap of rubble that had still not been cleared up from the Vernichtung would block their path and they had to backtrack. It seemed that there were very few people on the streets here; they saw only a few crippled beggars, who did not even ask them for a coin but shuffled on by. Distantly, they could hear urchins laughing and fighting, but other than that it seemed eerily deserted.

"What are we looking for?" Alaizabel asked.

"We would not find it if we tried," said Thaniel in reply. "We are waiting for them to notice us."

"Why is it so quiet here?" Alaizabel pitched the question to nobody in particular.

"The beggars go into the city during the day," Thaniel answered her, rubbing one bloodshot eye with a knuckle. They were healing fast, thankfully, and did not pain him any more. "Those who are left behind are good at not being seen. Wait till nightfall; then you will see what the Crooked Lanes are all about."

"You do know what you're doing, don't you?" Cathaline asked cheerily.

Thaniel shot her a bearish look, then spoke to

Alaizabel. "I have a friend here. His name is Crott; he is one of the four Beggar Lords that run this place. He can help us. We need to hide, and we need to get to the bottom of this mystery. Something dark is going on here. The Fraternity are up to something. They managed to summon the spirit that you carry inside you, and they also managed to raise a Draug and something else — only the Almighty knows what — in an attempt to either kill you or get you back."

Alaizabel blinked, not really knowing how to respond. "What are the Beggar Lords?" she asked instead.

"To be a beggar in London is as much a trade as being a thief or a carpenter," he said. "The carpenters have their union, the thieves have their guild; the beggars have the Beggar Lords. I think that there used to be only one Beggar Lord in the past, but now the beggars have split into four gangs, each under a different leader. The gangs help out their members in return for a percentage of the profits, and they see that anyone begging who is not a member of a gang is quickly seen off." He shrugged after a moment. "I really don't know all that much about it."

"And what about Crott? Who's he?" she asked.

"He and my father knew each other," Thaniel replied. "Crott's wife was afflicted with an Incubus. It is a wych-kin that hangs on to a person's back. You cannot see it or touch it, but it is there, weighing you down, making your heart sick and your soul heavy and your body tired. Slowly, you lose the will to live, and one day you sink to your knees and never get up again."

Alaizabel's eyes were sad as she looked back at him. "That's horrible," she said quietly.

"Fortunately, they are easily removed; the trouble is, nobody knows they are there. Crott's wife had seen every kind of doctor before he took her to my father in desperation. He removed it, but it was too late. She died, but Crott was always grateful to my father for making her last days happy ones. They had remained friends until my father died. I am hoping Crott remembers me fondly."

It was just past three o'clock by Thaniel's pocket watch — and the tolling of a distant church bell — when the Crooked Lanes finally acknowledged them. They were tired, having not slept enough, and they had been walking about in random directions for hours. It was almost a relief when a pinch-faced man wearing a tatty brown cloak approached them in a narrow alley, and suddenly said in a shrill voice:

"Are you lost?"

"Are you of Crott's gang?" Thaniel countered immediately.

"Hmm. You'll be wanting one of Crott's? Not mine; I'm Rickarack's man." The stranger looked them over like a magpie examining a potential treasure. "Wait here," he said suddenly, and hurried away around a corner.

They waited, as they had been told, none of them speaking, each wrapped up in anticipation. It was less than three minutes before a new arrival turned up. It was a bent old man, horribly scarred on one side of his face, as if he had long ago been mauled by some kind of wild animal. He wore a multitude of tatters and rags; his neck sagged and his bare forearms were covered in liver spots.

"They call me Grindle," he said, his voice low and

phlegmy. "What business do yer 'ave with Crott, strangers?"

"My name is Thaniel Fox, wych-hunter," came his reply. "And this is Cathaline Bennett, a wych-hunter also. The lady is Alaizabel Cray."

"Aye, I've 'eard of your father, Master Fox," Grindle said, squinting at him. "No wych-kin in the Crooked Lanes."

"We're not here for wych-kin. I seek an audience with Lord Crott," Thaniel replied.

"Do yer now?" said the old man, with a rancid smile. "Do yer indeed?"

It had been a long day for Ezrael Carver. There was no particular reason for it, no special circumstance that made this day any more difficult than the rest. He was just tired, and his patience was thin, and so he had to work hard to keep up a veneer of unflappable politeness as he trawled around Cheapside Police Station looking for files that their hopelessly inept secretary had scattered around various cabinets.

He didn't like the bustle that filled the main body of the building. It seemed like every day there were more people crowding around the reception desk, or sitting on the hard pews in the waiting room. The city of London was going to pot, all right. It had been sliding gradually downhill ever since the Vernichtung. Ever since those blasted Prussians had bombed it, twenty-odd years ago. Ever since the wych-kin came.

The requisite papers finally found, he returned to his office and shut the door on the noise outside, noticing that Maycraft was not back yet from wherever he had gone. He sat down in his chair and put the papers on the desk before him.

Truth be told, he quite liked Maycraft. He'd had plenty of run-ins with the older man in his time, when he worked in Holborn; but when he'd heard that he'd been given the commission by Parliament to work on putting an end to Stitch-face, he'd had no qualms about accepting, even though it meant working with a man whom he'd only ever antagonized in the past. Now, after two years of collaboration, they knew each other well, and accepted each other's foibles. And he certainly enjoyed the privileged position that he held, being able to pick and choose his departmental assignments around his work on the Stitch-face problem.

Well, he thought. *All that aside, what am I to do about these Green Tack murders?*

He tapped a pencil against his teeth, gazing into space, conscious of the light dimming towards another cold, dark and undoubtedly foggy evening. Inspiration was not readily forthcoming today, so to make himself feel useful he hit on the idea of calling Doctor Pyke up at Redford Acres to ask if he had had time to look over the documents they had given him. On Maycraft's suggestion, they had given him the details on the Green Tack murders for his professional opinion on whether the killer was indeed Stitch-face or, if not, then what kind of person could do those things. Carver had been against sharing information with those outside the police force, but Maycraft insisted that Pyke was trustworthy. In fact, it would have made more sense to wait for Maycraft to return and have him call Pyke, since the two of them were friends, but Carver did not want to wait.

Picking up the earpiece of the upright telephone, he suddenly realized that he had no number for Doctor Pyke. He asked the operator to connect him to Redford Acres, but she had no listing for it. He apologized and replaced the earpiece in the cradle.

How silly of me, he thought, and went over to Maycraft's desk, opening the drawer in which was the Inspector's address book. Maycraft would have the number. Opening it, he began to look. Maycraft's handwriting was shocking, and he had a habit of doodling on the edges of the notepaper that was most annoying and distracting to the eye. Additionally, he had not put the numbers in alphabetical order, and when Carver finally did locate Doctor Pyke's address, there was a small note beneath that said: *Telephone number: see Lucinda Watt, secretary.* It was while flicking through on a search for Miss Watt that he suddenly slowed the turning of the pages, a frown appearing on his face. He turned back two leaves and stared at the thing that had caught his eye.

Maycraft, not an imaginative man on the outside, was nevertheless extremely creative in his doodles. There were dragons, over there a sketch of a muffin-man (obviously drawn in a state of great hunger, as he was depicted as the Second Coming), and numerous Union Jacks. But there, in amid a clutter of other absent-minded scrawls, was a tiny shape. It looked something like a jagged seashell, or a heavily lashed eye. . . No, no, it was more like an odd malformed octopus or a seal or . . . he didn't really know. It was drawn within a circle, like a badge or a symbol. Ordinarily, it would not have attracted his attention, but for the vaguely unpleasant feeling he got from it; however, his quick brain had made a connection immediately upon seeing it.

He looked from the map on the wall to the symbol and back again. Then, drawing a small-scale map of London from his own drawer, he marked the spots where the Green Tack murders had taken place. And he joined them up, like a constellation, and drew a shape around them.

"By Heaven," he breathed, as he stared down at the map on his desk.

Stretched over London, with only a small section of its body left incomplete, was the tentacled thing in Maycraft's address book. The sites of the Green Tack murders formed the primary points of its shape; tips of tentacles, the top of what might be the head, and so on. He estimated that only two more points were needed to complete the shape, and he put dots where they would have to be.

A cloud passed before the sun, and the room dimmed.

"By Heaven," he said again. "Maycraft."

Lord Crott's feasting hall was huge, an immense stone room with tall, rough pillars that shouldered up to the great arches overhead and held them aloft. Everything was bare stone, made of massive blocks, and there seemed to be no real doors into the room; rather, it was almost completely open, with the peripheries yawning into blackness where no light shone.

Between the pillars, however, there was plenty of light, and sweltering heat. Metal troughs stood along the centre of the hall, filled with burning coals and topped with all manner of grill and spit, stringy steak and tough pork and chicken. Bubbling cauldrons — yes, cauldrons, even in this day and age! — bobbed with potatoes and vegetables. Cooks wandered around the perimeter of their domain, turning and tasting the food.

All around the lighted area were tables, at which sat men and women and children, the beggars of the Crooked Lanes. They were filthy and unkempt, most of them bearing some deformity or affliction, for it was common practice for poor parents to cripple a child so they could evoke sympathy in passers-by and gain coin from it. And yet, they were laughing and talking, exchanging bawdy humour or thumping each other playfully, and eating their fill at the tables, with jugs of wine to wash down the meat. The room was all noise and movement, the sound echoing up to the great roof and multiplying across the cavern, and merriment filled the air.

The man who Grindle pointed out as Lord Crott was sitting in no special place, at no specific table. He sat on no high chair or dais; he was feasting between a thickly muscled ogre of a man with a simple face that bespoke some brain deficiency, and a small boy who sat with his eyes closed and his long, dirty hair in knots and tangles all over his face. As they looked, he laughed heartily at some unseen joke and slapped the back of the ogre, who took it as his cue to emit a gormless, slow chuckle.

Grindle brought them over to where Crott was sitting, and he looked up as they neared. He was a lean man of perhaps forty years, and he would have been handsome were it not for the vicious sword-scar that crossed his cheek and made his lip curl unpleasantly, or for the deep smallpox pitting that hid beneath a thin, scratty beard. He looked little like a beggar, Thaniel thought; more like an outlaw of some kind, Robin Hood perhaps. He chastened himself for being fanciful.

But it was the boy next to him that dominated his attention. There was one detail that he had not been able to see from a distance, that was now overwhelmingly obvious. The boy was not sitting with his eyes closed out of choice. A twin line of dull brown dots linked with wire ran along just above and below his lashes. His eyes had been sewn shut.

"Thaniel Fox!" Crott exclaimed. "My, my, it's

been a time. You were half that height when I saw you last."

"Ezekien Crott," he replied, smiling. Crott stood and they shook hands heartily. "Still king of your castle, I see."

"Of course, of course," he said, then turned his attention to Grindle. "Some food for our guests, then." With a wave, he ushered away the people sitting opposite him, and they picked up their plates and left, so that there was now an empty bench on one side of the rough-cut table. "You must sit down," he said. "Ah, the enchanting Miss Bennett. It is a pleasure to have you at my table."

She nodded her head and smiled as she sat.

Grindle returned with a companion, and placed four plates of chicken, potatoes, gravy and cabbage down before them. It was only at that moment that they realized they were ravenous. Cathaline began eating hers immediately; the others waited for Crott to wave them permission to begin. Grindle sat down on the right of the boy with the sewn-up eyes.

"I am honoured to present my companions," Crott said. "Old Grindle you already know. Here to my right is Devil-boy Jack, an advisor of the highest calibre. And this mountain to my left is Armand. He's French, but otherwise a very fine fellow."

Armand made his slow *hur-hur-hur* again at the sound of his name, then picked up a piece of chicken in his fingers and began to chew it.

"I imagine you have something of a problem that I can help you with, Thaniel," said Crott, after a time. "Your father and I were always great friends; a service to his son is a service to him."

"I imagine I will be able to return the compliment," Thaniel replied. He was watching Devil-boy Jack uncomfortably.

"Tell me your troubles, then, and I will tell you mine," Crott said genially. "And we shall see what we shall see."

Thaniel told him then, leaving out occasional details here and there but being truthful in the main.

Crott leaned forward when Thaniel was done. The feasting had reached a freshly raucous pitch around them, but he seemed not to notice the background noise that almost drowned out their words.

"You seem to be in a dire predicament, my friends."

"I believe," Thaniel said, "that what we are involved with has much greater repercussions than we have yet seen. The Fraternity wants this girl, I'm convinced of that. It may be that the story behind her will affect us all."

"Thaniel Fox is right," said the Devil-boy, his voice a flayed, hoarse whisper. Everyone at the table shifted their attention to him, expecting him to elaborate, but he said nothing more. Crott did not even look at him, only tapped his index fingers together in front of his face.

"You need me to shelter you all," Crott said slowly. "You need me to shelter *her*, when things will come looking for her. And you want me to find out what I can about her past, and about what she is involved in now. Am I correct?"

"You are," said Thaniel.

"You ask a lot," he said.

"I know," Thaniel replied.

There were a few tense moments, and then Crott

clapped his hands. Armand clapped as well, aping him, and laughed his feeble-minded laugh. "Anyway, enough of your problems," he said. "I think we should discuss exactly what you can do for me."

"Things are dark, here in the Crooked Lanes," Jack said unexpectedly. Crott subsided almost immediately, deferring to the young, blind scrag. "I see a pestilence in the stones of our cellars, and the sewers are fouled by something unnatural. We are surrounded by portents of evil." He turned his sightless face to Alaizabel. "Do you not feel the city's death throes? We are on the brink of an unhallowed age. The aged spirit inside you is the key, Alaizabel Cray. She will bring about the darkness."

"Who is she?" Alaizabel asked.

"Her name you know," the Devil-boy replied. "Her purpose—"

"Will be revealed to you in time," said Crott, interrupting. "After you have done a small favour for me."

Thaniel's face was stern and blank. "What would you have us do?"

Crott chewed on a cold, greasy chicken thigh. "We have an unwelcome guest in our sewers," he said round a mouthful of muscle. "Get rid of it."

Thaniel nodded. "Of course," he replied, but any further comment was forgotten in the wake of the scream that came from the far side of the feasting hall. The beggars were on their feet in a flash, none quicker than Crott and few slower than Armand. The sound came from the darkness outside the pillars that surrounded the feasting area. Torches were brought, and by the time Crott arrived at the source of the disturbance, a circle had already formed around it. They made way for him and his guests, and in moments they stood looking upon the thing that lay at the edge of the vast feasting hall.

Five black rats, each the size of a small dog, lay dead. Their vicious incisors showed over cold lips and their thick tails were entwined, woven in and out of each other in a complex tangle, forming a hub around which the bodies of the rats were loosely scattered.

"What is it?" Alaizabel asked, noting how the beggars were gazing fearfully at the conjoined creatures.

"A Rat King," Cathaline replied.

"It is a portent of evil," Devil-boy Jack said in his scratched, hoarse voice. "The signs are unmistakable. A catastrophe is approaching. The darkness awaits."

THE STRANGE DEATH OF ALISTA WHITE
A CARRIAGE AT REDFORD ACRES

11

The great Gothic arch of St Pancras train station loomed out of the rain-mist, spectral in the faint moonlight. There was no fog tonight; the torrential downpour had torn it to tatters and it had retreated to the hollows, lurking in thin shreds around cold graveyards and derelict wasteground. Few people trod the streets, for the rain was enough to chap the cheeks with its fury, and those who did were surrounded by a private haze of moisture as the droplets exploded over every centimetre of them.

But for some, the necessity of travel was great enough to force them to brave the elements, and cabs still rattled back and forth through the deluge. For an unfortunate few, however, there was both the necessity of travel and the lack of wealth. Alista White was a woman with three children to support, no husband, and a good heart which would not allow her to condemn them to the workhouses. She made enough money at her weaving to eke her way through a tough, leathery life, but not enough so that she could frivolously afford a cab when Shanks's pony would do just as well. So she walked on, unaware that tonight there was something stalking her that would take her life before the dawn rose again.

A carriage creaked slowly through the downpour, forging through the sheets of rain, pulled by a black stallion and a white mare. Its hunched driver wore a top hat, with the collar of his voluminous greatcoat turned up, so that only a narrow band of shadow was left for his eyes, and nothing could be seen of his face.

Insidiously, the dark carriage moved through the streets around St Pancras, heading to a destination known only to its driver, an appointed time and an appointed place. Gradually, it was swallowed up by the rain, until it had passed from view and was gone.

The onslaught slashed down, the walls crawling with rivulets that shifted their routes restlessly back and forth down the rough stone. The kerbs had become river banks, and the street-gutters gaping caves that drank them in greedily. Spuming water-falls careered off slanted roofs, plummeting down to burst on the ground below. Under the feeble protection of her black umbrella, Alista continued on her way, hurrying to Doctor Roach's house. Of course he wouldn't appreciate being awoken at this late hour – it was half past one in the morning, she guessed – but her boy Jip was down with the shakes and the chills and the fever, and she'd seen what had happened to his best friend Tomas when *he'd* had the same thing a week ago. She'd seen those horrible red cracks appearing all over him, as if he had been shattered like a dropped vase and the blood beneath was welling up a millimetre beneath the skin. She'd seen it on the noses and cheeks of old drunkards many time; burst veins from a lifetime of alcohol. But this was *all over*, and now Tomas was lying somewhere, in a Poor Pit no doubt, with maybe fourteen others who couldn't afford a proper burial. And her Jip had it now. Crimson Fever.

She pulled her cloak tighter around her and bent her bonneted head down into the driving rain. It was a walk of over three kilometres, but the life of her son was at stake, and she thought nothing of it. She was even gratified to notice that the rain was slackening. And then, with eerie suddenness, it stopped, the curtain of rain slipping from its rail and collapsing to the ground, leaving only the persistent, chiming trickle and splatter of the water running through the drowned streets. Without the racket of the deluge, the streets seemed preternaturally quiet; and the moon emerged fully to paint everything in shades of steel.

Yet there was a creeping sense of dread in Alista's breast, and it began to gather slowly as she tramped along the wet pavement. Something was wrong, something . . . but she couldn't place her finger on it. A frown settled on her frumpish, weather-beaten face as she tried hard to think what it might be. She had never been very bright or educated, and she was frankly in awe of those who were; so she blamed her own slow wits for failing her, and was becoming increasingly frustrated when suddenly it struck her.

She stopped in the light of a dripping lamp-post. Yes, she heard it. She began walking again, listening hard. It was still there. Could it be a trick? An echo? Perhaps, but something told her that it was not. A chill was worming into her marrow.

For every two steps she took, she heard *three* footsteps.

She stopped again, looking behind her. Once more, the third footstep succeeded her two, a quick noise as if someone had been following her and had been caught out by her sudden halt. Like someone was trying to walk at the same rhythm as her, and failing. There was nobody on the street.

She watched for a time, but only the splashing of the run-off water came to her ears, and nothing crossed her gaze.

Wasn't there something, something she heard? About this? Why did it remind her of something? Ah, curse her muddled head. No time now, anyway. She had to get to Doctor Roach.

She set off again, but the sound was still there: *step, step(step), step, step(step)*. Was it something flapping about her right ankle? Or the tail on her coat? Experimentally, she tried grabbing and holding different parts of her clothing as she walked, so that she was sometimes comically holding one edge of her skirt as she went, sometimes her boot. After a time, she gave up. If there was anything flapping about her person and making that tapping sound, it would not be silenced by her grip.

Another glance over her shoulder at the long, well-lit street she walked along, and once more there was nothing there. There was something nagging at her, an old rhyme Tomas's mother had told her once, harrying her insistently, but in amid the chill of her strange, creeping fear and her concern for Jip, she could not recall it. With a snort, she turned back and continued on. But the fear and the nagging would not go away, and indeed increased, and there was something she ought to remember, but she could not for the life of her think what. And that damned footstep was *still* there, seeming louder now, almost as if someone was walking right behind her.

She could not resist a third look over her shoulder, and it was her last.

Lucinda Watt was a severe-looking woman, bird-like in her movements, pecking at her stenograph with her fingers or scratching with a pen at some paper while her head bobbed about like a sparrow's in an attempt to see what she was writing. She was the receptionist, secretary and personal assistant to the head doctor at Redford Acres, and she expected to be treated with the respect and dignity that she felt her position afforded her.

Redford Acres was an unpleasant place to be after dark, but at least one night in each week Doctor Pyke would require her services, and usually more. She was handsomely paid, and dedicated, and had little else in her life to distract her but her small flat in Islington and her two cats, both called Cat – her imagination was as limited as her flair for fashion. During these night vigils she would accompany the Doctor on his rounds, as he walked from one dingy cell to another in the lower vaults, making observations on the patients' nocturnal activities in a low, dry voice as the screams and laughter and gibbering echoed up and down the dank and mouldy stone walls. Mad eyes glared out from tiny windows in the steel doors, sometimes whispering obscenities which Miss Watt would not have wished upon the ears of the most common street whore. The Doctor seemed not in the least perturbed by the insanity that surrounded him, but Miss Watt had to firm her chin and quell the horror that crawled from the semi-lit darkness of the vaults to nibble and gnaw at her.

The rain had briefly stilled while she was making

ready to leave, but it had only been pausing for breath, and with a bellow of thunder it unleashed its full might upon the capital. Miss Watt had, in her meticulous way, a spare umbrella in a cupboard beneath her desk in case she should be caught out like this. A flash of lightning stunned the foyer into a white bas-relief as she emerged from her desk with the black umbrella in her hand. Gazing out at the rain, she considered it a sensible idea to call for a cab, but no sooner had she picked up the earpiece of the upright telephone than she heard the creaking of wheels outside. Puzzled, she opened the great front doors of Redwood Acres, and there, just beyond the porch, was a dark carriage pulled by a black stallion and a white mare.

The driver, hunched up against the elements and wearing a top hat and high collar to protect his face, raised a hand as she emerged.

"Miss Lucinda Watt?" he called over the chatter of the rain.

"I am she," came the reply.

"Carriage for you, madam."

"I ordered no carriage," she said, peeking into the darkness on either side of the lighted porch. A yelping shriek from one of the inmates on the upper storeys was accentuated by a fresh flash of lightning to the south.

"I believe it was called by a Doctor Pyke," he said. "Am I mistaken?"

Miss Watt glanced back at the stairs that led to the Doctor's office, where he was compiling reports at this very moment. It was certainly out of character for him to be so thoughtful, but he was capable of such things from time to time. "No, you are not mistaken," she said, opening her umbrella for the short few metres between the lip of the porch and the carriage's door, which the driver now reached down and opened for her.

"Bad luck to open an umbrella inside, madam," the driver offered, for Miss Watt had not yet stepped on to the porch, but was pulling open the front door fully with her free hand.

"Pish posh," she replied, closing the door. "I don't believe in such superstitious nonsense."

The driver's hidden eyes followed her all the way to the door, where she got inside and folded her umbrella as she drew it in after her, like a black flower retreating into its bud.

Inside, the carriage was cold but blessedly dry, and she settled back into the comfortable seat as the driver urged the horses into action. The Doctor would have given him a destination, so she had only to relax. It had truly been a beastly night, and this carriage was a stroke of good fortune. She settled in, listening to the roaring storm outside as it gathered in strength, and was thankful that she was in here and not out there.

It was only as the carriage began to slow, creaking to a halt, and she knew they could not possibly have gone even half the distance to Islington, that she began to feel the first inklings of trepidation.

"I say, driver," she called, opening the carriage door. She was immediately struck by the sense of space around her, unfamiliar to one used to the narrow streets and lanes of London. It was some kind of heath they were on, or a park, but the obscuring rain made it hellishly difficult to see to the edge of wherever it was. There was only the path they rode on, and the endless grass, and a few ghostly trees.

"I say!" she repeated. "Why have you stopped?"

There was only silence as her reply.

She called once again, and received no answer a third time, before deciding to open her umbrella and step out into the rain. Part of it was a desire to give this so-called driver a piece of her mind, another was fearful curiosity as to what was occurring.

"Should this be some kind of joke," she said sharply, as she got out, "I can assure you that you will not be employed much longer."

She walked around to the driver's bench. It was empty.

For a few moments, she did not know what to do. She was alone, in the midst of this great expanse, surrounded by the dashing rain that was already soaking into the hem of her dress. She cast a few quick glances about herself, her neck turning left and right with the speed of a starling, and then took a short step backwards. The horses stamped and snorted restlessly, shaking their manes in a shower of moisture.

"Driver?" she called.

Nothing. She stood, indecisive, for a few moments. She did not know London well enough to guess where she was, and she could not see far enough to discern any kind of exit or direction. Distantly, she heard the drone of an airship as it ploughed through the night, no doubt heading for a safe port from the storm.

Profoundly disturbed, she decided to climb back into the carriage and wait for help or for the driver's return. Walking on a night like this would be inviting pneumonia.

Back inside, she shook off her umbrella, cursing roundly at the carriage driver. She could be stuck out here all night, in this foul rainstorm. What had the man been thinking? What had—

Her eye fell on what was lying on the opposite bench of the carriage, something that had not been there before. It was a piece of paper, with a crude sketch drawn on it, of a many-tentacled thing within a circle. Reaching over, she touched it reverently with her fingertips, as if to see if it was solid.

"*Chackh'morg*," she said to herself.

She turned sharply as the door of the carriage opened, and threw herself back in her seat with a thin cry of terror. For it was he, Stitch-face, the ghoulish effigy of a sewn-up corpse gaping from beneath the wet strands of lady's hair that stuck to the grey sacking of his skin. A glistening knife was held in one hand, tiny droplets of water gliding along the blade.

She was paralysed as he closed the carriage door behind him and sat opposite her, picking the sketch up as he did so. Slowly, he leaned forward and scraped the tip of his knife along her trembling throat; with the other hand, he held the sketch up in front of her eyes.

"*Chackh'morg*," Stitch-face said, and having expected a hollow death-rattle to emit from that mouth, she was surprised that it sounded perfectly normal, though there was a chill edge to it that terrified her as much as the knife. He leaned further forward, until his mouth was so close to hers that it seemed he might kiss her.

"You know who it is that is killing in my name," he whispered huskily. "Won't you tell me, Lucinda Watt?"

It was approaching dusk of the following day when Thaniel and Cathaline found themselves in the company of the simple giant Armand and the elderly Grindle, descending down a rusty ladder from amid the rubble of a collapsed pumping station. They had slept through the night, exhausted after their flight from Crofter's Gate, and there had been no visitation this time. Alaizabel slept soundly, under the alternating watch of her companions. It appeared that the charm she had been given was working, at least for now.

Alaizabel they had left in the care of Crott, for there was no sense bringing her on a wych-hunt; she would only be in danger.

"Thaniel?"

He looked up. They stood in a dank antechamber, with a circular manhole above them through which the light from the pumping station spilled down the rungs of a rusty ladder and splayed across the bare stone room, illuminating a single archway that led to a downward slope.

The voice had been Cathaline's. "Pardon me?" he said.

"I asked if you had any ideas on what the wych-kin might be," she replied lightly. "Though evidently your thoughts were elsewhere."

"Sorry," he said. Armand said sorry too, in a thick, dull voice heavily slurred and tinted in French. Grindle poked him and told him to be quiet.

Thaniel raked his hair back and chewed his lower lip in contemplation for a moment, then looked back at Cathaline. "Well, from the description Crott gave us of those who had seen the thing and lived, and the necrotic state of those who did not; I would say it was a wight."

Cathaline smiled to herself.

"And how do we deal with wights?" she said.

"Is this a test?" he replied.

"You never stop learning, Thaniel," she grinned.

"And you never stop teaching, it seems," he replied. "Wights exist only in light; they cannot harm you in total darkness, but too much light destroys them. It takes a lot of light, however." He frowned. "Actually, I have never dealt with a wight. Do we drive it out into daylight? But how can we do that, if they do not come out till dusk?"

Cathaline rattled the heavy bag she was carrying. "We make our own daylight."

Crott had told them earlier that day about the sewers beneath the Crooked Lanes. What lay on the surface of the Crooked Lanes was only one-third of the whole; beneath the streets there was a labyrinth of old vaults, hideouts, and a network of sewers and half-finished tunnels for the underground trains. Each of the four gangs had their territory and held it jealously, for underground was where the real fortresses were. The Crooked Lanes were all but unassailable if the Peelers or any other force should for any reason decide they wanted to reclaim the streets. Underground, it was a warren, with dead-ends and sealed doors, hatchways and crawl-spaces, even traps. And like the wych-kin, the beggars could only be driven back, never defeated; they would always return in greater numbers. The begging trade was a prosperous one in these days of industry and wealth, as evinced by the feast they had witnessed, and they would not give up their niche easily.

But recently, there had been something in the sewers that had slipped past the talismans and superstitious artefacts traditionally used to keep wych-kin away. Thaniel suspected their talismans didn't really work, anyway; it was just that the Lanes were so far north from the river that the wych-kin had not reached there yet. Until now. For several beggars had gone missing on a certain stretch of sewer, and their bodies later found in a terrible state. Necrosis, the death of body tissue, came from the touch of a wight. Skin shrivelled and blackened, arteries seized and knotted, decay raced with rigor mortis to see who would gain the body first. It was truly a horrible sight, and for this reason wights were treated with extreme caution by wych-hunters. But if they wanted Crott's help, then they had to deal with it.

So Crott had sent his men to get whatever they needed, which was presumably what was in the bulging bag that Cathaline carried, and as dusk fell they had begun.

Grindle led them downward, to another antechamber lit by gaslight. This one was circular, with a man-hole in the centre from which protruded a crowbar that had been wedged underneath one of the handles.

"Light yer lamps, if you want to see," Grindle said.

"Be ready to turn them off the moment I say," Cathaline added.

"Eh?" Grindle replied, as he was slapping Armand on the shoulder and directing him to raise the manhole lid. "Turn them off? Yer must be mad; it's black as pitch down there. I'm not turnin' nothin' off with that *thing* runnin' around."

"Didn't you listen?" Cathaline said. "A wight is made of shadow; it can't hurt you in the dark, because shadow needs light to give it shape. If it comes for you, turn out your light."

Thaniel had already become distracted again, his mind restlessly returning to Alaizabel and prowling round her like a wary wolf.

The sewers beneath the Crooked Lanes dripped and stank and stewed in their own murk. The darkness down here was total; if not for the light from the gas lamps that they held aloft, they would be in a blackness so complete that they would be utterly blind. The sludgy water lapped unceasingly past them, its murmuring a constant background to their footsteps and the scurry of rats. Thaniel found himself thinking back to the Rat King that they had found, and he shivered. There had been numerous sightings of the curious phenomenon that was the Rat King: four or more rats joined together at the tail so tightly that they could not be untangled even in death. It was thought that the combined minds of the conjoined animals formed the Rat King, and they communicated by whatever unpleasant way that rats did. The idea that the invisible scurrying all around them might be coordinated by a verminous intelligence made Thaniel uneasy.

"Could be anywhere up ahead now," Grindle said. "This is the edge of the cursed thing's patch, as far as I know."

"Here, then," said Cathaline. "We'll set it up here."

She placed the bag down on the stone walkway upon which they had been travelling, and unzipped it along its length. Inside, bundles of short sticks jostled with each other.

"'Ey, you're not usin' dynamite down here!" Grindle cried.

"Boom!" Armand said, and laughed at his own joke.

"Not dynamite," Cathaline said, pawing through the bag with a grin on her face. "Fireworks."

"Flash bombs?" Thaniel asked. "Lovely."

"We will set up a network of flash bombs here, and you will be responsible for firing them, Grindle," Cathaline said brusquely. "Thaniel and I will drive the wight into this spot, using the remainder of the bombs. Once it is here, the bright flashes from all sides should be enough to destroy it as effectively as daylight."

Cathaline began setting out the flash bombs in sequence along the sewer, trimming the fuses with expert precision. The others could not help without getting in her way, so they stood about in the light of their lamps and glanced nervously at the darkness beyond, or covered their noses against the awful stench that hung about the sewer tunnels. Grindle muttered to Armand, who listened vacantly. Thaniel blinked and rubbed his bloodshot eyes.

Grindle was getting noticeably more agitated now. "How much longer are yer goin' to be?" he grizzled at Cathaline, who ignored him. The elderly beggar held his lamp up and peered warily at the shifting shadows. That thrice-plagued wight could be anywhere; any one of those shadows might suddenly become something demonic.

It was with a sense of relief that the group heard Cathaline's announcement that she was ready. She handed out the remainder of the flash bombs, and showed Grindle the fuse that would ignite the first firework and thus begin the sequence. And so, leaving Grindle and Armand behind, the wych-hunters began to make their way into the dank throat of the wight's stalking-ground.

"The moment you see it, throw a firework," Cathaline advised. "Wights are slow, and your Wards will protect you for a few seconds, but it only takes a touch. . ."

Thaniel ran his finger along the jingling array of small metal charms that hung beneath his shirt. They were the wych-hunter's last line of defence; if everything else failed, you could only hope that one of the Warded charms about your person could fend off whatever wych-kin was coming at you. Sometimes they all worked, sometimes none. With the Cradlejack, because it was hosted in a flesh-and-blood body, they were ineffective. With a wight, who could say?

The spread of their lamplight seemed terribly small as they moved away from the small island of illumination in which Grindle and Armand waited. Soon, they had rounded a curve in the sewer, and then there was only the two of them, the shutters on their lanterns thrown open and their eyes darting about. The soft sliding of the water to their right seemed to increase in volume as the silence settled.

They had only the width of the slippery path between the moist wall and the foetid sludge of the sewers, and the stink that surrounded them was enough to keep Thaniel on the verge of retching.

Minutes passed, marked only by the sound of the water and their near-silent footsteps. Thaniel felt his nerves tautening like the strings on a cello, twining up to the point of snapping.

"Ssh," Cathaline hissed, and Thaniel froze.

For long moments, nothing. Then they heard it. A tiny rattling noise, as of teeth chattering very faintly. Cathaline held up her arm, pulling back her sleeve to reveal a bracelet of tiny coloured squares of bone threaded together by catgut. She pulled it off and held it up. Sure enough, the bones were jittering, clacking against each other.

"Have you ever seen that before?" she asked Thaniel.

"What Ward did you use on the bracelet?"

"Manderil's Paradigm."

"That is for detecting deildegasts," Thaniel said.

"And apparently it works on wights, too," she said with a grin. "Who would have thought it? Another piece of lore goes down in the name of Cathaline Bennett."

"Congratulate yourself later," Thaniel said, as the rattling got more pronounced. "It is on its way."

The darkness was congealing around them, and the hairs on their necks were standing on end. All wych-hunters – or at least those who had survived long enough in the profession – cultivated a wych-sense, recognizing the telltale signs of a presence that were too subtle for most to notice. Now that sense was shrieking at each of them, telling them that something invisible was near, something that would only show itself as it passed into the range of their light.

"There! Thaniel, to your left!" Cathaline cried, and she thrust the fuse of her flash bomb into the flame of her lamp at the same moment.

Thaniel whirled to face the blank, stony curve of the sewer wall, his eyes catching the faintest movement, and in the merest fraction of a second he registered the shadow reaching down the wall towards him, five hideously long fingers of darkness on either side. With a cry, he dropped and rolled aside, his lantern smashing as he landed and sending a flaming slick of oil racing over the edge of the path and on to the water. A moment later, the flash bomb ignited, and the tunnel was blasted with blinding white. Thaniel was looking up at the wight as the bomb erupted, and the image of the thing was burned on to his already beleaguered retinas.

For long seconds, he was blind. Something shrieked a terrible howl, the cry of the wight as it was caught in the light, but all he could see was the shape of his attacker, descending with its long body, hands with spindly fingers half the length of the entire shadow, reaching towards him with a spidery grip of decay.

"Thaniel!" called Cathaline, and he felt her arms underneath him, pulling him to his feet.

"I am all right," he insisted, blinking. The flash was receding to the edges of his vision now, and he could see again. "Which way did it go?"

"That way," Cathaline said. "Back towards Grindle."

"*Grindle!*" Thaniel cried, the volume of his voice making Cathaline flinch. "*It is coming your way!*"

He ran up the path, Cathaline following. There was no time to waste on recovery; Thaniel was not even quite clear on what had happened, but he guessed that the flash had made the wight flee. He stayed close to Cathaline, for she held the lamp that was all between them and complete darkness – and perversely, safety from the wych-kin that they chased.

"*Grindle! Light the fuses!*" he shouted, but as they rounded the corner the answer came back as a strangled wail, a howl of utter horror as the wight fell on the elderly beggar. Thaniel felt his blood turn to ice in his veins as they came into sight of Grindle and Armand, and saw for the first time the wight in full.

It was a terrible, shifting, amorphous thing, stretching thin and breaking and reforming like liquid as it moved, a clot of darkness that bled along the walls and path of the sewer, darkening the lantern light. Each hand was fully the size of its narrow body, impossibly out of proportion, and it had no head to speak of, only a pair of smouldering dots that approximated eyes and were buried in what might be called its chest. Great long legs with sharp knees completed the mockery of a shape that it possessed, such as those stick-figures cast by humans at the end of the day, when the sun is low and the shadows lengthy.

The wych-kin was on Grindle, holding him, enwrapping him, seeming to go *through* him with its blade-like fingers. Thaniel averted his eyes to preserve his sanity, but the single second that his eyes had lingered on the unfortunate beggar was enough to shake him to his heart. Flesh crinkling and blackening, teeth coming loose and falling, Grindle *rotting* before them. . .

"Armand!" Cathaline cried, as the simple-minded giant got up from where he had tripped and fallen in fright some distance away, intending to throw off the horror that held his friend. "No, you idiot!"

Thaniel was fumbling with a flash bomb. He pulled Cathaline to a halt so that he could light the fuse on her lamp, and flung it down the path as far as he could, hoping to reach the dark thing that now dropped the husk of Grindle and turned on the giant. Cathaline raced past him, heading for the master fuse that would ignite the network of flash bombs. Thaniel's bomb skittered towards them, hit a kink in the stone path, and bounced into the sludgy sewer water, extinguished.

Cathaline had reached Grindle's body now, and she touched her lamp to the fuse of the flash-bomb chain that Grindle had been too slow to initiate. The wight, occupied with Armand's approach, ignored her as the short fuse began to fizz, and a second later the fireworks went off.

Thaniel and Cathaline had averted their eyes this time, but the light was so bright that they could see the traceries of red capillaries in their lids. The wight shrieked, a noise that sawed through the marrow of the wych-hunters and made them shudder, but it was caught in an illumination too intense to escape this time. With a fading wail, it was annihilated and as the flash faded, so did the wight.

Two lamps still burned; Cathaline's, and one that Armand had left on the floor when he went to aid his companion. As the dazzle faded to the gentle glow of the lamplight, casting its moist sheen across the rank sewer, a sound could be heard, a quiet sobbing.

Armand was kneeling next to the necrotic remains of Grindle, pressing his cheek next to the shrivelled skull of his dead friend and hitching up great sobs from his chest.

C rott's chambers nestled at the centre of the labyrinth that comprised the Beggar Lord's territory. The route to them was under dripping stone arches, up through basements and down through trapdoors, through tunnels and gates guarded by burly, unkempt sentries, and without a guide they would have been impossible to find. Here was the heart of his small empire, and the seat of his power, hidden where no other Beggar Lord might find it. There was scarcely the need to blindfold the wych-hunters as they were led into Crott's presence; they could not have found their way back if they had tried.

The chambers themselves were plush treasure troves, the stone walls draped in furs and finery, a monument to over-decoration. Crott seemed to have a fully fledged magpie instinct that led him to collect anything shiny and gaudy, and the four interlinked rooms that formed his home were so cluttered with cheap vases and ornaments that there was scarcely space to walk through them. The room where he sat now was lit by gas lamps, and contained an assortment of odd furniture sat around a low table, with a stuffed leopard snarling out from behind one arm of the settee and rugs tangling the feet and hanging along the walls. It was quite unlike any place Thaniel had ever seen, with the possible exception of Cathaline's attic.

There were five of them here now. Crott in his favourite chair of polished wood and dark-green cushions; Cathaline and Thaniel on a settee together; Alaizabel sitting in another chair of mismatched green; and Devil-boy Jack, standing. They were arranged in a loose circle around the table, on which sat decanters of wine and spirits. All of them held a glass full of rich red Chianti, and as Crott raised his glass in a toast they followed.

"To Grindle," he said. "A sad loss." With that, they all drank, and when the toast was over, they waited expectantly. Crott had summoned them all, directly after they had emerged from the sewers.

"Business, then," he said. "I believe it is time we had a meeting of the minds, my good friends. It seems that all of us are up against something. Indeed I don't wonder if London has not been up against something ever since the Vernichtung, and there's a sight too many secrets being kept around here. So I have brought us together to talk, to discuss . . . to *plan.*" He drank from his glass, and then leaned forward to his listeners. "Even I can see that something dark is afoot in London. The signs are all around us. And what is bad for London is bad for me and my men. I would like you to share with me what you know, and after that . . . I have arranged a meeting with a friend of mine who will be able to tell you all you need to know about Miss Cray's past and the whereabouts of her parents."

Alaizabel looked up.

"He will meet you at five o'clock tomorrow, in the

Green Angel inn, south of the river. In the meantime, you are my guests. Thaniel, you may accompany her. That is all. He's very nervous when it
comes to meeting new people. That's why he's still
alive."

And so it was that Thaniel and Alaizabel came to be
crossing the great sullen gush of the Thames, its
waters a putrid green-brown murk as it flowed
beneath the great old bridge that spanned it. The
day was bright and almost warm, and sailors rolled
up the sleeves of their shirts and stood on the decks
of their steamers as they laboured upriver towards
the docks. The gates of Battersea Bridge stood open,
as they always did during the day, the Peelers at
guard on either side, in their taut black uniforms.

Thaniel cast a critical eye over the defences, examining the double row of spiked railings that ran
across the midriff of the bridge. The last line of resistance between north London and the Old Quarter,
there was one on every span crossing the Thames.
The Peelers stood here every night with their swords
and pistols, minding the gates, but it was really a
pointless task now. The wolves were canny enough
not to try and cross the bridges, and wych-kin had
other ways. Thaniel suspected they were using the
Underground, travelling the tunnels beneath the
river. Ironic, really; everybody hailed the subter-
ranean trains as a masterpiece of city planning. Then
the wych-kin came. Nobody with any sense went
down into the Underground after sunset now. For
anyone but a wych-hunter it was literally suicide.

They passed over Battersea Bridge and into
Battersea. It was odd how the Old Quarter was still

a teeming bustle of life during the day, yet deserted at night. The residents of London refused to cede their territory completely, and the preposterously cheap rent in the infested streets south of the Thames meant that people swarmed there. Goods were cheaper, because the shopkeepers and market sellers had lower overheads to pay. There were less police; the Peelers — so named after their founder, Sir Robert Peel — staying mainly on the north side. The Old Quarter had become a haven for those who tiptoed on the thin end of the law. It was not a respectable area of London, and considerably more dangerous than the streets across the river — for muggers and cut-throats did not stick to the night hours like wych-kin did — but for those willing to take the risk, it was a place brimming with opportunity.

"Where did the wych-kin come from?" Alaizabel asked, as they headed towards Lambeth.

"What do you mean?" Thaniel replied, only half-listening as he jostled his way past an aggressive apple-seller.

"Well, they have always been here as long as I remember. But there must have been a time that they weren't. I'm sure I read about it somewhere."

They turned on to a quieter thoroughfare, between two high terraces of crumbling buildings, where only a few people hurried about and the odd juggler or muffin-man plied their trade.

"Nobody knows for sure," he said. "It was not long ago. Twenty years maybe."

"That is all?"

Thaniel nodded. "I do not even know how it began. Few people talk about it. Some dispute over naval territory with the Prussians, I believe. Things were looking like war, then. . ."

Alaizabel frowned briefly. "The Vernichtung."

It was a seldom-spoken word in Britain; nobody liked to be reminded of failure, and Thaniel was careful never to mention the Vernichtung around people he didn't know in London. In fact, he was a little surprised that he had spoken of it to Alaizabel, and he was relieved that she chose not to take offence.

It meant *destruction* in the language of their aggressors. The Prussian Empire was particularly strong at the time, fresh from having crushed France; they were full of swagger and strength. A minor dispute with the British – the only nearby Empire of comparable muscle – was escalated to a major incident. Historians suspected that the Prussian Chancellor was merely looking for an excuse to test his new technology, the secret pride of the country. Airships.

The first that the British public knew about them was when a fleet of the dark, silver shapes arrived one night over London, coming in along the estuary and fanning out over the capital. It was too dark to see them, but people woke and looked fearfully to the sky, seeking the source of the dull, sinister drone that surrounded them.

The bombs came afterward, crude bundles of explosives that blasted the city and shattered buildings. The noise was terrifying, sending people screaming into the streets or huddling paralysed in their beds. Never before had anything so destructive been witnessed by the folk of London, and to have it turned on them was enough to make them quail.

The bombing went on for two weeks before Parliament capitulated and allowed the Prussians to win their dispute. British pride had been crushed; they did not even dare declare war for fear of the airships that hovered above them. The airships returned to their home, but the scars never healed.

"That was when the wych-kin came?"

Thaniel rubbed the back of his neck. "That is what they say. Some people think they were imprisoned deep underground, and an explosion set them loose. Some say they are God's revenge for letting the Prussians bomb St Paul's Cathedral into rubble."

"But what do you think?"

"It does not matter where they came from," said Thaniel. "All that matters is how to get rid of them."

"I think it *does* matter," said Alaizabel. "You need to know the nature of your opponent if you want to defeat it."

"Be that as it may, you are correct; that was when the wych-kin came. At first, nobody believed they were there at all. Doctors said they were merely ghosts of the brain, things witnessed by bomb-shocked survivors of the Vernichtung – it was especially savage around the area of Camberwell, where little was left standing."

He talked to her as they followed the streets to the old inn where they were to meet Crott's acquaintance, telling her of how the wych-kin thrived in the broken streets of bomb-torn Camberwell, how they benefitted from Parliament's reluctance to believe they existed. The Prime Minister was more concerned with repairing bomb damage in the centre of the city; the less prosperous south side could wait. That was a mistake. In a year, Camberwell was called "the dead walk". In two, it was uninhabitable. A plague of rats struck the city then, bringing with them a cruel disease called trench fever, characterized by a drying of the skin on the face and hands so that it split into little gullies, at the bottom of which was raw pink flesh. The epidemic rampaged through London for the next eighteen months, until a particularly vicious winter killed it off, and the rats with it.

Scholars of wychlore today argued whether the rats were somehow connected to the wych-kin, or whether it was merely an unfortunate coincidence that they arrived at the same time that the wych-kin did. Maybe, if there had not been a city-wide epidemic to deal with, the wych-kin could have been contained. But Parliament had their hands full, and so the wych-kin multiplied and spread, moving subtly, unnoticed. By the time the trench fever had been brought under control, the wych-kin had permeated the greater portion of south London, and there were now too many to shift.

But it was not only London that suffered under the attentions of the wych-kin, though London was the first and the worst of all the cities. Manchester, Liverpool, Newcastle and Glasgow were now burdened with the same yoke, although they had the problem adequately under control. New York, Philadelphia and New Orleans already had their own thriving population of wych-hunters. Almost every country's capital had some kind of infestation. The Vernichtung might have marked the start of it, but the wych-kin had spread since then, growing where the population gathered thickest. The world's best scholars of wychcraft couldn't explain how it had happened. Why was it that they only appeared in the biggest cities? Were they being spread like a virus, or appearing spontaneously? Nobody could say.

It had been early superstition that had bestowed the name of wych-kin upon the things that plagued London. Demons, devils, ghosts, spirits . . . none knew what they were, but all agreed on one thing: they were kin to the wyches, those who conspired with the supernatural. It was a credit to the Age of Reason that new wych-hunts had not begun then, of the kind such as they had seen all across Europe in the previous centuries; but the British were too reserved now, too mannered to act on such foolishness. In their hearts, they needed wychcraft to account for the wych-kin, but they would never admit to such a thing.

Wych-kin, then. It was as good a name as any to place on the unnamable.

With the new horror came those who desired to exterminate, adopting the somewhat misleading title of wych-hunters. Not like the wych-hunters of old, who sought out scapegoats for disease and illness that had long been explained by science; these were a new breed, men and women who hunted the darkness that spread across London. Wych-hunters.

The inn that Thaniel and Alaizabel came to was a low, squat jumble of dark timbers with a stout wooden board hanging outside, swinging in the evening light. It was painted with the faded image of a winged lady wielding a sword, wearing a dress of lime. The Green Angel stood on the northern edge of Battersea, not far from the Thames, and it crouched down a side street where the shops and warehouses leaned in over the cracked cobbles, so close that they nearly shut out the sky. Alaizabel looked it over doubtfully, listening to the raised voices from within. Shadows lurched and swayed across latticed panes of smoky glass.

"The sun will be down soon," Thaniel said. "I mean to have you out of the Old Quarter by then. We shall not stay here long."

Alaizabel steeled herself. "Let us go inside," she said. "I must know." And yet, curiously, she was once again struck by her own lack of enthusiasm at the prospect of finding out about her parents.

The interior of the Green Angel was hot and dark and reeked of smoke and sweat. The people that drank and ate there were swarthy and unshaven, laughing through rotted teeth, their skin dark with dirt. Cold eyes fell on Alaizabel as she followed Thaniel inside, and she felt a threat from each of them; but she held herself tall, and did not shrink from their gazes. Thaniel led her without hesitation to a round table in a dim corner, where a squat, fat man chewed on a turkey leg. He drew out a chair for her to sit on, and then sat down himself. The fat man never looked up at them.

Alaizabel glanced uncertainly at Thaniel, but Thaniel simply waited. She looked back at the man at the table. His jowls were covered with a patchy map of bristly stubble, and one of his eyes was filmed with a milky cataract. He snorted as he ate, and turkey juice dripped down his chin on to his belly. Alaizabel had seen people as repulsive before, but she was sure that she had never been so close to one out of choice.

"You better not have been followed," the man grizzled suddenly, without looking up at them.

"We were not," Thaniel said calmly.

He tore another chunk from the turkey leg and cast his good eye at Alaizabel. "This her?" he asked around a mouthful of flesh.

"Alaizabel Cray, it is my pleasure to introduce Perris the Boar," Thaniel said. He knew this man by reputation.

"Boar like the pig," their host added.

"Really," Alaizabel said blandly.

"Oho! She thinks she's clever!" he said, with a nasty edge to his voice. "Think you're better than me, do you?" He jabbed his turkey leg at her. "You won't think so when I'm done."

"Crott does not pay you to give us cryptic hints," Thaniel said. "You have the information he asked for?"

"Indeed I do. Though why this fine lady couldn't tell you herself, I can't imagine."

"That is not your business," Thaniel replied. "Talk."

Perris the Boar harumphed and snorted, wiping his mouth with his cuff. He glanced around the room to be sure nobody was listening, and then began.

"Elisander and Sanforth Cray married young. They were middle class and not so well off, with a newborn child to support, but Elisander was a talented musician and Sanforth was the heir to a merchant shipping company. They were young, full of life, but they were troubled. See, Elisander's talents were wasted in small orchestras, and she was beginning to despair of ever getting noticed by anyone who mattered; and Sanforth's father wouldn't give control of his company to his son until he himself had died. Sanforth had spent his youth making

154

merry with the allowance his father gave him, and it was generally thought that he was something of a rogue and a wastrel. Hope this is meeting with your satisfaction so far, Miss Cray."

Alaizabel showed no reaction, sitting there as cold and still as a porcelain doll. It was evident that beneath the disgusting exterior of this man beat the heart of a storyteller, but the story he was telling called up memories that she was not sure she wanted back.

He continued nonetheless. "But those very features captured Elisander's heart, and they were deeply in love. And when finally Sanforth's father succumbed to consumption and died, their future was assured . . . or so they thought."

Thaniel glanced at Alaizabel, his heart sinking a little. He had always surmised that there was something dark lurking in her past, but he had hoped he might be wrong. He wanted her to be made happy by the news.

"For a time, everything was wonderful for them," Perris said, pausing to take another bite from the rapidly diminishing turkey leg. "The business was doing well, although Sanforth had little interest in running it; and now that he had money, a word in the right ear got Elisander the audition she deserved, and within a year she was playing cello in the Queen's own orchestra. Miss Cray, you'd have been six or seven at that time."

"I remember," she said, her voice flat.

"But it was not to last. Sanforth simply didn't possess the temperament to be a businessman. He left his father's legacy in the hands of inept managers, content to take the profits while doing none of the work, and soon the lure of so much money began to take him over. He gambled and debauched, and his lady with him, while leaving their child in the care of nannies, to be educated in the ways of a high society she would never reach."

Thaniel looked at Alaizabel again. Her face was impassive. He felt uncomfortable that Perris should be talking about her as if she were not here, laying her life open to them like an autopsy. But that was his way. The man might have been repulsive to look at, but he could find things out.

"That was almost ten years ago," the Boar continued, "and it was not long before tales about the two of them began to circulate throughout society. Dark stories, whispers and rumours: opium dens, terrible perversions, things a respectable person would flinch at, and—"

"That's enough, Perris," Thaniel said quietly. "I will not have you gloat."

"Oh, but you can't say you aren't curious to hear the rest!" Perris said with a rotten grin. "Let me assure you, it gets worse!"

"Thaniel," said Alaizabel calmly. She smiled faintly at him. "I must hear."

Thaniel hesitated. He was beginning to wish he had not brought her, so that she could be spared this. "Miss Alaizabel, I—"

"Please, I insist," she interrupted, her green eyes searching his. "Some things must be faced, no matter how unpleasant."

"May I continue?" the Boar asked eagerly, surveying his audience. Without waiting for a reply, he went on. "Well, anyway, the two of them lost their jobs and fortunes in quick succession; Sanforth through neglect and Elisander through scandal. Sanforth had chosen poorly the people to run his empire, and they embezzled from him until his father's business collapsed. Elisander was too steeped in dark rumours to hold a position in the Queen's orchestra, however great her talent. Had it been just the narcotics and the dubious virtues of the lady, she might have survived there by dint of her great skill. But there was other talk, too. For, as their tastes for sin increased, the bland debaucheries of the upper class began to bore them, and they turned to darker pleasures. Talk abounded of a coven that they had joined, an unholy league of aristocrats, politicians, lawyers and other powerful individuals."

Perris's voice dropped and he leaned close. "They are known, as I'm sure you are both aware, by the name of the Fraternity."

Thaniel's eyes closed and his head dipped slightly. It was the one name he had not wanted to hear.

"He's right," said Alaizabel suddenly. Thaniel turned to her. "He's right," she repeated. "I remember now. All of it. The name was never spoken to me, but . . . it was the Fraternity. I know it."

"Ah, of course, I was forgetting the beautiful Alaizabel," Perris said. "While her parents were indulging in activities that would put Sweeney Todd to shame, she was becoming increasingly distant from them. Her parents' fortunes took a remarkable upswing after joining the Fraternity, and they were soon moneyed once more. But she was still much the same as she had always been: cared for by a succession of nannies, living in expensive boarding schools. She was a troubled adolescent, causing all kinds of mischief wherever she went, but Sanforth and

157

Elisander scarcely noticed. And no matter what she did, she could not seem to get the attention she craved from them."

Thaniel glanced again at Alaizabel, wondering at her reaction to such impertinent statements about her character. She had reverted to her impassive stillness, and showed him nothing.

"That was all there was. Until a week ago," Perris said, rising to a crescendo. "For at that time the whole Cray family disappeared, without trace, from their manor house in Kent. It was one of the rare times when the three of them were together. They went to bed one night, and when the sun rose . . . they were gone."

"And what then?" Thaniel asked.

"Nothing," said Perris. "Nothing for days. It was never reported in the papers. The police did not act on it. A prominent society family disappeared without trace, and nobody knew a thing."

"How can that be?" Alaizabel asked. She felt curiously distant from the whole affair, as if she was hearing about someone else's life rather than her own.

"This is the Fraternity I'm speaking of," the Boar said, scratching the side of his nose. "Police, newspaper editors, businessmen . . . believe me, miss, they decide what the public gets to know."

Alaizabel gazed into the Boar's gimlet eyes. "There is more," she said.

"There is," he said, and even he seemed to sadden a little then. "There is an unhappy postscript to my tale. Four days ago, the bodies of Elisander and Sanforth Cray were fished out of the Thames. They apparently jumped from Tower Bridge."

*

Inspector Maycraft slumped down in his seat at his desk, his stomach still turning cartwheels, the rank smell of bloodied rain in his nostrils. Damn it all! He had seen some vile things in his time, but . . . well, this time he *knew* her! It was different when it was some faceless wretch or distant aristocrat, but this lady he had seen less than a week ago, had talked to her, had tried in vain to make her laugh with a little pun about the Peelers.

He shut his eyes, but the darkness only gave him a better canvas to paint the mental image of what he had seen, so he opened them again. He went to the window, leaving a trail of drips on the floor, and looked out over the foggy lanes of night-cloaked London, imitating Carver's habit of doing the same. The thought of Carver led him to the telephone. He should call Carver, let him know about this. . .

No, he thought, changing his mind. No, he'll find out in the morning, right enough. Best keep him out of it for now. He didn't want Carver to see him like this; the man was a bright spark, and he'd make connections. It was hard to hide things from a man like Carver; he had an intuition bordering on phenomenal.

The phone rang in front of him, making him jump. He picked up the earpiece hurriedly, to shut off the infernal clattering tinkle of the bells.

"Inspector Maycraft," he said into the mouthpiece, wiping his rain-dewed face and slicking back the few wisps of hair that still clung to his pate.

"Someone is on to us," came the reply.

It took a moment for Maycraft to puzzle out who was calling him. "It was a message," he replied, when he had established in his mind who the other voice belonged to. "A warning, I think."

"Who would dare to warn *us*?"

Maycraft paused for a moment, then answered. "Stitch-face."

"*Stitch-face?*"

"I know Stitch-face. This is his work. It's unmistakable."

"What business does he have with us?"

"I don't know, do I?"

Silence.

"No matter. He may know about us, but he's too late. By the Sabbath, the first ceremony will be complete. After that, there'll be nowhere the girl can hide from us."

"Sunday? That's two bloody days from now! I thought we'd have a week to prepare!"

"Two days, Maycraft. I suggest that you be sure any family and friends you have that are not part of our little circle are not in London at that time. You, of course, will stay like the rest of us, and partake of the amusement."

Maycraft held his tongue, stilling the retort he wanted to make. "What about Stitch-face?"

"Do what you can. I trust he'll remain as evasive as always. In the meantime, you might be interested to know that I've enlisted a little extra help in the search for our erstwhile lady Thatch. Who better to find a wych than a wych-hunter?"

"Him? You called *him*?" Maycraft cried. "I hope you remembered to tell him we need the girl *alive* when she reaches us."

"Oh, he's quite clear on that," came the reply, and the phone went dead.

Maycraft slammed the earpiece back into its cradle with a force that nearly broke it. Getting up, he stalked agitatedly around the room. A cigar; a cigar would calm his nerves. He sat down, drew one from his inside pocket, clipped it and lit the end. He let the smoke drift around the inside of his mouth, trying to relax, but nothing could so easily dispel the unquiet that he felt. In frustration, he poured himself a stiff whisky from a decanter that he kept in his desk, tipped it down his throat in one swallow, and poured another.

Stitch-face! That damnable fiend! In his own strange way, Maycraft had felt something for the lady whose sundered corpse he had just laid his eyes on. An affection, a longing for the cold, stern woman. Maybe if things had gone another way, they might have become closer. Maybe.

But no matter how he tried, he could not shake the image from his mind. The wet, dank alley. The pouring rain. The rickety, corrugated shelter. The symbol of the *chackh'morg*, painted thickly in blood on the dry bricks of the wall. And then there was the victim, scarcely recognizable as human any more, and the nails and the knives and what he'd done to her *face. . .*

Maycraft downed the whisky to prevent himself from retching. Don't think about it, don't think. Carver had been right, as usual. That deaf woman had got away from him, so Stitch-face had killed again in the same area. Only this time it was Lucinda Watt, Doctor Pyke's secretary and the woman the lonely Inspector might have loved.

Stitch-face knew about the Fraternity. He had known Lucinda was part of it. That meant he might know about the rest of them.

Maycraft looked at the map of London behind

him, his face a grimace of hatred. He scanned the pins that dotted its surface, interspersed with the green tacks.

One more of those green tacks, my friend, and nothing can stop us. But I wish you hadn't chosen her, Stitch-face.

awn was breaking over the Crooked Lanes, the low, furious yellow of the sun shining through the haze, the edges of its disc broken in little waves as it climbed. The chill of the night was still upon London, but where the sunlight touched it brought a promise of an unseasonable warmth to come.

On the flat rooftop garden of a tall, narrow building that used to be an apothecary, Alaizabel stood and looked out over the opening eye of the city. She was leaning on her elbows against the chest-high stone wall that circumscribed the rooftop, her hands bunched distractedly in the sun-tipped blonde fall of hair on either side of her head. Behind her, rows of low greenhouses were a riot of colour, and troughs of potatoes and carrots were hidden under strips of coarse leaves.

She sensed his arrival even though she did not hear him come up the stairs and out into the open air. Pretending she was unaware, she kept her gaze on the jumble of rickety streets below her.

"Miss Alaizabel?"

"Hello, Thaniel," she said, turning around. He looked a little dishevelled, but the clouding of broken capillaries in his eyes had all but disappeared now, and he looked immeasurably better for it.

"You must be tired," he observed awkwardly.

"It has been a trying night," she said. "But I do not think I shall be sleeping soon. You?"

"I sleep very little," Thaniel said. "I've seen too many godless things to rest easy at night." He paused. "May I stay here with you for a while?"

"It would be my pleasure," she said.

They stood together for a time, taking in the strange beauty of the urban panorama before them.

"I feel nothing," Alaizabel said at last.

"Sometimes grief begins that way," he said quietly.

"No," she replied. "This is different. I hated my parents. I knew nannies, many of them. But my parents . . . they were giants, and my job was to stay out from underfoot. Am I truly that wicked, Thaniel?"

"Love sours easily to hate," Thaniel replied. "I do not think you wicked. Perhaps it was they who were at fault."

"I have an estate, then," she said at length. "Money. I should thank them for that, if the Fraternity has not already taken it away from me." She paused, and looked up at him. "But what else do I have? I do not recall any friends, any loved ones. Do you know what is frightening, Thaniel? I remember almost everything now, and yet there are still gaps. Places where warmth should have been, I remember only blanks. Thaniel, what did I *do* with my childhood?"

Thaniel didn't reply.

"I am all alone, Thaniel," she said quietly. "I know that now; I think I always did, really, even when I could not remember. I never . . . I never made much of an effort, did I? To find my parents. Do you think I knew?"

"Perhaps," said Thaniel. After a moment's pause, he added, "But you have us now."

Her small features curved into a smile, her hair limned in the brightening dawn light. "I was lucky you found me," she said. "No-one else would have done for me what you did."

"Anyone else . . . would have done the same," he said, feeling a little mawkish.

"You really believe that?" she asked, and suddenly she embraced him, softly. Surprised, he let his own arms fall across her back. With her cheek to his shoulder, she murmured, "You have a good heart, Thaniel. I have seen enough rotten hearts to know the difference. There has been little but horror in this city for me, but you. . ." She paused, "you are like the diamond at the heart of the coal."

"Alaizabel, I. . ." he began, but his throat closed on the words he wanted to say.

"Say it," she said, drawing back a little and fixing him with her soft green gaze. "Say whatever you feel. It is not so hard."

"I. . ." he said, then averted his eyes in defeat. "I am honoured by your compliment," he finished, and they both knew that it was a pitiful substitute for what he was intending to confess.

She drew back from him, a small measure of hurt and not a little disappointment written on her features, and changed the subject.

"The Devil-boy says he can draw Thatch out of me," she said, a rising morning breeze making the tips of her hair dance against her dress. No – Thaniel's mother's dress, like all the other ones she had been given.

"Will you be free then?" Thaniel asked. "When the foreign spirit is gone from your body?"

Alaizabel began to wander through the rows of vegetables that were being cultivated up here, occasionally letting her hand trail on a rough green leaf. Thaniel followed.

"I do not know," she said. "He says that Thatch is calling out to her kind; that is why they hunt me. She sleeps inside me now; the charm that Cathaline made has exhausted her. At any rate, it will take him at least three days to prepare the ceremony."

"It is terrifically complex," Thaniel said. "Beyond the range of most wych-hunters. The Devil-boy must have some great talent." He paused; Alaizabel stopped with him. "Who is she, really?" he asked. "Did the Devil-boy tell you?"

"She is a wych," Alaizabel replied. "Two hundred years old or more. She is a friend to the wych-kin, and a powerful one. When she died, her spirit was still strong. The Fraternity summoned her . . . and I was the host. She has a great purpose. The Fraternity have a plan, and she is essential to it. But while she is within me, they cannot act."

"Do you remember what happened that night?"

She shook her head. "Hardly at all. I remember clearly going to sleep that night, and next I knew I was in your house."

"You were drugged?"

"I do not know," she said. "But now that I know . . . now I know who I am, what I was . . . I am stronger now. Stronger than *them*."

"I believe you are," Thaniel said quietly.

*

166

Lord Crott had a lot to think about. The day had come and gone, and the beggars in his gang had gone about their business as usual while he slept, everything running like a clockwork timepiece. Everything smooth, everything nice. As usual, his troop returned to the fold, handing their takings to the accountants and receiving them back when they had been logged and twenty per cent deducted. Twenty per cent of their takings in return for the brotherhood and the contacts and the safety that his gang provided. It had always been that way.

But things were changing, and Crott felt an uncomfortable stirring deep in his gut that told him they were changing for the worse.

That girl. . . If it had been anyone other than Jedriah's son, he might be tempted to just get rid of her. Sent out of the Lanes, maybe; or perhaps a more permanent removal. If she was that precious to the Fraternity, she was dangerous to everybody else. Devil-boy Jack certainly thought so. He counselled having her killed, and he was rarely wrong. "The spirit she harbours is not the dangerous one," he said. "But she is the key to something, of that I am sure. If we destroy the key, the door stays locked."

But Thaniel had second-guessed that particular possibility. He had come to Crott after they had returned from their meeting with Perris the Boar.

"You promised us your hospitality if we removed your troublesome guest in the sewers," he said. "I hope that extends to guaranteeing our safety from you and your men."

"Of course," said Crott, smiling genially.

"And your women and children, and any other

tricks you might have up your sleeve now that you realize what danger we – and you – are in."

"Of course, Thaniel," Crott repeated, a little colder this time. Thaniel had rightly surmised that Crott did not consider some of his more murderous womenfolk to fall under the title of his "men", and would have considered sidestepping his promise if Thaniel had not caught him.

So, they had his word. And a beggar's word was as ironclad as a thief's. A strange irony, Crott reflected, that the most base and lowly of London folk were the most honour-bound of all, and that the value of honour diminished in direct proportion to the heights of society a man climbed to.

He was locked in contemplation when Millenda the Scot knocked on the doors of his inner chambers and was admitted.

"Millenda," Crott said. "How's your boy?"

Millenda smiled a gap-toothed grin. Despite her name, she had been born near Leicester, and begged around the market until she had moved south to London. Her outrageously false accent elicited extra sympathy from the London aristocracy, who believed that the poor woman had enough trials in her life without being Scottish too. Crott liked that; she played on their old notions of Britain as an Empire, and they felt benevolently towards one of their "subjects".

"He's just fine, Lord Crott, just fine. Listen 'ere, though. Some blighter's been caught wanderin' about upstairs, if yer know what I mean. One o' us recognizes him as a Peeler, right, 'cept one o' them fancy ones, not a reg'lar uniformed one."

"What have you done with him?"

Millenda scratched an earlobe. "We was goin' to just send 'im on 'is way, like always; but then he starts saying he's got to see the big cheese o' the place, that he has somethin' important to tell yer."

"This *is* interesting. What's his name?"

"Carver, he says. Ezrael Carver, Detective wiv the Cheapside Peelers."

"Well then, bring him to me. Let's hear what he has to say."

Millenda nodded and disappeared through the door again.

Crott leaned back in his chair and steepled his fingers. "Curiouser and curiouser," he muttered to himself, unconsciously quoting from the book he had just read.

It took fifteen minutes for Millenda to return with Carver, by which time Crott had prepared the room in which he had met with Thaniel and the others early that morning. Though he was far underground, he could sense the gathering night without looking at his pocket watch. There was brandy, sherry and wine in crystal decanters waiting when Carver was shown in, for Lord Crott always took his title seriously, and unlike Rickarack and the other Beggar Lords, he believed that a certain amount of dignity was necessary when dealing with the outside world.

He was pleased to see that Carver was a neatly dressed man, his black hair slicked back immaculately and his moustache maintained with exactitude. He knew of Carver, though he had never had to deal with him before. He couldn't be worse than Maycraft, whom he had run into several times now.

"Detective Carver, welcome to my home," he said,

ushering him towards a seat on the other side of the low table.

"Lord Crott, it's a pleasure to meet you at last," he said, without a trace of irony in his tone. He sat down.

"Brandy, sherry, or wine?" Crott asked with a smile. "Or are you on duty?"

"Even if I were, I should ask you for a sherry," Carver replied. "I have had a harrowing few days."

"Ah, yes; Millenda mentioned something. . ." he said, pouring the sherry. "What can be so important to bring an Inspector − off-duty, no less − into the Crooked Lanes? Surely you know better."

"I need your help, Lord Crott," Carver said bluntly.

"Doesn't everyone?" Crott smiled, his scarred face twitching in amusement.

"I'm at a loss," the Detective said. "I have no-one else to turn to except you, a Beggar Lord, and only then because I know that you cannot possibly be involved in this and I have no other recourse I can imagine."

"Then tell me what has happened, and what you need, and we can talk terms," Crott said.

So he told his story. He began with the Green Tack murders, then spoke of how he had discovered that Maycraft was withholding information from him, that he must have known what the Green Tack murders really were, and was involved in them somehow. He spoke of how he laid the strange, tentacled shape that he had found in Maycraft's address book over the map of London, and found only two points left to complete the shape − and he spoke of how a lady named Alista White had been killed only yesterday at one of those points, leaving one more to go. Then he talked of Maycraft's close friendship with Doctor Mammon Pyke, and how it was Pyke's secretary Lucinda Watt who was brutally murdered last night, with the same symbol drawn in blood on the wall behind her.

Crott sat back and drained the brandy he had poured for himself. "You think this is all connected. Tell me how."

"Maycraft, Pyke and Miss Watt are all part of something," he said. "Something to do with that symbol; and that symbol is something to do with the Green Tack murders. Now Stitch-face has got involved, and he killed Miss Watt and left her as a warning, or a message."

There was a pause. "Would you like another sherry, Detective?" Crott offered, and when Carver agreed, he poured them both refills of their chosen liquor.

"You have come to me because you believe I may know something that your police colleagues can't tell you," Crott observed, as he gave Carver the sherry glass. He paused as Carver took it. "Or is it that you don't trust them?"

Carver looked at him levelly. "I came because you are the man that people come to when they have no other way to find out what they need to. And because I dread to think what might happen when the last of the points on that cursed symbol is completed. This is not just a matter of murders, Lord Crott, nor of catching the murderer. There is something greater here, I know it. I need to know what I am facing." He leaned closer. "I hear you have a friend called the Devil-boy, who can divine answers from objects.

I have brought something from one of the Green Tack victims, and I—"

"This symbol you described. . ." Crott said suddenly, reaching behind his seat and unrolling a piece of coarse paper. "Did it look anything like this?"

It was the *chackh'morg* – the symbol of the tentacled thing, unnerving to the eye – etched in scratchy ink.

Carver blinked, looking up at Crott in sudden alarm.

"I'm not one of them, don't worry," the Beggar Lord said. "My advisor Jack drew it for me after talking with Alaizabel. He's a particularly talented artist for a blind boy, don't you think?"

"Who is Alaizabel?" Carver asked.

"A girl you should meet," Crott said. "Well, as I was saying, the Devil-boy saw it all over her thoughts. He is . . . *gifted* in that way. I showed this symbol to Thaniel Fox, and they told me it was tattooed on Alaizabel's back."

"Thaniel Fox? The son of the great wych-hunter? It is all connected, somehow," Carver said. "All of it."

"Have you heard of the Fraternity, Detective Carver?"

Carver frowned. "Heard of them, yes, but . . . aren't they. . ."

"From what you have said, I think you could better choose your partners in future." Crott spoke gravely. "You are in Fraternity business now. Inspector Maycraft, Miss Watt and undoubtedly Doctor Pyke . . . you can be sure that they are all involved in whatever plan is unfolding."

"But the Fraternity don't exist," Carver said.

"They're as real as Stitch-face," Crott replied. "Perhaps it is time you and I joined forces, Detective. There are things afoot greater than each of us, and I shiver to think what will happen when the great *chackh'morg* of murders that covers London is finally complete."

"Do you think it is that bad?"

Crott held his gaze coolly. "I will take you to Devil-boy Jack and the others, and you will see. The darkness is almost upon us, Detective. We are the only ones who can prevent it."

PART THREE:
THE FRATERNITY ASCENDANT

The chill breath of the London night stirred and swirled in the gas-glow, curling with a serpentine malevolence through the islands of man-made light. The mists from the Thames were stealthy at this hour, hiding at the edges of the clutter of Whitechapel streets. It was relatively clear for November, and the usual murk had been tattered into eddies by a sharp northerly breeze that cut through to the bone without being warmed by the intervening flesh.

The city is turning evil, Alaizabel thought. *You can feel it too, can't you?*

This last was directed at Thaniel, who walked by her side with his arm in hers, stiffly playing the role of the husband escorting his wife through the deepest hours of the dark. He glanced around with a frequency that betrayed his nervous alertness. He was a little afraid, she knew that. But fear alone did not account for the whole of his manner. Like her, he could feel the rot at the heart of London, could feel the cancerous tendrils snaking through the veins of the metropolis.

The sensation was not a new one, even to people such as Thaniel and herself — he with his highly developed intuition, honed over years of wych-kin contact; she, harbouring a slumbering spirit in her breast. Everybody in the city felt it to some degree, something so subtle as to be almost unnoticeable. Always, it had been there on the edge of perception, lending speed to the footsteps of those who walked London's streets, making eye flick away from eye in fear of contact with another who might be an agent of that nameless dread. In the last few days, however, it had gathered in strength until it was like a dull throb in the stones of the terraces, bleeding through the cement.

Today was the date that the Devil-boy predicted would bring the final Green Tack murder, and the brooding sensation that enwrapped the capital had shifted to palpable eagerness. The air was charged, like lightning straining to jump the gap to earth, desperate to complete the circuit and fulfil its promise.

The meeting with Carver had been a strange affair. Alaizabel had been initially uneasy at the sight of the neatly dressed Detective, with his trim moustache and slicked-back hair; it had taken her some time to work out why. It was an odd sensation that had seized her, as if Carver's appearance was not so much coincidental as predetermined. He had come holding missing pieces of their jigsaw, and suddenly all had become clear.

He had brought with him a knick-knack from one of the previous Green Tack victims, for he knew the way of wychcraft. He knew where the next killing would be, but not when. Jack performed a Rite and divined what he could. What kind of opponent they faced, he could not say. But it would strike, tonight, in Whitechapel.

There were forces at work here greater than anyone had guessed at. Alaizabel had a terrible notion that her meeting with Thaniel had been a little more than luck, and that they were not finding each other by chance but being assembled. Thaniel Fox, Cathaline Bennett, Lord Crott, Detective Carver: all united in a cause that they had not even known existed a week ago.

"Are you warm, husband?" she asked gaily, attempting to introduce some levity into their lonely walk.

"Warmer for having you by my side, wife," Thaniel replied, then offered her a wry smile and a wink.

The streets of Whitechapel appeared to be deserted at eleven o'clock this Sunday night, but the truth was a different matter. Those who watched the tortuous lanes and darkened alleys were masters at the craft of hiding, observing unseen. Lord Crott and his minions were here tonight, slinking from shadowed doorways or peering over gutters from tiled roofs. Among them walked Carver, strolling nonchalantly alongside the slender frame of Cathaline Bennett. They patrolled Whitechapel just as Thaniel and Alaizabel did, pushing through the sparse tendrils of mist with their eyes darting about, knowing that, somewhere nearby, something was waiting to strike. In all of Whitechapel, there were perhaps fifty men and women whose sole aim was to spot the Green Tack murderer and prevent the kill. But Whitechapel had many streets and many alleys, and in the final analysis, would it be enough?

A cart clattered past Thaniel and Alaizabel, returning from some late-night delivery. Thaniel, a night-creature by trade, knew well how the heartbeat of the city sped and slowed in the dark hours, and he knew that even on a Sunday night it still pulsed dully with traffic and commerce. People still visited, lovers stalked home after arguments, favours were called, urgent business was concluded. London never slept, but only dozed with one eye open.

"What do you think the wych-kin are, Thaniel?" Alaizabel asked. They had walked a long time now, and she craved distraction.

Thaniel's face was neutral. "They are just wych-kin, the way a cat is a cat and a dog is a dog."

Alaizabel frowned briefly. "But we know why a cat is a cat and a dog is a dog. We know where they came from. Darwin has explained them in his theory of evolution. They have been with us for ever." She paused, then looked up at Thaniel. "But what of the wych-kin? Why do they disobey science? How do they exist in a world where everything lives by the same laws except them?"

Thaniel did not reply.

Alaizabel felt the cold breath of the breeze across her skin, a chill rippling in its wake. They turned on to Crawley Street and strolled onward, Thaniel touching the tip of his top hat at a couple coming the other way. With his youth concealed by the shadow of its broad brim, and his lean frame disguised by his heavy coat, Thaniel made an entirely convincing gentleman.

They had been walking for perhaps two hours now, making random paths through the streets, not knowing what they were looking for or if they could even deal with what they found. The Green Tack murderer had never been seen, never failed to kill. Even

Stitch-face had been spotted several times in his life, and his knife had missed its mark more than once.

"Sir?" came a voice at Thaniel's elbow, and he looked around to see a small, pale-skinned lady in a black dress. She had slipped out of the shadows of a stone stairway. "Sir, could you help me?"

Thaniel glanced at Alaizabel and then nodded. "How can we be of service?"

"I'm being followed, sir," she said. He felt Aliazabel's grip tighten slightly on his arm. "At least, I believe I am."

"Who is following you?" Alaizabel asked, her doll-like features creased in concern.

"I do not know," the lady replied. "I cannot see him, but I hear his footsteps. Oh, maybe I am only letting the night play tricks on me." She seemed less than convinced with her own rationale.

"We could walk with you to your destination," Thaniel offered.

"Oh, I couldn't, you see. . ." she trailed off, averting her eyes. It was obvious that her journey was intended to be secret. Certainly, it was difficult to imagine why a lady would risk being out alone at this hour, even without the ever-present threat of Stitch-face.

After a moment, she came to a decision and spoke. "Could you wait here for a few minutes?" she asked. "If someone is following me, they will pass by here and . . . sir? Are you all right?"

Thaniel wore an expression of pain on his face, his head inclined as if facing a stiff wind. His wych-sense had suddenly blossomed with a painful intensity, a pressure inside his skull such as he had never felt before.

"Thaniel?" Alaizabel queried, seeing him cringe.

"Perhaps I should . . . well, thank you for your time," said the lady, eyeing Thaniel nervously. Her frayed nerves were evidently not up to any more strangeness. "I shall be going."

"No, wait a moment," Alaizabel said, trying to prevent her from leaving while simultaneously attending to Thaniel, who was scrambling inside his coat for something. The lady was having none of that, however; she saw only a man reaching for a knife or a gun, and was retreating as fast as she could without running. Alaizabel seemed about to follow, to keep her from slipping away, but Thaniel gripped her arm. From his pocket, he withdrew a phial of pre-prepared sulphur, glowing faintly from the Ward that he had laid upon it, and tipped it on the ground.

The lady had already made a good distance away from them, and had turned a corner into a side street by the time the liquid splashed on the cobblestones. Thaniel straightened, having managed to get over the initial shock of the sensation in his head, but Alaizabel's eyes were on the sulphur compound that was spreading through the gullies and valleys between the cobblestones, creeping away from them with a life of its own, branching and dividing slowly to follow several paths. And as she watched with increasing horror, the sulphur began to form a shape in the road, a vague yet unmistakable outline of a two-toed footprint.

"Oh," she said.

Thaniel broke into a run, his hat toppling from his head and his hair flying free as he sprinted after the woman. It was impossible, it just *couldn't* be. . .

Do not look behind!

Thaniel projected the thought at the lady as he turned into the street where she had gone, still not quite believing what he was allowing himself to think, what the thing they were facing would be. But he already knew nothing could stop it now. He saw her, hurrying away from him, alarmed by his pursuit and thinking that *he* was the one she had to fear. She cast a terrified glance over her shoulder.

It was her third backward look since she had started to notice the extra footstep in her walk, and that was all it took to make visible the thing that trod behind her.

There was no shimmering as the creature revealed itself to the eyes of its victim, no gradual unveiling as of the moon from behind a cloud. It was simply *there*; one moment not, the next it was lunging at her, a huge and terrifying bulk of claws and metal teeth that dwarfed her as it reached to open her up.

The roar of Thaniel's pistol sounded like a cannon on the still of the night, blasting the creature aside at the same moment as its claws made contact with their target. There was a scream as the lady was pitched bodily across the street; she slammed across the cobbles and rolled to a stop in a storm gutter, dark blooms of blood moistening her black dress and seeping from her hairline to inch down her face.

The creature staggered, turned a baleful gaze on Thaniel, and he felt his heart shudder under its glare. What he was seeing was inconceivable.

Rawhead.

When he was a child he had stared for hours in horrified fascination at the carving in the sanctum at his home in Crofter's Gate. Rawhead and his companion, Bloodybones: they were a tale to frighten youngsters, the things that lived in cupboards and hid in the dark beneath the bed. Now he stood facing the creature that had haunted his childhood nights, when he had lain awake in terror at the thought of what might reach up and grab him. No myth any more, but real, as if the carving that had so scared him all those years ago had come to life.

Rawhead was huge, grotesquely muscled and hunched, a heavy brow shadowing small, louring eyes that sat above a wide mouth in which small, pointed teeth of brass gleamed faintly in the light of the gas lamps. He was an exaggerated mockery of the human form, terrible and fearful, and Thaniel felt himself suddenly wishing that he was not alone, that the others who must have heard the gunshot would arrive soon.

A slow snarl came from the throat of the thing as he took his stance to deal with the newcomer. Thaniel's pistol had done no discernible damage, even though he was quite certain he had struck the creature in the side of the neck.

Rawhead came at him like a bull, roaring as he charged; Thaniel levelled his pistol and shot him square in the face. The creature's forward momentum was checked violently, as if by a hammer blow, and he was lifted off his feet to collapse heavily to the cold stone of the road. Thaniel was already holstering his pistol, tugging free from his belt a long string of charms, an array of Warded artefacts linked by wire. Cured snakeskin wrapped in hay; vulture feathers; a depiction of the evil eye carved in a coin-sized piece of wood – there were perhaps twenty in all. It was the wych-hunter's first line of defence against an unknown foe: a broad spectrum of Wards and charms that had proven effective in the past against other forms of wych-kin. The theory was that at least a fraction of the arsenal would work against the enemy.

Rawhead had already regained his feet by the time Thaniel had the charm-string ready, his heart trip-hammering against his ribs and cold sweat slicking his hands. No mark showed on the creature's face from the bullet, but he was certainly enraged. He lunged again, bellowing mindlessly, and Thaniel threw himself aside as the enemy thundered towards him. But Rawhead had moved faster than Thaniel had credited, and his dodge was clumsy. One foot snagged the other, and he felt himself trip. He lashed out with the charm-string as he fell, praying that fortune was with him.

This time, it was.

He crashed to the ground, Rawhead missing him by centimetres, and the charm-string snagged on the creature as he passed. It tore free from Thaniel's hand, wrapping itself loosely around the body of his enemy, and as he rolled he felt the wave of force wash over him that was the Wards flaring into life. There was an animal howl of fury and pain, and then Thaniel was up and ready once more.

In the steely moonlight between the gaslights, the charm-string lay on the floor, blackened and smoking faintly. Of Rawhead, there was no sign.

"Thaniel!" came the cry, and there was Cathaline, appearing from a side street with Carver, attracted by the sound of gunfire. Two others, Crott's men, were with them.

Thaniel blinked, realizing by the fading intensity

of his wych-sense that Rawhead really was gone. A moment later, he was rushing to the lady, whom he had all but forgotten. The others reached him as he crouched by her bloodied form to check her pulse.

"Are you all right?" Cathaline panted. "What was that you—"

"Never mind me," he said sharply. "She is still alive. There is hope yet. The *chackh'morg* has not been completed while she still lives."

"Get her help!" Carver barked at one of Crott's men. The pair of them ran to comply.

Thaniel was beginning to shake now, the adrenalin leaving his body and making him weak. Cathaline crouched next to him and put an arm round him.

"It was Rawhead," he said quietly.

"Rawhead?" Cathaline asked.

"When I was a child, late at night, when the lights were out. . ." he said. "If I had to visit the bathroom, I had to walk along the dark landing."

"I know," said Cathaline. "You can't look over your shoulder more than twice."

"They used to sing it in the playground," he said. *"Rawhead close behind you treads, three looks back and you'll be dead."*

"But close your eyes and count to ten, and Rawhead will be gone again," Cathaline finished.

Thaniel laid his hand over his face. "How could he be here, Cathaline? He is not real. Stories of Rawhead go back long before the wych-kin came. How could he be here?"

He heard the tread of Carver's shoes behind him before she could reply.

"Thaniel," came his puzzled voice. "Where is Alaizabel?"

Thaniel felt a flood of ice wash out from his heart. In the heat of the chase, he had forgotten her, assuming she was right behind him. Now he realized that he had not seen her the entire time he had been fighting Rawhead.

Alaizabel.

She was gone.

The room was dark and cool, tiled in faded green ceramic from ceiling to floor. Three figures busied themselves around the centrepiece by the glow of a single gas lamp set against one wall. By the doorway, several more clustered, watching, their expressions blank in the darkness.

"There is little more I can do," said the doctor, and stepped away from the hospital trolley on which his patient lay. "We shall have to wait and see."

Leanna Butcher, the last of the Green Tack victims, struggled for life beneath the Crooked Lanes, and only her heartbeat held back the tide of disaster.

Cathaline stepped into the light, holding the letter that they had found in her pocket, the declaration of forbidden love from a married man that had brought her to this point. She was still now, the great rent in her chest bandaged and treated, her head in a clamp to set the crack in her skull. If not for that letter, she would not have been hurrying to a secret rendezvous that night. If not for Thaniel, she would not even be alive. Cathaline slipped the letter into Leanna's limp grip.

"I hope he was worth it," she murmured.

"It is in fate's hands now," Crott said. "She will be safer here than any hospital, and better cared for."

"Leave us now," the Devil-boy croaked. "I will set Wards. There may yet be other wych-kin to finish the job."

Cathaline and Thaniel drifted away, heading for the cluster of rooms that Crott had assigned them as quarters. They were furnished well enough with scavenged chairs and beds and rugs, a chaotic blend in which nothing matched. In other circumstances, Thaniel might have found himself missing his home by now, and wondering what had become of the place they had abandoned. But for now, he had greater worries.

"She'll be all right," Cathaline said as they walked, correctly guessing the reason for Thaniel's silence. "You're not to blame."

Thaniel was a slender obelisk of shadow, radiating suppressed anger and frustration.

"We should have left her here," he said.

"She insisted upon coming," Cathaline replied. "Couples are less threatening at night than lone men; we talked about this. That woman would never even have talked to you if Alaizabel had not been at your side."

He made no reply.

They reached their quarters through a cracked and peeling corridor that used to be the basement and boiler room of a schoolhouse. It was cold and damp, with an oil lamp burning in an alcove. Thaniel lit the fire in the small wood stove and set about blowing on it to kindle the tinder.

"She may have left of her own accord," Cathaline suggested, as if they had not already thought of every possibility. "If she——"

Thaniel snorted. "Either Stitch-face has her or the

Fraternity do. If the latter, then they have Thatch back and things have just gone from bad to worse. If it is Stitch-face. . ." he paused, "at least we need not worry about Thatch any more."

"Thaniel," said Cathaline, a little shocked at his callousness. "You sound like your father now."

"My father would not have failed to protect her," Thaniel said.

"Of course he would," Cathaline replied, sitting in a chair. When Thaniel was silent, she looked up at him and saw him staring at her in disbelief.

"How can you say that?" he asked.

"Oh, Thaniel, did you think you were the *only* person who knew Jedriah? I hunted with him dozens of times. He was good. *Exceptionally* good. But he was not what his legend makes him out to be. And you should stop trying to live up to something impossible."

"I do not know what you mean," Thaniel said, but the blaze in his eyes indicated the opposite.

"You had a choice," Cathaline said, infuriatingly calm. "If you hadn't saved Leanna Butcher, we'd all be in a whole lot more trouble that we are now. So which was it to have been? To keep Alaizabel and let the Fraternity complete their plan, or lose her for the sake of saving that woman and buying us all some time?"

Thaniel's face was shadowed. "You know the answer to that one, Cathaline."

Cathaline looked at him levelly. "Then don't pretend that you don't care she's gone."

Despair was not an emotion that society would have a gentleman show, so Thaniel found his own dark place to despair in, alone. It was an old bell tower, the upthrust arm of a crumbling church that rose high enough above the tumbledown roofs of the Crooked Lanes to let him sorrow in the pure moonlight, unhindered by tethers of fog.

He sat with his knees against his chin, hugging himself in the spectral light of the gibbous moon. The cool stone pressed into the curve of his spine. All was silent. Through the Gothic arches of the tower, he watched the distant, ghostly cigar of light that was an airship turning slowly and heavily over Finsbury Park. Somewhere far away, he heard the dull boom of the bombs being dropped on the Old Quarter. Tonight was one of the monthly forays by the fleet into Camberwell, dropping explosives on to the already ruined areas where the wych-kin bred, in an ineffective attempt to keep the population down. Bombing their own city to destroy the heart of the cancer.

He was thinking about his past, about the time when things were simpler. When his father was alive, and he was not a wych-hunter but only a child. He had been too young to understand his mother's death; most of his recollections of her were half-formed sounds and feelings that fled his memory as he tried to take hold of them. But his father; that was different.

He was missed by few when Jedriah took him from under the wing of Her Majesty's educational institutions and into his own nest. He had always been quiet at school, and did not make friends easily. Jedriah took him away from that, and taught him the trade of the wych-hunter, and Thaniel loved him for it. How to set and bait a soul cage; how to administer a Rite; what kind of hollows to look in for a stumpfoot; how to recognize a Black Shuck; how to look at a marshlight without being drawn in. And the boy, wide-eyed, worshipped his father, who was the greatest wych-hunter of them all.

Then Jedriah died, and Cathaline took his place. The boy, distraught, threw himself into the one thing he knew, immersed himself in it completely. He was a wych-hunter first, foremost and always. It would have been what his father wanted. But being a wych-hunter left little room for anything else.

Father, he thought. *If you hadn't died, perhaps I would have seen you as Cathaline sees you. How can I live up to a legend, Father? How do I beat a ghost?*

Jedriah had been lonely after his wife died. He had never loved again, and never wanted to. That was the man with whom Thaniel had grown up, and the lessons he had unconsciously absorbed. To be solitary. To be alone. To need nobody.

But then Alaizabel had arrived.

All it had taken was Alaizabel to destroy the walls of silence in his life. Without really doing anything, just by being there, she had awakened in him feelings he did not know he had. She had unravelled him, unknotted him. And it was not until now, now that she was gone, that he realized the depth of it all.

He despaired. He despaired, because Alaizabel was gone and no matter how he racked his brain, he could not think of how to find her. The charm that Cathaline had made for her for the purpose of protecting her from the wych-kin was now preventing them from trying to locate her. He had spoken with the Devil-boy, and the Devil-boy had confirmed his worst fears. No Rite could locate her without a token of hers, something like hair or a fingernail or a treasured piece of jewellery. It had to be something dear and close to her; nothing else would do. And even if they had such a thing, Cathaline's charm would hide her from them.

"She is lost to us," the Devil-boy husked. "Leanna Butcher has perhaps a week to live. All we can do is hope that it is Stitch-face and not the Fraternity who have her; for if the Fraternity can draw out the spirit inside her, then we must prepare for the end."

For a time, there was only blackness, an absence of mind. Then Thaniel stood in the moon-silvered darkness. "Alaizabel," he whispered. "Come back to me."

A GATHERING **17**
CURIEN BLAKE

Pyke's mansion was a block of darkness against the November night. Dusk had not long passed, and lights burned inside against the gathering blackness, tiny spider-eyes glowering from the gloomy monolith. It sat in isolation amid a ruff of evergreens, which soughed in the wind and rustled to each other in disapproval of anything and everything. A winding country road led to a gate with wrought-iron creepers twisting between its bars, and from there the great driveway ran in a circle around a flower bed, whose hardy winter blooms had turned to ice and velvet in the moonlight.

It was perhaps an hour from Redford Acres by carriage, the lone occupant of a hill of many trees. Usually it sat silent, its colonial curves gilded in the glow of the tall lamp-posts that guarded the driveway. But tonight its halls rang with voices, the chime of decanter to glass, and the mutter of plots and seduction.

"Maycraft," said Pyke, the single word combining a greeting and an introduction for the benefit of the tall man who stood with him. "You're late."

"Mammon," the Inspector replied, purposely using Pyke's forename because he knew how it irritated his host. He glanced around the room, still flustered from his ride. "I was dealing with business. I hope you know they'll fry me for being away while another Green Tack murder shows up."

"I think you'll find you need not worry," Pyke said, blinking his heavy-lidded eyes. It occurred to Maycraft for the first time that the Doctor resembled nothing more than a vulture, with his pinched, balding head perched on a scrawny neck. He turned his attention to Pyke's companion. With his long coat and stetson clashing terribly with the elegant dress of those who surrounded them, he was the only other one in the room apart from Maycraft who was not dressed for the occasion.

They stood in one of Pyke's reception rooms, which had been decorated in a style befitting the atmosphere of the house. Powder-blue walls, wooden settees with floral designs on their thin cushioning, white plaster edging on the ceiling; heavy gold frames circumscribed grim portraits of elder statesmen all around them. Pyke had once described it as "Independence-era Philadelphian" and Maycraft, being no critic of interior design, was happy to take his word for it. The Doctor had always had a curious affinity for America. That explained the person standing to his left, who, under other circumstances, might have ended up in one of the Doctor's treatment cells.

"You seem distracted, Maycraft," Pyke observed blandly.

"Doesn't everyone?" he retorted, motioning at the small knots of people who stood about the room. High-society folk, talking about high-society things in which a man like Maycraft had little interest; but their façade was a poor one, and the nervous glances they threw towards Pyke betrayed their unease.

"What's going on?" he hissed, once Pyke had taken his meaning. "Why hasn't it happened?"

"All in time," Pyke said. "For now, I don't believe you two have ever met face-to-face?"

"Curien Blake," said the taller man, in a slow American drawl.

Maycraft shook his hand and introduced himself, mustering the bare minimum of politeness towards a man he already despised.

Curien Blake was a wych-hunter of great renown – some would say infamy – who hailed from Kentucky in the United States. He had emigrated to England seven years ago, no doubt fleeing the results of his habitual over-enthusiasm with his Remington six-shooters. There, Blake met Doctor Pyke, who was impressed both by his ruthlessness and his entirely mercenary principles. The Doctor used him on occasion to clear up little mistakes that the Fraternity made. Sometimes a Rite would go awry; sometimes a particular wych-kin would need to be captured or destroyed; and sometimes, a person knew too much to continue breathing. Blake was equal to every task.

Maycraft hated him. Perhaps he was a useful asset to the Fraternity, but he was an odious man with a penchant for violence that bordered on sickening. He had heard tales of Blake beating a victim to death with the butt of his pistol so as not to waste a bullet; he had heard also how he disguised the murder as a burglary by ransacking the house and shooting the man's wife. Then there was the Fraternity judge who had begun to take the quite unfortunate view that he wanted to leave the fold. Pyke told Blake to "persuade him otherwise". Blake kidnapped his eight-year-old daughter, trussed her up like a chicken and threw her in the Thames. He then reminded the judge that he had two more daughters and a wife, and if he should ever think of leaving the Fraternity again, they would follow his eldest child down.

Maycraft was not a man of principle, but Curien Blake's cold-bloodedness repulsed even him.

To avoid making conversation with the man, he searched the room again. Here, a portion of the Fraternity was assembled: judges, barristers, doctors, politicians, a mayoral candidate from Essex; the highest strata of society. They came beguiled by the promise of joining a group comprised of the most powerful men and women in London, bewitched by greed for success, knowing that with people such as these helping them out, they could not fail to get all that they wanted. Beneath them were the less affluent, those who were influential because of their jobs. Nurses, civil servants, nannies, secretaries, policemen, even postmen; all placed so that records could be changed, messages could be intercepted, people could be coerced. And there had been more than one occasion when a baby had gone missing from one of London's many orphanages, and found its way into the Fraternity's ceremonies.

People who were approached by the Fraternity were drawn first by the social advantages it offered. Indeed, it was Maycraft's disgust at being passed over for promotion twice that led him to join, after he was approached and promised he would not be passed over a third time. The initiation into the cult came after, once people had been "helped". They were indebted to the family by then, and most felt the ceremonies would be harmless enough. Atheism or a certain elasticity of religion were an important factor in the choice of people to approach. It was after they saw what the cult could do that they began to believe, and hunger for more. Those who were firm in their refusal to participate – and there had been mistakes in the past – were either blackmailed into silence or disposed of.

They were all here, waiting for Pyke to speak. Waiting for him to tell them why his promise had gone unfulfilled.

Why hadn't their gods been unchained?

A hush spread over the assembly as Pyke ascended the curved stairway. The stairway was part of a symmetrical pair; its twin snaked up to meet it from the dark stone floor of the main hall. Where they met, there was a short balcony with two oak doors on either side, leading deeper into the body of the mansion. It was here that Pyke stopped, leaning on the scrolled teak banister and looking over the upturned faces of his congregation, who had fallen silent in expectation.

Maycraft had been left standing with Blake. The American gave him an oily and entirely false smile.

"I see a portion of our number have decided to stay at home and decline my invitation," Pyke said, his steady voice knifing through the guests. It was a measure of his importance that he did not concern himself with introduction or preamble. The assembly murmured and looked about, trying to establish who was absent, who they could feel superior to. Pyke did not give them time.

"I will not prolong your agony of uncertainty by waiting until dinner to make the announcement you came to hear," he said, standing back from the railing and surveying them with vulpine interest.

"Many of you have travelled some distance from your retreats. Those of you who decided to stay in London have had a shorter trip, but such are the benefits of the faithful."

He smiled coldly. It was no secret that Pyke thought little of those members of the Fraternity who had chosen to escape the capital in the face of the impending cataclysm. London would be the epicentre of the Fraternity's ascendancy, and the cautious – the faithless, Pyke would say – feared to be in the heart of the furnace until they had tested its heat.

"The *chackh'morg* was due for completion yesterday. The first stage of our victory should have come into effect. What you all want to know is: *why not?* What went wrong? That's what you all want to know."

The congregation looked faintly guilty, even though it was they who had been summoned by Pyke. Curien Blake examined the fingernails of his left hand.

"Let me enlighten you, then," Pyke said. "Yesterday, the final sacrifice in the sequence of the *chackh'morg* was interrupted by an outside influence. Wych-hunters, to be precise."

The congregation was overtaken by a tide of mutters. Pyke waited for it to subside, the final whispers draining away into the corners of the room and fading to nothing.

"Our agent was able to fatally wound his victim," he continued, "but inconveniently, she has as yet failed to die. It is, however, only a matter of time before she succumbs to the injuries dealt to her. When her last breath has been drawn, then the *chackh'morg* is complete and the first stage will begin. This is a minor setback only; the greatest minds in medicine could do nothing to save her now, and besides, as I'm sure you'll agree, most of them are right here in any case."

His joke was met by a smattering of laughter, easing considerably the tension in the room.

"There is, however, another reason that I summoned you here. I have need of you all once again. A complement of sixty must attend for a recitation of Chandler's Distillation. I expect volunteers by the end of dinner. The recitation is tonight at one hour past midnight. I will supply you with details of the venue."

Tonight? Maycraft thought in surprise. *But that means. . .* He turned to Blake automatically, his eyes asking the question. Blake smiled languidly and touched the brim of his stetson.

By thunder, how Maycraft hated that man.

THE GIRL IN THE WHITE SHIFT 18
AN ILL MEETING

The room was low and square, shabby and derelict, with bare stone walls roughly carved. Firelight sent slivers of shadow darting through the crevices and grooves, jabbing and retracting like rapiers. It was swelteringly hot, and the scent of sweat and blood was thick and heavy enough to choke. The walls were a chaos of symbols, here thick lines of dark, flaking red, there a close press of sigils drawn with the same stuff. Handprints vied with neatly scribed Wards for space on the dirty stone, spreading across ceiling and floor until it seemed that the room was a dark womb of crusted gore.

They were there, the people masked in mirrors. Robes of plain crimson, cowls that drooped over smooth ovals of reflective glass that were their faces. Each one of the cultists wore a picture of the scene before them beneath their hood; the bright pit of burning coals, the loose crowd of their companions. They were chanting in a low monotone, a harsh, guttural language that was ugly and repellant to the ear.

There was a grid over the firepit, and an iron framework above that, a tall assemblage of supports that formed the hollow outline of a cube. Hanging inside the cube was a hammock of thick ropes, each rope dark with Wards; and inside the hammock, wrapped like a fly in a spider's web, was Alaizabel Cray.

Her eyes focused and unfocused uncertainly on the blurred sea around her. She was unbearably hot, her skin trickling with sweat, her entire body seeming to be melting like wax. Cradled in the hammock, her veins drenched with drugs, she was only barely aware of who she was, let alone where she had ended up or how she had come to be here.

The monotone grew in volume, swelling around her. Beneath her, on the grille above the firepit, a wide iron bowl was catching the sweat that dripped constantly from her body, soaking through her thin white shift. Her throat and lips were dry; her blonde hair clung to her face in wet strands; her breath came laboured and heavily. She remembered nothing, knew nothing, except the heat and the incomprehensible strangeness all about her. A newborn babe, looking at an unfamiliar world through bewildered eyes, completely at the mercy of others.

There was something stirring inside her, a presence, a voice that radiated a sinister glee. It was saying something, something, something . . . the sounds would not gel into coherence. She frowned briefly in consternation, trying to concentrate her way past the fuzz that surrounded her.

!!Yes!! Yes!! Oh, you thought you were so clever, my pretty thing!! But who's clever now? Eh? I said, who's clever now? You've been a troublesome thing to old Thatch, a most troublesome thing. I'll see to you, oh yes, I'll see to you!!

Who are you? she asked herself.

!!Thatch, I said!! Are you deaf? I said, are you deaf??

Alaizabel thought about that.

I can hear you. Does that mean I'm deaf?

!!Stupid girl!! the voice snapped, and fell silent.

The chanting was rising in pitch now, speeding up little by little. She did not like the sounds that were being made; they reminded her uncomfortably of some other time that she wished to forget.

What is happening? she asked the other voice.

!!Idiot girl!! They're taking me out of you, aye, and not before time neither. And they'll put me in another young girl, and this time they might do it proper!! She'd best die when she's supposed to this time!! Not like you, you little scratchy sparrow. Not like you, my horrible. Ugh!! How I hate you!!

Why are you saying that? What did I ever do?

!!Silence!! Silence, you mean thing!!

Alaizabel obeyed. She felt that she should be frightened, but the cosy warmth that seemed to flow outward from her heart to her extremities would not let her get excited. And she was so tired, both from the soporific effect of the heat and the dehydration that it produced.

Now she could see something moving out of the corner of her eye, and she managed to twist her neck to observe what it was. Blurrily, she saw a girl in a white shift being brought into the room. She was drugged — Alaizabel knew that somehow — but still she struggled weakly against the mirror-faced figures that were pulling her towards the firepit.

No, not drugged. Poisoned.

A savage moment of clarity seized Alaizabel at that moment. That was her, a short few days ago. A different ceremony, but similar. When they joined the Fraternity, her parents had not bargained on the sacrifices they would have to make. They may not have loved their child, but they would not let the Fraternity use her as a receptacle for the spirit of Thatch. So the Fraternity kidnapped them all, killed the parents and took her anyway. Poisoned her, put her in a cradle like the one she was in now, chanted the chants. This was not quite the same; this time they were taking the foreign spirit out of her and putting it into someone new. But the girl still had to die and, even through the poison, she fought against her fate.

Alaizabel felt a great sadness overwhelm her, and tears began to course down her cheeks. She could barely see the girl through the drug-haze, but she could feel her fear, feel her slipping away and weakening.

??What's this?? What's this?? Sad, are you?? Don't worry, my dear. The ceremony will probably kill you too!!

The words were swept away by a tide of rage that boiled up from inside Alaizabel. The Fraternity! How could they play with lives like chess pieces, pawns to be sacrificed for the kings and queens and rooks? With *her* life? Oh, she hated them; *how* she hated them then, for everything that had been done to her, for the humiliation and fear and degradation and pain, and she felt the drug-haze draw back from her as clouds part for a bright shaft of sunlight, and she swore then that she would endure, she would survive this trial, and she would make them pay for what they had done to her, and to the girl who they now pushed to her knees at the edge of the firepit, and to them all.

!!Still feisty, sparrow!! Well, you—!!

Be silent! Alaizabel commanded with a force that stunned the other. *I will not hear another word of yours, you evil, long-dead abomination. I am alive, and I will stay that way, and you will return to whatever part of Hell from which you came!*

Thatch quailed and retreated, seeming to recede within her. She was but a shade, a frail spirit. Alaizabel was still the mistress of her own mind, and anger lent her muscle to overcome the persistent effects of the drugs enough to think clearly for a short time.

The chanting reached a crescendo and suddenly stopped. Alaizabel felt a sudden tautening in the room, the heat-baked air stretching thinner and thinner. She felt suddenly as if she was being crushed, but the crushing was coming from within, as if someone inside her were squeezing her lungs and her heart. She screamed in pain and at the horror of it, the unnatural sensation. It was a tearing of the soul, as if the core of her self was being mauled by some clawed thing. She screamed, but her throat was sandpaper and it brought fresh agonies. She screamed anyway. These agonies, at least, were natural.

Inside her head, Thatch was screaming with her. The hammock seemed to have embedded itself in Alaizabel's skin, sinking through her flesh as if it could dice her and she would fall in pieces into the bowl below. The Warded ropes burned, and she writhed, drugged and helpless. She bit her lip in the throes of pain, and salty blood trickled down her throat, tasting of metal.

Then came the wrench, and it brought pain beyond imagining. The drugs that kept her quiescent were the only thing that stopped Alaizabel dying of shock. It was like she was being drawn by horses, ripped apart in every direction at once, a torture that stole her breath and flayed her mind and made her retch and spasm and weep all at once.

The pain continued long after she thought she could not conceivably suffer any more. If she had lapsed for a moment, if she had for one second thought that she wished to die and have it done with, then she would surely have done so. It was only her will that kept her body going, her anger, her need to survive so that they would not win. And finally, finally, after aeons and eternities piled upon each other, the pain stopped, and there was a void of such bliss that she thought she really had died, and here was her reward.

Below her, the girl was drinking the bowl of her sweat with a dagger at her throat, made to swallow, helpless to resist. She was dying, and Thatch was inside her now. Soon they would give her the antidote to the poison, but by then her mind would be too weak to resist the old wych.

Alaizabel could not see her face, could see nothing but darkness, and finally she went limp and unconsciousness claimed her.

The padded walls of her cell were familiar to her by now, though she had not been at all certain that she would wake up again after the ceremony. It was with a sense of relief that she looked around the soft squares of dirty white, the gridwork of flat buttons that formed their edges, row upon row surrounding her on all sides.

Still here, she thought. She had survived the ceremony, and the Fraternity had not killed her yet.

Distant shrieks forced their way through the cushioning of the cell, a cacophony of anguish from some of the asylum inmates nearby. She lay where she was, her cheek pressed to the gently yielding floor, and let a tear slide from her eye. At least she was clear-headed again. They had kept her drugged ever since that American wych-hunter had brought her here. He had snatched her off the street that night, striking like a cobra the second Thaniel's back was turned. One moment she had been pursuing him as he chased after the final Green Tack victim, the next she was being pulled into an alley, her mouth muffled by a handful of cloth, and the sharp smell of chloroform was the last thing she knew before she awoke in this cell, deep beneath Redford Acres.

She had no idea how long they'd kept her here. Probably not very long, she guessed; they would have wanted Thatch out of her as soon as possible, and into a host body with a spirit that was a little more willing to leave. They had conversed with Thatch several times, sedating Alaizabel before each session so that her conscious mind was powerless and the spirit within her could speak through her mouth. She could not recall the content of the conversations. Maybe Thatch was making requests; maybe the reason she was alive now was because Thatch wanted her to be. Certainly, she was of no more use to the Fraternity now that they had Thatch. She recalled the words of the spirit during the ceremony: *You've been a troublesome thing to old Thatch, a most troublesome thing. I'll see to you, oh yes, I'll see to you!*

She feared to think what Thatch had in store for her.

Tenderly, she levered herself up and sat with her

back against the padded wall, facing the door. She was wearing a coarse cotton shift of drab white, the uniform of an inmate. Her throat was still dry, but she was not as dehydrated as she might have expected to be after the ceremony. Perhaps they had made her drink afterwards? Possibly she had been awake at some point between the ceremony and here; she could not be sure.

A faint smile forced its way on to her haggard features. *But I am my own again. I am Alaizabel Cray, no other. And if I should get away from these people, I promise to God that nobody but I will ever have a hold on my mind. Not by drug or by wych.*

It was true. It was only when Thatch was gone that Alaizabel realized how noticable her presence had been, a weight on her mind, making her head heavy. She felt lighter now than she ever had, liberated and free.

But you are still in a cage, Alaizabel, she pointed out to herself.

She would not despair. She was herself again, and her staunch will had always been strong. She would wait, and see what happened.

In the hour that followed, she thought of her parents and felt little remorse for their deaths. They were too far away; they had always been strangers to her. They had joined the Fraternity; they had been the instruments that had drawn Alaizabel into this chaos in the first place. They deserved what they got, floating downstream in the murky Thames.

She thought of Thaniel, too. How did he feel now? Was he worried about her, searching for her? Did he want her back because he wanted to keep Thatch from the Fraternity, or did he just want her back?

Did he want her back at all? She could not fathom the way he reacted to her. Sometimes he was warm, sometimes cold. But she liked his smiles, and the way he sometimes turned his words, and the odd flash of his eye. She would like to be back with him again. He was the only honest thing she had ever had.

It was while thinking of him that she began tracing patterns in the grime that lay on the white fabric of the cell padding, carving little lines of clean white through the dirt. Her doodles were at first idle shapes, then more complex pictures; and finally, in the midst of a depiction of a steam-train, she was struck by a thought that froze her with its possibilities.

Could it really be that simple?

She got to her feet, hunger and weariness making her head light, then crossed the cell to the door and knelt in front of it. It was blank, with no handle on the inner side, a section of the quilted wall outlined by a dark, narrow rectangle. She closed her eyes, remembering. How elusive memory was, and yet the image of the shape she wanted burned in her mind with a definition and solidity so strong as to be unnatural. She had seen it only once, and yet she could remember it more perfectly than her mother's face.

With her finger, she began to draw in the dust of the quilting, her fingertip drawing a track. Lines met and linked, curved and swept, seeming to form themselves before her. When she was satisfied, she sat back on her heels, and there in the dirt was a perfect Ward of Opening. The same as she had drawn that night when Thatch had first taken control of her body, when she had been locked in Thaniel's room and seeking escape.

Nothing happened. She pushed the door experimentally. It was still as locked as it had ever been.

Her heart sank, no longer buoyed up by the hope that she had felt for a time. It had been foolish, anyway. The foul spirit inside her had been drawing the Ward, not her. She had hoped, perhaps, that some small part of that power might have remained inside her by some arcane osmosis. Apparently she had been wrong.

She squinted at the shape she had drawn. Like all Wards, it seemed a little *too* real, as if the rest of the world were faded slightly by comparison. And yet . . . did it not seem as if the fabric was somehow thinner where her finger had passed? As if she had worn a little way into the padding of the door?

Suddenly excited, she ran her finger over the lines she had already made, forcing herself to go slowly and carefully, willing the Ward into existence. Her first trace of the shape produced no effect; undeterred, she tried again. This second time, she thought she could see something, but she could not be certain it was not her imagination. By the fourth time, she was no longer in doubt. It was not the padding that was thinning beneath her fingers, but some invisible gauze in the air, wearing away steadily to open into another place, the place where the Wards existed.

Her heart began to race, her eyes to widen and glitter in astonishment. Heat was building in her gut, like it had the first time, when Thatch had been in control. There was some technique to this, some drawing of the power, but it was so natural to her that she did not even know how she was doing it. She had seen Thaniel drawing Wards in pig's blood, but the blood took treatment and preparation, needed Rites and mixing with other reagents. She was drawing a shape with her finger, and it was working, actually *working!*

Thatch, you festering thing, I may have something to thank you for yet, she thought, and beneath her finger the glowing red of the Ward welled through like blood from a surgeon's incision, and she made the final pass and took her hand away. It lay on the door for an instant, a fierce glow of red, darkening the room around it; and then it was gone, leaving its imprint on her eyes like the after-image of the sun.

There was a soft click, and the door drifted open a few centimetres.

She wasted a few moments in silent disbelief before standing up shakily. She pushed the door open and peered out. An empty corridor, dank and echoing with distant shrieks, gas lamps marking the way and reflecting from the wet stone floor. Out here, without the muffling effect of the padding, she could hear the muttering, the crying, the thump and scuffle and yell of her neighbours in their cells. A thousand mad voices whispered in the air all around her, echoing and multiplying in the corridor. No wonder there was nobody here; a sane jailor would quickly join his inmates if he had to patrol this corridor day after day.

Barefoot, she stepped out and on to the damp, cold floor. Small puddles and runnels of water crawled across the corridor. She shut the door of her cell behind her, then looked either way. A door was at one end. She began to run.

Weak though she was, the thought of getting away from the voices in the corridor was enough to push her on. Mercifully there were no windows on the doors of the cells, so she could not see the tortured souls that made such awful sounds; but her imagination provided more than adequate substitutes. Reaching the end of the corridor, she found the door unlocked, and hurried through with little regard as to what might be on the other side.

She found herself in a treatment room. A trolley stood in the centre of the room, with straps at wrist, waist, ankle and neck for restraining the patients. To her right, a tall thing like a cabinet stood, cold and forbidding and covered with dials and switches. It hummed with electricity, no doubt from some generator deep within the guts of the asylum. There was a metal cap on the trolley, attached to the cabinet by thick wires. Alaizabel felt a thrill of disgust, not wishing to know what went on in this room. She hurried past, leaving the noises of the inmates to fade behind her.

She found herself in what appeared to be the staff quarters. Within, she found a small kitchen with a burned copper kettle, and a table in a nearby room with the remains of a meat pie on a chipped plate. She stole the pie without a second thought, and was relieved to find it cold. The fact that the pie was old enough to cool suggested that whoever ate three-quarters of it had not been by this way for a while. She ate what was left, as she was ravenous and needed the strength it would give her. It was not at all unpleasant.

A search revealed a narrow set of stairs leading upwards to a short, dark corridor ending at another door. This one was locked, and there was no dirt on which to draw. She frowned briefly, then raised her hand and traced the shape of the Ward in the air before her. The shape stayed, nearly invisible, hanging in the air, sketched in deeper darkness.

Why is it that I can do this? she thought to herself, and traced it again. Each time, she expected to find that it was a trick of her eyes or her mind, but it never seemed to happen. It was more than simply drawing in the air; it was as if her finger were following a groove, a pattern that it would take more effort to get wrong than to draw correctly. She was remembering, but it was *more* than remembering. Thatch had cleared out of her mind, but she had left things behind; experiences, memories that were now Alaizabel's. The old wych had unwittingly shown Alaizabel the art of drawing a Ward, and once it had been achieved it could not be forgotten, like the riding of a bicycle. Alaizabel did not even know how she was doing it, but it was working, and that was all that counted at the moment.

The Ward completed, the door clicked softly and popped open. Alaizabel allowed herself a smile of pure, childish pleasure and pushed the door. It was immensely heavy, but she put her shoulder to it and shifted it.

Here the room that faced her was not dank like the others but furnished beautifully, an attractive study with a picture of Queen Victoria above a stone fireplace and a phrenologist's model on the desk. Through a window, she could see that it was deep night outside. She stepped inside and saw why the door was so heavy. It was a section of a bookshelf; and when she closed it behind her, it was indistinguishable as an entrance.

Were there passages like that all over Redford Acres? Was this Pyke's study, or someone else's? She did not have time to find the answers. There seemed to be nobody about in the asylum tonight, and she did not intend to waste the opportunity to get out. She checked outside and then made her way onward, listening for sounds, hearing none. The asylum had its own electricity supply, and light bulbs glowed inside little brass lamps. A shriek echoed from somewhere in the depths of the building, loud enough to penetrate the walls. She jumped, cursed, and continued to where a balcony looked over a wide reception hall. Ahead of her was a dark mahogany door, with an unmanned desk next to it. There was no sign of life.

Why is nobody here? she thought, and crept her slow way down the curving stairs, ready to spring away at any time. Her bare feet padded over the carpeted floor, making not a sound. When she reached the bottom, she looked around. Several interior doors faced her, all closed. The one which led outside was obvious, and she went for it, glancing over her shoulder as she crossed the hall. This glut of good luck could not hold out. She had to hurry.

The door was locked, as she thought, but she drew her Ward over it. It was done with a little more haste than it should have, but the effect was the same. The door clicked and opened, and she looked through on to the porch of Redford Acres. The electric lamps held back the night a short way, and beyond that she could see the dark lunge of the walls and the gate; but there was no light in the gate-keeper's hut, no sign of movement anywhere. Of course, she would not expect a lot of staff at this time of the night, but surely all hospitals kept a skeleton crew around the clock? Lunatics did not respect office hours.

She had no way of knowing that the ceremony involving the transference of Thatch involved more than one Rite; it would take until the dawn to complete the necessary preparation of Thatch's new body, to fix her there and prevent her soul from straying. Most of the staff of Redford Acres were in the Fraternity, and those who weren't were given the night off. Pyke wanted no interruptions for his business tonight. He trusted to his locks to keep Alaizabel where she was until he decided what to do with her, and the inmates could fend for themselves for a night.

So Alaizabel stepped out into the freezing November night, feeling her skin goosepimple under the cotton shift that was her only clothing. It was mortally cold, but she dared not stay a second longer than she had to. She shut the door and ran barefoot down the gravel drive, fleeing from the light to the safety of the darkness beyond the gate. It could not be more than a kilometre or two to London, over the fields. She would be able to see the lights of the city and head for them.

But by the time she reached the gate, her teeth were chattering and she was shivering uncontrollably. The soles of her feet were scratched and bleeding from the gravel. Doggedly, she climbed the gate, nearly fainting from the exertion. She dropped down the other side and slipped off the road. She could indeed see the lights of London, but they would do her no good. She would freeze to death in half an hour. It was a choice between dying out here, or going back into Redford Acres.

Die here, she thought. *Better that way.*

No. She would try. She would try to make it, hopeless as it was.

She had no sooner come to the decision than a sound came to her ears. It was the distant rattle of a carriage, coming down the road towards her. Hunkering down to the grass, she drew herself out of sight, concealing herself behind a row of bushes that edged a field. The flare of hope that had ignited within her caused her to forget the cold for a moment.

It might be Pyke, a cautionary voice warned.

It might not! she replied.

A distant blot of white resolved itself into the shape of a horse down the road, with the body of a dark carriage behind. Then she realized there were *two* horses pulling, one as black as the night it cantered through. The carriage showed no sign of slowing as it approached her. If it was not going to Redford Acres, then perhaps it would be her saviour. She held her breath as it came closer, still not slowing; and when she was sure that it was going to pass the asylum, she leaped out with a cry.

"Sir! Please help me!" she called, the volume of her voice overcoming the juddering of her jaw. "Take me to the Peelers, please! I was kidnapped, but I have escaped!" She knew the Peelers could not help her, but any other destination would be too suspicious.

The driver, his collar high and his hat low and his face in darkness, reached around and pulled open the carriage door. He took a blanket from the back of one of the horses and threw it to her. "Young lady, this is no place for you. Get inside. I will take you wherever you want to go."

Too relieved to thank him, she threw open the door and clambered into the dark carriage, wrapping herself in the blessed gift, which was still warm from the horse and smelled of its previous owner.

"Go, please! Go!" she called urgently from the inside of the carriage.

"Of course, Miss Alaizabel," Stitch-face said under his breath, and urged the horses into motion.

"**D**o you sense it?" said the Devil-boy, making Lord Crott jump as he appeared like a spectre at the tableside.

"Whore's blood!" he swore in shock, then rounded on his aide. "Why aren't you in your sanctum trying to find us that girl?"

Crott had been more and more agitated of late, and his calm, roguish exterior was slipping. Some in the feasting hall looked over to him with concerned expressions on their faces, then returned to their platters. Crott was cracking steadily under the strain of his responsibility; he had hundreds of men, women and children under his protection, and he was damned if he could do a thing to prevent whatever the Fraternity was doing, the darkness that he knew would come. This interminable waiting had sanded his nerves raw.

"Do you sense it?" Jack repeated, and this time it was obvious he was addressing Cathaline and Thaniel, who sat opposite Crott and Armand.

"Sense what?" Crott demanded before she could reply.

"The Fraternity have got Thatch," Cathaline said, paling. "I felt *something*, but . . . I didn't know. Have they done it?"

"Unquestionably," croaked Jack. "Chandler's Distillation. I would never have expected to feel the force of it. The Fraternity have more power than we had guessed."

"What about Alaizabel?" Cathaline asked, pushing her plate of food aside. "Did you find her?"

The Devil-boy turned towards her. "She matters nothing now."

"She matters to *me!*" Thaniel cried, jumping up.

Cathaline laid a hand on his arm, not taking her eyes from Jack. "Do you know where the Distillation was performed?" she asked.

"I could not locate it," the boy rasped. "It does not matter. Alaizabel was taken by the Fraternity, and the Fraternity have their spirit. Leanna Butcher's death will bring their plan to fruition. We must prepare."

Armand laughed his mindless laugh. *Hur-hur-hur.*

Crott looked distractedly around the feasting hall. It was the same as any other night in the high-vaulted stone hall. Laughter, food, carousing; the high life of the beggars. He was their guardian, and he took his post seriously. The rest of the world could slide into the abyss for all he cared, but not *his* people. Their faces might be scarred and deformed, their limbs twisted or missing, but their hearts were the same as any. He felt himself failing them. The omens, the Rat King, the Crimson Fever . . . all symptoms of the evil that was to come. He was not a man who believed in God, but he believed in the Fraternity, and he believed in wych-kin. And he knew what they could do.

The word went out at dawn. Messengers were sent to the three other Beggar Lords, telling them what was occurring, warning them to be prepared. Crott's gang were informed, ordered to forsake their begging duties for the coming day and prepare for a war. Traps were checked, fortifications were built, doors were bolted. Guards were sent to the sewers, lookouts to the high-ground, spies out on the streets. Crott had not wanted to give the order until the very last, because he knew that panic and disorder were never far away when people were scared, especially when they did not know what to be scared of.

The evil is coming, was the whisper around the Lanes. *The evil is coming.* But what the nature of the evil was, no-one knew.

It was enough for the people of the Crooked Lanes that their Lord had given them an order; and being superstitious folk, having witnessed for themselves the foul portents that had spread across the city, they believed in the evil. The Crimson Fever was spreading fast outside the Lanes, and several had already fallen within, though mercifully they had not infected any others as far as anyone could tell. They knew dark times were upon them, and many of them were relieved to be doing something about it.

The warrens that ran beneath the streets had always been ready for a war. The beggars lived in a state of permanent alertness, for their enemies were many. There were the Peelers, who had always wanted to clear the Crooked Lanes of her festering inhabitants; there were the other Beggar Lords, whose constant struggle for territory and advantage meant that conflict was never far away; and of course there were the wych-kin. In less than twenty-four hours, the Lanes would be as fully prepared as they could be, and their deeper recesses would be as impenetrable as the Tower of London.

*

Cathaline returned to the cold, sterile room like a moth to a flame. She had stolen short hours of sleep here and there, but the tiredness that had draped itself across her shoulders would not be shifted by such half-hearted remedies. Here, time seemed to slow, measured by breaths rather than seconds. Leanna Butcher's breaths, becoming progressively more erratic as she neared the end. She had the smell of death on her.

Leanna Butcher: utterly insignificant in every way. Unhappily married to a callous and uncaring husband, a worker in a tin-packing factory, she was a pale and frail thing. All that Cathaline knew about her was that she had embarked on an affair, a forbidden love somewhere in London. She had divined that much from the letter in her pocket, a tender and heartfelt confession of one man's feelings. It was the one shining light in Leanna's dreary life, and it had been snuffed out when she became the final mark in a demonic join-the-dots puzzle.

She had been kidnapped and taken in secret to the Crooked Lanes. Nobody knew where she was. She had disappeared. That was the way it had to be. No hospital could protect her from the wych-kin.

So she lay; alone, dying. There were guards outside the door, and the occasional visit from the doctor, but beyond that . . . nothing. Only Cathaline, for hour after hour, sitting with her. Something about the woman provoked a terrible sadness in Cathaline, the woman and the letter. *Why didn't you leave your husband? Why didn't you try to be happy? Why did you stay crushed and downtrodden?* She felt as if she knew this woman, knew her by her pinched features, her mousy shape, her drab clothes and bonnet. She had read the letter many times, drawn many details from it. It pricked her heart, for reasons she could not explain. Insignificant Leanna Butcher was now the most important person on Earth to them. She was dying for them, and only one person cared enough to be with her when she did.

What cruel, foul things people are, Cathaline thought. *With their ambitions and their greed and their ignorance. This whole city will go about its affairs this morning, and not one hundredth of them even know that their lives may be preserved one more day because of this woman. And those who do know don't care. They only care that her heart keeps working. If she never awoke, if she kept on breathing but never awoke; why, that'd be just perfect for them.*

Sometimes she hated the city. The factories spewing filth, the endless new inventions, the strict manners, the criminals . . . this was the face of the Age of Reason, the new world of science. Muck and soot and horrible, horrible greed. Murder and spite and hatred. The factories brought the money, and where there was money there were the businessmen, and who gave a shilling about the life of a poor woman like Leanna Butcher when there were a million like her to pack the boxes, work the looms, stir the lye? Cathaline longed for days she had read about, days of country folk, days of villages and honest work and a warm hearth. Days where people cared about each other, and it was only the aristocracy who spent their days debating how to kill each other while the common man got on with his business.

Such days probably never existed, she told herself, but she could dream. Dream of a place that was not like this, this soulless, polluted, seething mass of humanity's worst. Dream of a world without wych-kin.

She held Leanna Butcher's cool, dry hand, and read the letter to her for the hundredth time. She hoped that somewhere, Leanna could hear and be glad that there was someone who loved her. Somehow, she knew Leanna was going, going soon. She finished the letter, and looked up at the ceiling of the dim room, as if she could see through it to the dawning sky. Tears sprang to her eyes. What would become of them now, now the darkness was poised to swallow them? What would become of them all?

She was still holding Leanna's hand when she died.

PART FOUR:
THE DARKENING

The catastrophe came slowly on to London. Morning had broken, sheeting rain down on to the dirty streets, turning everything dark and glistening. People got up as usual; the tram drivers, the muffin-men, the cobblers and solicitors. The night-folk took their rest, the prostitutes and the gamblers and those who ran the opium dens in the Docklands. One shift off, one shift on, the city went on as normal, unaware of the horror bearing down upon it. Only the innocent and the sensitive felt what was happening. All across London, babies cried incessantly. Palm-readers and fortune-tellers – those who were genuine, anyway – shut up their shops and huddled fearfully in their homes. Dogs howled, cats wailed, and people commented that it was most odd, how, even in the centre of the city, the cacophony of animals was to be heard in the distance.

It was in Margate that people noticed it first. There was a stiff west-to-east breeze blowing, curving the rain as it fell. Why, then, was the high, bobbled blanket of cloud moving west, *against* the wind – towards London? Similar observations were made in the north and south, where the clouds were rolling perpendicular to the bluster, crawling steadily inward in the direction of the capital.

The storm began at mid-afternoon, doubling the fury of the rain and jabbing forked sparks of lightning down on the city, the sky flashing and booming with terrible rage. So heavy was the downpour that it masked the clouds above, and consequently few were aware that the thick grey mass looming over them had begun to slowly circle.

So immense was the scale of the phenomenon that it would only have been possible to fully appreciate it from high above. If a person could have ridden a hot-air balloon high into the stratosphere, higher than anyone had ever gone, they might have looked down and seen a sight never seen before. The British Isles were covered in cloud, as was usual for this time of year, but never had it behaved in such a way. It appeared that London was sucking in the cloud in a great spiral. The vast, louring bulk was circling massively, like water down a plughole. London was the centre of a huge, rotating monstrosity of cloud. The eye of the hurricane.

By now it was only the most ignorant or those best versed in denial of the unknown that could not feel the unease and faint dread which settled upon them like ash. Something primal in their souls spoke to them, telling them that something unnatural was happening, made their spines prickle and their hands jitter. Only the women discussed their fears; the men kept it to themselves. That was the way of things.

The gas lamps were lit at four o'clock, so dark had it become. They glowed pallidly, reflecting in waving lines on the rippling rivers that chased each other down the streets. By six o'clock, people had begun noticing the reddish glow from the sky, strongest in the south, across the Thames; but the rain was still too strong to see through.

Just shy of eight o'clock, the rain thinned and stopped; and finally, the people of London realized that their unease had not been mere fancy, but terribly real. For there, hanging above the Old Quarter, was the centre of the spiral of cloud that stretched across the land, and at its core the sky glowed a foul arterial red. Like a slow whirlpool of blood it stirred around and around, rumbling and growling, flickers of dry lightning lashing from the maelstrom and darting down to the ruined, bomb-torn streets below.

Behind the clouds, night fell, deepening the already dark day to black. The fog gathered in the alleys and roiled out on to the streets. And with the fog came the wych-kin in their hordes.

They came from the Underground, pawing their way through the locked doors of the stations. They came across the Thames. The bridges across the river were guardless all of a sudden, and the gates hung open. They walked like ghosts through barriers, slipped from the shadows, slid beneath doors. They stalked and shifted, half-seen things, and the wolves stalked with them. Unhurried, they passed into north London, quietly, stealthily, and there they spread like a plague, finding new hollows to dwell in, new streets to roam. New lives to take.

It took time. First to suffer were those areas which nestled close to the Thames. Wych-kin moved subtly, each with their own urges and intentions. Perhaps two hundred were afflicted in that first night, but nobody had any idea of the insidious tide that was washing foetidly beneath their window sills until it was far, far too late.

*

In her bed in Chelsea, the copywriter's wife Claris Banbury woke with a shriek to see her husband rising from beneath the sheets of his own bed, lifting silently into the air. As the white shroud fell free, she saw in terror that his eyes were closed, that he was lying perfectly straight in sleep. Still shrieking, she saw the thing lurking in the shadows of the corner of the room, visible only in the murk of sleep-fogged eyes. Naked, twisted, an old, old crone with her long straggly hair cloaking her bent body, she crouched on all fours with hooves for feet and a long tail twitching behind her. Claris's heart had always been weak; it stopped altogether at the sight of the Night Mare taking her husband, and she sighed and lay back in her bed as if returning to slumber. She did not see her husband continue his smooth rise to the ceiling, dreaming of flying, until he was swallowed by the shadows up there. She was spared the slow, steady droplets of blood that began to spatter the beds, *drip, drip, drip*, painting the white sheets in shocked flowers of red.

Stepney Cemetery, a sprawling patch of walled-in grass scattered with tombs and markers for the victims of the Vernichtung. The fog that gripped the city was only a wispy mist here, due to some trick of geography. Corbis Tallow, grave-robber of no mean reputation, was in the process of procuring a fresh corpse for the experiments of one particularly ambitious doctor when he walked between the moon and the grave of Kitamina Forrest, a young aristocrat's daughter who had fallen to polio, aged eight. It was a little-known fact even to scholars of wychcraft that ghasts preferred the tombs of children to hide in, but

Corbis had never even heard of a ghast, and so he walked on, leaving his moonshadow behind him in the clutches of the wych-kin, not realizing that he had already died.

Barrow Smith, real name Boris Dunkel, an immigrant from the Teutonic states, had not found life in London easy. Experience had taught him to curb his accent, for Londoners were not fond of his people after the Vernichtung, and he lived under another identity to prevent the random beatings that he had suffered in the years following the bombing of the city. Bitterly now he hated the city to which he had come fifteen years ago. It had steadily worn him down, taking first his dignity, then his job as a secretary to a Bond Street lawyer, then his home. Fifteen years, and what was he left with? Only himself, a tattered rag of a man, tramping dismally over a heath in the undeveloped areas of Poplar, unable to sleep because the awful cold sent arthritic needles through his joints. So he walked, not knowing where, fog swilling around his ankles, hoping that somewhere on this wet, desolate patch of land was the long-awaited upturn in his fortunes that would make him feel a little bit human again.

He had not been witness to the strange and evil-looking phenomena over the Old Quarter, having spent the late evening huddled in an alley, screened in from the sky. Only after the fog had fallen did he decide to wander.

The yelp of the dog echoed eerily across the ghostly heath, making Boris start. He listened, and once again it came, a pitiful whine as of a mangy creature pleading for something. Boris looked, and he could faintly see a place where the earth folded over itself, leaving a small earthen cave with the roots of a near-by tree holding it up. A third sound, and he realized that the dog was inside the hollow.

There might have been a time when he would have imagined finding a hurt dog, nursing it back to health, having a companion to brighten his days on the streets. But his imagination had long since withered, and so he could think of no clear reason why he headed to the hollow, except that he felt a strange yearning for whatever was within.

"Here, boy," he said, in perfect Cockney. "Let's 'ave you. Where are you, then?"

He crouched down in front of the hollow. Eyes glittered back at him. The yelp deepened to a growl, and Boris realized that whatever had been making that noise, it was most certainly not a dog, and that mistake was to cost him his entirely pointless life.

Jimley Potter, master pickpocket at the age of twelve, street-urchin in the employ of Pete the Knife. He slept, twitching, in his cot in an empty warehouse, along with six other boys his age who formed the rest of Pete's gang. It wasn't a bad life, stealing other people's purses, keeping a bit and giving the rest to old Pete. Apart from the occupational hazard of being hung, it was really quite rewarding.

It was of the hangman's noose that he dreamed now, a gallows standing alone on the Yorkshire Moors, the rope swinging steadily. He often dreamed of the noose, but he never remembered, just as he would not remember this one, which was remarkable because of a new element in it. There was a small child standing by the gallows, a little girl wearing a black funeral dress, and a black cloak with a hood set halfway back on her head. He could see she was entirely bald. Her eyes were downturned at first, but when they looked up at him he could see that her irises were red as blood, and her face was as cold as the grave.

He awoke as normal that morning, stretched, and got up to have breakfast. It was only later that day that the Crimson Fever began to make itself felt.

Frannie Best, prostitute and mother, lived on the top floor of a two-storey house. It stood alone, a little island in the centre of a particularly tight muddle of back streets. The property was the result of a helping hand from an appreciative client, who was also a landlord and who lived on the bottom floor with his wife. He had made a fortune from unscrupulous dealings in the developing areas of London, fiddling property boundaries to make a profit. Downstairs, he was sleeping soundly. Upstairs, Frannie did not know what to do. For twenty minutes now she had been watching the wych-kin circling her house, listening to the soft scrape of its feet, watching it lumber slowly and awkwardly along with the great, glowing round stone held in its big hands. Three times now it had stooped to put the stone down, each time at one of the corners of the house; three times it had walked away and returned with a new stone. It was a tall, mournful, dreadful thing, known in wychlore as a deildegast. It took the shape of a narrow, lanky man in rags, his head bowed, his shoulders drawn as he carried his burden. Shuffling like a sleepwalker through the fog, it made a slow circuit of the house, and if Frannie had counted she would have noticed that it always made three circuits before dropping its stone.

Now, as it approached the fourth corner on its third trip around, Frannie panicked. She rushed into her two-year-old daughter's room, swept her up, and ran. Down the stairs she went, her infant starting to squeal in her arms. Out of the door, her fear of the wych-kin overwhelmed by her fear of staying in that house when the final stone was placed.

The deildegast placed its last stone on the final corner, and vanished. A moment later, the house gave a groan and collapsed, burying the landlord and his wife, leaving only the stones, their glow dimming until they had faded to grey rock once more.

The great steelworks at Fulham never slept, its forges never allowed to cool. Great pots of molten metal seethed like lava, hissing as they were tipped down long trenches and funnelled into enormous casts. Men wore only vests, helmets and stout trousers, all grimed with sweat and dirt. The darkness was thrown back by the hellish light from the furnaces, but the price to be paid was a constant and fierce heat that made the workers' bodies run with perspiration. Long shadows fell against the black walls, of hammers rising and plunging, of great chains pulled and clanking pots rattling along on runners.

Word of the evil thing that brooded over the Old Quarter was all over the factory, but the workmen were a hardy breed and not given to idle talk, so the speculation was limited at best. As long as the forges kept burning, and the Union watched their backs against the businessmen who would have their jobs and cut their wages, then they were content, which was as close to happiness as most of these men got.

It was past three in the morning when Bertlin Creel approached his foreman with a worried expression on his face. He was pudgy and balding, but his arms were like logs and he was as strong as any man in the works.

"What is it, Bert?" the foreman said, without taking his eyes off the beetle that was scuttling across the metal at his feet. He stamped on it, crushing it beneath his boot. "Well?"

"It's the melting pot, Amon."

"What *about* the melting pot?"

"I should come 'ave a look if I was you. You wouldn't ne'er believe me."

Amon scraped the remains of the beetle off his shoe and followed where Bert led him, back through the clanking and darkness and industry to where the vast melting pot hung like some idol to a fire-god. It was an enormous cauldron of black alloy with a pooched lip like a jug, and chains hanging from it; several trenches beneath it waited for it to be tipped, to carry the molten metal to the casts.

They climbed the unsteady metal steps to the top, where the heat was fiercest, and there Bert pointed into the heart of the glowing mixture.

Amon stared hard. At first, all he could see was the black islands of impurities that floated on the top of the furnace; but then something stirred deep inside the pot, and his vision was drawn to it.

"You see it?" Bert asked.

"I see something, all right," Amon replied. "I

should think it's — hold yer horses! Did you see *that?*"

"Course I did," said Bert. "The blessed thing's been movin' about down there the better part of five minutes now."

Amon studied it further. Other workers were there too, watching him for a reaction. He examined it for a time. It was only a vague black blur, impossible to tell what it was, but he could see by the way it was moving what was happening. It was swimming like an otter or a seal. In molten metal that was several hundred degrees in temperature. Which was impossible.

"The boys think it's a salamander, Amon," Bert said.

"What's a salamander?" Amon asked.

"It's a thing that lives in fire. They get so hot that when they come out, they cracks like when you put a hot glass in cold water."

"What 'appens then?" Amon inquired.

"Nobody lived to tell the tale," Bert replied.

Amon tutted. "You tell 'em there's no such bloody thing as a salamander. Get the moulds, pour that metal and get whatever that thing is out of there. You hear?"

"Right," Bert said, glad that someone had decided what to do.

At five o'clock, the Fulham steelworks exploded in a rain of flame, sending burning meteorites as far as Chelsea, Battersea and Hammersmith, starting fires that spread hungrily towards the dawn.

By the morning, London had realized that the boil of the Old Quarter had burst and spread itself. If indeed a morning it could be called, for the sky was so thick with cloud that the sun's best efforts could only muster twilight. Smoke drifted in a pall from the blazing sections of the city, and faint coronas of firelight could be seen above the terraces and parks. The day provided no respite from the wych-kin now; of those people who walked out on the streets to go to work, many never arrived. Carriage horses were savaged by packs of wolves. Factories were panicked by the sight of crouching things in the rafters. Children who had squalled in the night that there was something under their beds were missing that morning, and only little dolls of them were left on their pillows. The Crimson Fever was everywhere, more and more people observing with horror as the cracked red lines appeared over their body, the delicate tracery of burst capillaries showing up to jigsaw their skin. It struck with no pattern and no logic, and did not seem to be infectious in a conventional manner; yet overnight it had afflicted more people than in the previous week.

People hid, or locked themselves in their houses, or left the city as fast as they could. Some made it; most didn't. Drivers on the way out seemed to become disorientated and find themselves on a road back into the heart of the city. Others found to their cost that there were things unmentionable waiting by the main thoroughfares out of London.

That was the first night, and the first dark day. As the twilight began to fade back to pitch without having ever touched brightness, London trembled and dreaded the night to come.

Alaizabel sat on the rickety wooden chair in the dark room, her head hung and her blonde hair lank across her face. Slats of grim twilight showed through the black rectangle of the single window, shutters letting in what feeble luminescence there was. Distantly, a wolf howled and was answered by another faraway pack.

Her wrists were chafed raw from rubbing against the ropes that tied them to the back of the chair. She was faint from hunger and exhaustion, and she shivered against the cold in the bare room. Clouds of her breath plumed raggedly from her mouth. She had been here for hours, it seemed; but it was still night outside, so it could not have been so long.

One horror to another, she thought to herself. *When will it be over?*

Stitch-face. How could it have happened, that of all the saviours that might have driven by in that freezing November night, the one to save her life would happen to be London's most voracious serial killer? What manner of force conspired against her? What had she done to bring such evil upon herself?

Perhaps I am suffering for the sins of my parents, she thought.

But no; she would not give in to despair. The

terrible weariness that had sunk into her bones was weakening her resolve, but she was stronger than self-pity. Stitch-face had her, but she still breathed. There was that.

She thought of Thaniel then, and for a time she entertained notions of him rescuing her; but they were false hopes. Nobody knew where she was, not even her. Alone, once again.

She heard the sound of a heavy key in the lock, and she looked up, her chest tightening. The thick wooden door opened, and Stitch-face stood there, a huge bowie knife in one hand, sharpened to a gleam.

"Good morning, child," said the sewn corpse-mask beneath the beautiful cascades of dead brown hair. He stepped into the room, his knife held before him.

Alaizabel suppressed a sound of fear that threatened to escape her throat. She kept her eyes fixed on him, never wavering. If she was to die here, it would not be as a cowering child. She was herself now, free from the dark spirit within her. Alaizabel Cray.

He locked the door, and pocketed the key. Drawing another chair up, he placed it before her and sat on it. He was wearing riding boots, leather gloves and a greatcoat, the collar turned down. Nothing showed of him but the bow of his lips and his cold, dead eyes.

She waited, not saying a word, hardly daring to breathe.

He leaned forward and reached out a hand, stroking it down the line of Alaizabel's jaw. She stiffened, frozen in horror and disgust. Stitch-face's knife was at her neck the moment she flinched.

"Where is the wych-spirit, Miss Alaizabel? Why is she not with you any more?"

"How——" Alaizabel began, but her throat was dry and she made only a wheeze. She began again. "How do you know she is not?" It was both a question and a bluff; pretending to have Thatch inside her could mean she kept her life. Or lost it. She had no idea what Stitch-face wanted yet.

It didn't matter. "I *know*, Miss Alaizabel. You just told me by the tone of your voice."

Alaizabel kept her face blank.

He removed his knife from her throat, tapped the side of his head with the point, and then withdrew to sit back in his chair.

"You do not have the wych with you," he said. "The Fraternity have her, I suppose?"

"What would you do if they had?" she demanded bravely.

"Please stop these games, Miss Alaizabel," Stitch-face said with a sigh. "Suffice to say that if you still had the wych inside you, I would gut you like a fish here and now, and then she would die and the Fraternity's plan would collapse."

He got up, leaving her chilled at the tone of his words. He walked over to the window, produced another key, and unlocked the shutters, throwing them wide. The sounds from outside came louder now: wolf-howls, running footsteps, distant pistol-cracks, high arcing screeches of unidentifiable things, and beneath it all a distant rumbling, almost too low to hear.

"Fortunate, don't you think, that I happened by tonight?" he asked, looking out of the window. "Or rather, ironic; for I had come to find you and kill you, but I was sadly too late. Have no fear, child. You are a little young for cutting, and the mood is not on me tonight. I have other concerns. Come. See for yourself."

He stepped away from the window and came up behind her. She winced in fear as he put his knife to her bonds, thinking only of that sharp edge so close to her skin. But the ropes fell free, and Stitch-face stepped back. She got up, rubbing her wrists, and went to the window as she was told. This side of her prison faced on to a wide patch of waste-ground, where rubble and pieces of junk lay scattered. Nobody within calling distance, even if she had got the shutter open. Beyond the waste was the city, and beyond that the awesome, fearful swirl of bloodied clouds that rotated gigantically in the near-darkness. The city itself was alive with shrieks and wails and ringing bells. One section was burning, the flames rising above the roofs and sending floating chunks of burning ash into the air. Lightning flashed and zagged, darting into the streets to light fresh blazes, and there was no rain to put them out.

"Is . . . is this the Old Quarter?" she asked in horror. She turned back to Stitch-face. "Have you brought me to the Old Quarter?"

"Oh no," said Stitch-face casually. "We are still a good mile north of the Thames. The Old Quarter is beneath that particularly pretty maelstrom in the sky."

She looked out again, numbed by shock. "Is it all like this?"

"Most of it," Stitch-face replied.

"You said it was morning," she said quietly.

"It is," he replied. "Ten o'clock, or a little past. Those clouds keep everything awfully dark, you know."

She slumped, moving away from the sight. "We failed, then," she said.

"You've *not* failed," said Stitch-face suddenly. "Not yet, anyway. This simply represents a small portion of what will happen if you *do* fail. The *chackh'morg* is complete; the sacrifices have been made, the gate is open. This is only the faintest breath of the power of what the Fraternity are bringing through that gate. They can be stopped yet."

Alaizabel frowned, puzzled at this new turn. Of all the things she had expected from her first meeting with Stitch-face, she had certainly not expected *this*.

"I had a talk with a lady named Lucinda Watt. She was really quite knowledgable about the workings of the Fraternity, once I had persuaded her enough." He grinned, a horrible death-rictus. "The *chackh'morg* is the beginning. The preparing of the way. A great Ward, shaped with murders. The Fraternity have spent decades preparing for the summoning of Thatch. The Rite to summon Rawhead alone took seven years to procure all the necessary ingredients and knowledge. The gate is open now, the way prepared. But there is another ceremony yet. Thatch is the guide; a spirit who has died and been brought back. In life she had great power, which allowed her to overcome death." He paused, examining the edge of his knife. "Where the dead are, it is not easy to find a way back to the land of the living. Now Thatch knows the pathways of the dead, and she can lead the Fraternity's god to us. She is like the tug that pulls a great ship into harbour. She is the key. She is mortal. She can die."

Alaizabel could barely take it all in. "Kill Thatch?"

"The ceremony will take a few days," Stitch-face

242

said. "When it is finished, all is lost. As is London, so will the world be."

Terrified as she was, Alaizabel heard herself speak. "Why?" she asked. "Why are you doing this?"

The ghastly face looked out of the window, tinged in red. "I am a monster, Miss Alaizabel. But even monsters want to live."

"I don't understand," she said.

"Someone was killing in my name," Stitch-face said. "Pretending to be me. I mislike imitators of my work, child. But I know something of the Fraternity, and I guessed their hand in this. So I found Lucinda Watt, and I talked to her, and she told me all she knew. And after that . . . well. The Fraternity plan to bring death upon us all." He fixed Alaizabel with a dreadful gaze. "And I do not wish to die. So they must be stopped." He paused. "And if I should come across the man behind the plan to mimic my artistry, one Doctor Mammon Pyke, then I may be tempted to do to him what I did to his secretary."

Stitch-face turned away from her then, walked to the door. He unlocked it and stepped through, then looked back. "You have friends. I suggest you find them. I shall not trouble to lock this door behind me."

And with those words, he was gone.

"Burn them! Burn their filthy hides!"

Matches were struck and held to alcohol-soaked rags that poked from bottles of London's most potent grog. The foetid air was full of shouts and howls, echoing along the tunnels in a constant throb. And above it all was the squeaking, the maddening chatter of the rats as they swarmed over the makeshift barricades, biting and scrabbling and scratching.

The dull explosion of the grog-bombs was accompanied by a surge of heat as long patches of fire raced along the sewer walls and spread themselves in burning slicks across the turgid, knee-high water. Rats screamed as their fur ignited, jumping for the water, but the water was aflame too, and they could only dive for so long before they returned to the surface to die.

In amid the horde lumbered the Dog-rats, the wych-beasts that were leading the masses. They were a metre long without counting the tail, all arched hindquarters and bristly black fur, with jaws that could have a man's hand off. Twisted from within, they were; possessed by wych-spirits that warped them and made them huge and foul. Their muzzles were leathery and dog-like in expression, their claws hooked and vicious, and their eyes glowed with a demonic light – little lanterns in the darkness.

Crott swung his own grog-bomb at one of them, smashing it dead centre on the creature's back. He took a moment to enjoy its shrieking and thrashing before turning his sabre on a nearby clot of rats that had attached itself to the leg of an old beggar.

The Crooked Lanes were under siege on all sides. Wych-kin stalked the streets and tunnels, heedless of the defences and not a bit confused by the mazes within; and down in the sewers, these damnable rats.

The hastily constructed barriers of metal sheeting and grilles were proving remarkably ineffective against the tide of vermin that had arrived that morning. The rats had undermined some blockage further up the tunnels, and had come riding on a deluge of junk and debris to pile up against the barricades and overwhelm them. Driven by a dark intelligence, they had effortlessly invaded the humans' domain, leaving the defenders flailing to keep them away.

Behind the barricade, dozens of beggars fought and thrashed in the stinking water, stabbing at the furred things that swam around their legs or scampered along the footway at the side of the sewer. Crott swept up a rat by the throat and shook it viciously, feeling its bones crack, then tossed the limp thing aside and waded away, back towards the tunnels that would lead to the surface. He could do no good here. Their efforts at defence were futile, yet it was necessary to provide some kind of resistance. He had never felt so helpless.

Beggars hurried and hobbled down the grimy stone stairway as Crott made his way up it, heading to the battle below. They scarcely recognized their leader in his bedraggled condition, reeking of sewage and slump-shouldered. He reminded himself that he should act according to his position, and he corrected his bearing so as not to look quite so defeated.

He burst through the door at the top of the stairs, suddenly possessed by a fury born of frustration, and collared a beggar-boy who was about to run down the stairs to where the rats were.

"Never mind them, boy," he said. "Go find me the wych-hunters, bring them to my chambers. Do it quick."

The boy obeyed, holding his lame arm to his chest as he scuttled away. Crott stamped his way through the dark underground tunnels, stopping here and there to issue an order, to offer support, to help his people in some way. All around him was scuffle and skirmish, distant cries. Things were the same in

Rickarack's territory, by all accounts. He didn't know what had become of the other two Beggar Lords; none of them had sent messengers in return, perhaps disbelieving his warning. He'd wager they believed him now.

He wanted to scream or kill something. Nothing he could do would hold back the invaders. He had no effective methods of dealing with wych-kin or Crimson Fever. The rats were the easiest to handle, and even they were beating the beggars hands down. He swore hard enough to make a sailor blush and stamped towards his chambers.

Cathaline and Thaniel were already there when he arrived. His eyebrows raised a little at the sight of Carver, sitting with the wych-hunters; the Detective should have had his hands full dealing with the chaos in the city. Closing the door, he sat down in an armchair that seemed to grow out of a heap of gold bedsteads and wooden dressers.

"So," he said. "This is a pretty little mess, isn't it?"

"Indeed," said Thaniel tonelessly.

"How are things, Detective Carver?"

"Bleak," he replied. He looked a mess; for a man of Carver's fastidious neatness, it said more than words could. "We're being overrun. And people can't get *out*. The bastards are penning us in for slaughter. The Army's on its way, but I'd like to know what they could achieve that we haven't."

"Have you achieved *anything?*" Crott asked out of spite, rubbing the sword-scar that curled his lip into a sneer and ran up his cheek. He was still feeling venomous, though not towards Carver specifically.

"We are keeping the panic to a minimum," the detective said. A rattling noise came from another room in Crott's chambers; he looked towards it for a moment, then disregarded it and continued. "Guarding the hospitals. It is all we can do."

"What did you want us for?" Cathaline asked bluntly. She was too tired to be polite. Her last few hours had been spent dealing with all forms of minor wych-kin; thankfully, she had not come across anything major yet.

"I want a battle plan," Crott said. "What we're doing is useless. They're swarming all over us. You two are the only real weapon we have against the wych-kin, and I suspect that you are running out of supplies and charms. We can't win by fighting them here."

"I have a proposition," said Carver.

"Ah. A proposition." Crott sat back in his chair and steepled his fingers. "I knew there was some reason why you had come."

Carver let Crott's unpleasant tone slide off his back. "We're up against an army, one that's much bigger than we are. There's no sense dealing with the foot soldiers. We'll lose. We have to strike at the generals."

"The Fraternity," said Cathaline. "You think we haven't considered that?" She waved a hand above her head, indicating the outside world.

"You know where Thatch is now?" Carver asked.

"*I* know where she is," said Devil-boy Jack, walking through the doorway from another chamber, as silent as a ghost. It was he who Carver had heard rattling; though what he was doing, the Detective had no idea. Crott was apparently used to the Devil-boy coming and going as he pleased. "I'm sure you all have guessed. The Old Quarter. The centre of the maelstrom."

"We know," Cathaline said irritably. "It's obvious.

You don't even need a wych-sense to feel where it's all coming from. Besides, I imagine you've already performed a Divination to be sure?"

"I have."

"Wonderful," said Crott. "And have any of you thought how we're going to get into the heart of the Old Quarter when to travel a mile above ground and remain alive is nigh impossible?"

"My point exactly," Cathaline said, settling back into her chair.

"By Heaven, are you all already beaten?" Carver cried, getting up. "I have never seen men and women fold so easily! I came here with a *way* to get into the Old Quarter. Would any of you care to hear it? Or would you prefer to declare your cause hopeless and give in?"

There was a moment of slightly shamed silence. Even Crott felt childish in his negativity.

"How do we do it?" Thaniel said at last, his eyes dark. His jaw was set in determination. He had become dour and menacing in aspect since Alaizabel had been taken from them, his every thought upon how to find her. But then the wych-kin had attacked, and he had been forced to stay and defend the Lanes. Cathaline could not do without him here. But if Alaizabel were . . . no, he dared not think that thought.

"West of here is the old Caledonian Road station," Carver said. "The Lanes stretch up close to that. If we can get there, we can go through the Underground tunnels and get to Finsbury Park."

"You want us to take an airship?" Crott asked in disbelief. "You want us to go through the *Underground?*"

"I can't pretend it isn't dangerous," Carver said. "But it can be done. In the Underground, there are not so many sides wych-kin can come from. I have telegrammed and commandeered a pilot; he is waiting for us there. The Finsbury Park airstrip is still held by the soldiers there, at least for a time. After that, we fly over the Old Quarter. Not many wych-kin can fly, I would guess."

"I don't believe I am hearing you right, Carver," said Crott. "What you are proposing seems to be suicide."

"Oh, don't be dramatic, Crott," Cathaline snapped. "It's the best idea I've heard so far. I'm in."

"I will go, too," said Thaniel.

"We shall all go," husked the Devil-boy. "Come into this room."

Puzzled, they got up and followed him to the room from which he had come. There, beneath the light of a stuttering gas lamp, a chalk circle had been drawn on the floor. A doeskin bag lay nearby, and scrying stones were scattered in the circle. They were flat, white and elliptical, and each bore a mark on it, carved and painted in black ink.

"Do you know of the stones?" he rasped.

"A little," Cathaline said, then privately added: *enough to know whether you know anything about them.* Scrying stones were a blend of old runic disciplines and tarot, a complex system of symbols that created pictures of great complexity when combined. Unlike runes or tarot, however, they were extremely specific and not open to wide interpretation. To a charlatan or an amateur, they would spell simple nonsense. It took long study to master them, and each had to be treated with its own Rite. Cathaline was sceptical of the Devil-boy; he was far too young.

Jack crouched down by the side of the chalk circle,

his hair straggling over his blind eyes. He never seemed to have the slightest problem finding his way about, even without his vision.

"See," he said. "This rune, fallen in that way, conjunct with this one. The King and his Boy. That is you and me, Lord Crott. Here, the sign for the Hunters, and its orientation towards the others means *two*. That is you, Thaniel, and Cathaline. Three more: the Yeoman, the Idiot, the Sacrifice. Detective Carver, Armand and Alaizabel."

He brushed a frond of hair back from his dirtied face and pointed elsewhere in the circle. "There. Journey, the Earth, and that one means Above and Below. We travel under and over the ground." He straightened and faced them. "I cast the runes before I came in here. It is fated, already decided. We go. It is the way."

"What do those other stones mean?" Crott said, motioning to several stones within the circle that Jack had not mentioned.

"They are irrelevant. Their location helps divine the meaning of the other stones," came the reply.

Thaniel looked at Cathaline, who shrugged. The Devil-boy seemed to know what he was talking about. Whatever and whoever Jack was, he was certainly possessed of great power and a knowledge far in advance of his years.

"So we bring Armand," said Crott. "What of Thaniel and Alaizabel?"

"Have you not realized yet? It is all being decided for us. We are the pawns of the higher powers, who want us to stop the Fraternity."

"You mean Alaizabel will find us?" Thaniel asked, a note of sudden hope in his voice.

There was a knock at the door. "Girl 'ere to see you, Lord!" hollered the guard.

"It appears," said the Devil-boy, "that she already has."

Thaniel sprung to his feet faster than any of them, as Crott motioned at the guard to let her in. He was at the doorway when she stepped through, bedraggled and exhausted, and her eyes rose to meet his. The two of them faced each other for a heartbeat, no words coming to either of them; and then they held each other, and words were not needed any more.

T ime was desperately short, and perhaps the hardest aspect of that day was the waiting. Once the decision had been made to go, nobody wanted to put it off; the fearful anticipation was almost unbearable. But Cathaline, Carver and the Devil-boy all insisted that they move at nightfall. Cathaline's reason was practical: they needed time to prepare new charm-strings, for the morning's battles had left them nearly out of weaponry. Jack declared in his annoyingly vague way that the alignment of the scrying-stones favoured a night departure. Carver said it "made more sense", but did not clarify why.

The fact was, they needed sleep. All were exhausted. The hunters and beggar-folk were nocturnal by nature, but most had missed at least one day's rest, and there had been precious little chance to lay down over the previous few days. They would need to be as alert and prepared as possible to stand a chance out there.

They slept in Crott's chambers, which were guarded and had several rooms large enough to accommodate them all. Crott himself refused to sleep; despite his acceptance of his companions' recommendation, he could not rest while his territory was under siege. He threw himself back out into the fray, and when he returned towards nightfall, he was plainly exhausted. Cathaline suggested he stay behind, but he would hear nothing of it, and nor would Jack.

"I live in a battlefield, Miss Bennett," Crott said, his smile turned leerish by the scar that ran up his pox-pitted cheek. "I've endured more than these creatures can throw at me."

Thaniel and Cathaline had spent most of the day with the Devil-boy in his sanctum, performing Rite after Rite, only sleeping when they were too tired to continue. It was gruelling work, but they were heading into the heart of the wych-kin's domain, and they needed every weapon they could. Knives were Warded, charm-strings were sewn, amulets treated and reagents prepared. Powder, sulphur, bullets and blades; their arsenal was an assembly of superstitions, myths and legends. The Devil-boy supplied them with what they needed, and offered them items from his own hoard; Jamaican feathered darts for use against jumbies, gris-gris from New Orleans to ward off dead-walkers, miniature Canadian forest-idols for wendigos. There was no way they could prepare enough, and yet they simply could not carry too much. In the end, they could only do the best they could, and hope it would suffice.

Alaizabel spent her time reading. Jack had provided her with a tome of simple Wards, and instructed her to study it. If Thatch's memories still resided in her, it would take little more than a reminder to awaken them again. Alaizabel read, her eyes blurring from staring at the arcane and disturbing shapes etched in red ink on the page. And each shape, once seen, stayed. She learned thirty of the most basic Wards that day, but they were thirty Wards that she knew would *work*.

What has she done to me? Alaizabel thought. *What am I supposed to do with this?*

Alaizabel had been left with a power, literally overnight, that could change her entirely. She was used to imaginary and impossible things happening in fairy tales; but here, the ability had been delivered into her hands. She was terrified of it. She had already come across Wards for the infliction of pain, for disorientation, for death. All of these had sprung from her mind like jack-in-the-boxes as soon as her gaze made contact. She dreaded to think what else she might remember if she spent a month, a year in the study of wychcraft.

I am a wych now, she told herself, and the thought brought her to sudden tears.

All of them snatched a few hours' sleep, sheer exhaustion overcoming them. Armand, who did not need the rest, was away with Lord Crott. Only Carver slept the whole day through, untroubled, like a baby.

Outside, the Crooked Lanes gave itself up slowly but surely to the wych-kin.

Night fell.

The storm burst from the clouds with typhoon fury, a raging dragon of lashing rain and thunderous roars, striking out with forked barbs of lightning, setting fires and extinguishing them just as quickly. The blazes that had raged across London quailed and choked under the onslaught, leaving wet and blackened patches of char kilometres wide, hulking skeletons of buildings that ran with water and wept for the human corpses within.

On the edge of the Crooked Lanes an old church

sat, a creature of weathered stone and high Gothic arches. Soot from a nearby fire had blackened its face, but the rain was washing its stained-glass windows down, pummelling the dirt away with cleansing savagery. Its great doors were locked, for it had lain unoccupied for a dozen years now, ever since the Crooked Lanes crept up behind and claimed it. It was the westernmost point of the slums, the limit of Lord Crott's territory.

Inside, the Hallow Ghoul walked as it had always walked, shuffling between the mighty sandstone pillars, through the cloisters, past the altar to the apse. The baptismal bowl had long been dry; the altar was an abandoned slab. High above, a mighty wooden crucifix hung from chains, one worn and snapped so it tilted at an angle, Christ's carven eyes watching the unholy thing as it dragged itself past the pews.

It was a creature that thought itself alive, though it was little more than a shade, a ghost of a ghoul. To human eyes, it was visible only where light struck it directly; all else was invisible, unsolid . . . not there at all. But somewhere in whatever could be called its mind it believed itself the keeper of the church, the defender of the stones, and so each night it walked. It had claimed trespassers before, but those that had escaped its grip had warned others, and there had been no visitors for nigh on six years now. Until tonight.

The shifting of the stone trapdoor in the crypt of the church was no easy task. Once, perhaps, it might have been the escape route for priests still nervous about the religious persecution that drove the British to America. Since then it had joined the network of tunnels and alleys left over in the wake of the Vernichtung, half-discovered and half-constructed by the enterprising beggars that called the Crooked Lanes home. There had not been cause to ever use it until now.

It took all of Thaniel's might to heave the trap-door up, revealing a square of light in the floor of the silent, dusty black void of the crypt. He raised his lantern, spilling unwelcome brightness into the empty dark, filling it with rows of stone shelves and ledges, cracked coffins, scattering spiders.

He looked about warily before clambering through the narrow tunnel. Cathaline followed, then Alaizabel, Crott and the others, finally squeezing Armand's massive frame through. By the time they had all got their feet under them, the lantern light had been multiplied by the addition of several others and the entire crypt was visible.

The musty, still decay surrounded them, seeping through the time-worn stone. Several stone oblongs dominated the floor, their legends brushed away by the passage of time, containing bones that had long since gone to powder. All around was the eerie sensation of movement, the rats and spiders and beetles as they hugged the corners of the crypt, fleeing the light. A low roof loomed in close, sandwiching them between the ledges of coffins on either side.

Armand's face was a childish picture of fear, plainly terrified. He made a strange moaning noise. Thaniel spared him a glance before raising his lantern towards where a set of narrow, crumbling steps led upwards.

"Keep alert," he said.

"The bastard's around here somewhere, I'll wager," Crott muttered.

They knew about the Hallow Ghoul. Most of the Lanes did; some were almost fond of it. There was never any reason to do anything about the creature. It was just an old church, after all. Let the ghoul keep it.

But now they had to deal with the warden of the church. Simply, it was a trade. The long northward tunnel clipped off a kilometre of dense and dangerous streets, but the downside was the thing waiting at the other end.

"Better the devil you know," Cathaline had said.

"Light it," said Thaniel, and Cathaline brought forth a small incense burner from her pack, a delicate globe of gold hanging from three thin chains. Carver did the same, holding a match to it and lighting the flammable mixture that lay beneath the powdered incense. Armand continued to bleat as the smoke wisped out from the globes. They both swung the globes gently side to side like pendulums, allowing the scent to rise up and surround them. It was earthy and dry and somehow flat, with an acrid underside to it.

"And this is what will keep the Hallow Ghoul from us?" Crott asked sceptically, keeping his voice to a whisper in the silence of the crypt.

"Ghouls hate it," Thaniel said confidently. "Powdered lilies, grass, dried earth, mixed with incense. The smells of a funeral." He looked at Cathaline, who nodded to indicate the burners were working well enough now. "You just have to remind them that they are dead."

"I'd hardly have imagined something so small

could defeat wych-kin," Crott said. "It makes them hardly fearful."

Thaniel gazed at him levelly. "I would not like to guess how many wych-hunters died at the hands of ghouls before someone discovered this," he said.

They ascended a set of narrow stone stairs and opened the door that led to the sacristy. It was a small room, where the priests prepared themselves for Mass. There was nothing there now, having been emptied when the church was abandoned; only a bench and a washbasin. It was as black as the crypt was, with no windows to let in the light.

They made their wary way across, and Cathaline pushed open the door that led to the church proper.

Silent cloisters greeted them as they emerged, pillared walkways covered by a balcony above. The church was not so dark as the previous rooms, and it echoed and roared whispers that told of the assault from the sky on its outer skin. The tall stained-glass arches let in a faint glow, slanting its hue with the robes of the saints and the wings of angels. The pews were thick with shadow, the great wooden Christ staring out across them, tilted.

"Where is it?" Alaizabel whispered.

"It's near," said Thaniel and Cathaline in unison, responding to their wych-senses.

"Keep moving," Crott advised.

Armand, considerably happier now that he was out of the crypt and away from the corpses, laughed his foolish laugh. They walked slowly along the cloisters, the pews on their right, heading for the arched double doors at the north end of the church. Thaniel felt the skin creep along his nape, his eyes searching the slices and patches of shadow that lurked in the hollow body of the building.

"There's our ghoul," Crott muttered suddenly, pointing.

They saw it then, slouching along the central aisle, their lamplight splashing across the left side of its body and showing it up in translucent white. Rags and tatters clothed it; a bony hand showed through a torn sleeve. Its head was half-fleshed, a white eggshell of skull showing through behind its eye socket, and its lips were withered to nothing, showing a skeleton smile beneath a collapsed nose and lidless eyes that stared endlessly. Half corpse, half skeleton, it managed to be neither. The portions of its form that were lit seemed to hang in the air, flat pictures supported by nothing, for its unlit parts were invisible.

It seemed not to have noticed them; rather, it was dragging itself slowly along and looking ahead, instead of to its left where they were.

"Does it know we are here?" Alaizabel asked.

"It knows," said Thaniel. "Do not be fooled. Keep walking. Slowly. It may let us by if we do not alarm it." They did so, none daring to take their eyes off the thing. It was perhaps five metres away, with only the length of a pew dividing them.

None of them had been above ground for a considerable time and, despite the rain, none were truly aware that there was a fully fledged storm raging until it decided to announce itself with a blinding flash and a simultaneous bellow of thunder loud enough to make Armand shriek and Alaizabel duck.

Crott swore. "It's gone!" he said, and he was right. The Hallow Ghoul, for one second illuminated all over by the lightning, had disappeared in the dazzling aftermath.

The brightness faded, leaving them in an empty church. The air prickled with tension. Their enemy had been bad enough when they could see it; now that they had no idea where it was, it was worse.

"We have the incense," said Thaniel. "Keep going."

Cathaline held her burner up high, swinging it around a little wider, sending the maudlin scent all around them. Carver did the same, and the others moved in closer around him. They were perhaps halfway along the length of the church.

Cathaline was considering making a run for the final stretch when a terrible shriek ripped through the cloisters, and from behind one of the thick pillars the Hallow Ghoul lunged at them, claws reaching for Alaizabel. She cried out and threw herself back against the wall; but the ghoul pulled up short as it encountered the fumes of the incense burner. Crott's pistol was out instinctively, firing a round into the rotting thing. The creature was already recoiling, pulling back with a hiss, and Crott's shot passed directly through it and through the great stained-glass window on the façade of the church. The glass shattered and came tumbling down in a riot of colour and sound, a disastrous waterfall of accidental destruction.

The Hallow Ghoul shrieked, appalled at the damage to its home. The noise sliced through them like blades, making them cringe as it turned its one good eye on Crott. It lunged again, thrusting its claw into Crott's chest, reaching inside and grasping his heart as if it were an apple in a basket. The Beggar Lord screamed, a noise higher than anyone would have thought could have come from the scar-faced man, and then suddenly Thaniel was there, a charm-string snaking towards the ghostly thing. Lightning flashed once more, shattering thunder bursting through the air, and then there was only the sound of the charm-string clattering to the ground and a disappearing wail as the Hallow Ghoul went to rest at last.

Everyone was shouting at once. Crott was collapsing into Armand, still screaming; Alaizabel was crying out in horror; Armand had joined his master by setting up an idiot wail of distress; Carver and Thaniel were shouting instructions, Cathaline too. Only the Devil-boy stood quiet.

"Stand back!" Cathaline commanded, her voice rising above all the others. "Lay him down, Armand! Stand back, all of you!"

Crott was like a wounded rabbit, wild-eyed and thrashing. He had run out of breath and had stopped screaming, and gaped instead, mouthing nothing. Armand lowered him to the ground. Cathaline shoved Carver aside, who was attempting to take control of the situation in his policeman's way, despite not knowing what he was doing. She tore Crott's shirt open while Armand knelt at his head and held it, a surprisingly intelligent move.

"Why didn't the incense work?" Carver demanded of the room in general.

"This fool made it angry," Cathaline said, pressing his hand to Crott's chest. It had gone grey where the ghoul had touched it. She held out a hand and opened her mouth to speak, but Thaniel was already handing her the golden incense globe. She tipped it into her hand, pouring burning hot ash on to her skin, and threw the globe aside before rubbing the ash vigorously into Crott's chest. Crott was still gasping for air, twitching and coughing.

"It should not have been able to. . ." Thaniel said.

"The wych-kin's time is at hand," Devil-boy Jack said. "They are more powerful than before." He walked over to the charm-string and picked it up, apparently unconcerned with his Lord. He studied it. Two Wards were smoking, having flared and burned out on contact with the ghoul. "Now we know how to deal with them next time," he said, holding the object out to Thaniel.

There was a heavy thump as Cathaline linked her fists and brought them down on Crott's chest, and the Beggar Lord gasped and coughed and then lay back, breathing heavily. Cathaline sighed and looked over her shoulder.

"He will live. For now. He needs to be treated. He needs a proper Rite. You can take him back, Devil-boy. You can perform the—"

"No," Jack rasped. "That is not the way. We go as the scrying stones ordained."

"You will take him back as I say!" Cathaline ordered.

The Devil-boy's soulless, sewn-up eyes showed nothing. "I have seen in the stones how this will end. If all goes as it should, we will be victorious. If we deviate from the pattern set, we change the course of the future. I will not jeopardize the world for Crott."

"The other stones, the ones you said were useless; they told you things, did they not?" Thaniel demanded.

"Who lives, and who dies, and where," Jack replied. "And in one case, how."

"You cannot keep that from us!" Thaniel said.

"I must," came the guttural reply. "I must, for if we change what we were to do, so we change the outcome. I could save one of your lives, and the rest would then die and that person would die later anyway and we would *fail!*" He barked the last word, making Alaizabel jump. "We have been set a path. How strange, don't you think, that both my stones and Detective Carver independently arrived at the same plan? A higher power than ours directs us against the wych-kin. There is no turning back."

"There is no *higher power*, Devil-boy!" Thaniel said angrily. He got to his feet. "And I am no-one's pawn, neither man nor wych nor whatever entity you speak of."

"I do not speak of entities," Jack said. "I speak of the force that created the physics of the universe, the force that makes time flow forwards and not allow everything to happen at once, the force that sets the patterns to which the planets turn. Its weapons are coincidence, unlikelihood, happenstance. It is there when a man stops suddenly to pick up a coin dropped by another man ten days before, and the woman who is to be his wife bumps into him, and five hundred years hence their offspring rules half the world. It is there when a chance comment causes a scientist to think, "*what if. . .?*" and ten years later a great plague is cured. It is so vast that what we call chaos is simply another part of its order, with a shape too big to see. It has no name, nor will it ever have, though man may hint darkly at *fate* and *destiny*. It is what it is . . . the pattern. We may choose our own paths, but the pattern is always ahead of us. It is a way. It is *the* way."

Carver was the first one to speak. "Who are you, Devil-boy?"

"I am a vessel, just like Alaizabel was," he replied. "I have glimpsed the way ahead, and I must accompany you on it. That is the pattern. Pick up Lord Crott; he will not die yet."

Armand lifted him up, and Crott stood shakily. He looked grey, and his chest was smeared with a dark, foul stain. He glared at Thaniel, and then at the Devil-boy.

"I can go on," he said. "I can go on."

There was nothing more that could be said. They had a task, and they set to it.

Caledonian Road station was a ruin, as if crushed under the weight of the pummelling downpour. It had taken a square hit from an airship-dropped bomb twenty years ago and the wound had never healed; yet astonishingly, its superstructure was still largely intact, and the bulk of the station was still standing. The low, square building that squatted among the terraced derelicts bowed inwards in the centre, having slumped in the aftermath of the explosion. Tears in the brickwork spewed rainwater out on to the pavement, and the broken roof seethed with a mist of wet impacts.

The hunters and their companions were soaked to the bone within a minute of leaving the Hallow Ghoul's lair, but they counted themselves lucky that they had come across nothing more threatening than a scared cat on the short journey between the church and the Underground station. And at least the rain had driven off the cursed fog. Crott's breathing was raspy and erratic, and he walked with Armand's massive arm around his shoulder, bearing him up. The hunters and the detective held their pistols at the ready, and the Devil-boy hurried with Alaizabel at the centre of the protective circle.

A dark pall had settled on the group in the wake

of Jack's announcement. One thing they had all divined was that some of them were to die. None of them were comfortable with the idea that their actions were following a plan that decided who should be sacrificed and who should not. Hadn't the Devil-boy already ruined the pattern by telling them what he had? Or was that a part of what he saw in the scrying-stones? Was he *supposed* to tell them? In their minds, each was second-guessing frantically, and no conclusions were drawn. Hateful glances were thrown at the blind child, the instrument of their manipulator. Was it possible that he was simply lying to be sure that they did what he said? And would they dare to go against him, to take that chance?

He had them snared, that was for sure. But whether he spoke the truth or if it was he alone who was playing them for puppets, there was no way to tell.

They approached the broken building, a crumbling gateway to the abyss beneath their feet. They had long become accustomed to the idea of the Underground being impassable at night, when the wych-kin came to take the tunnels. Most Underground stations were like fortresses, to keep the unwelcome visitors in at night and stop them spilling on to the streets. But Caledonian Road had been bombed during the Vernichtung, when the wych-kin were only just emerging and, fortunately for the wych-hunters, it had never benefitted from those defences, so it was easy to get in and out of. Wych-kin did not usually travel so far up the Piccadilly line anyway. At least, they had not in previous times. The stirring rose of blood over the Old Quarter had emboldened the wych-kin like never before, and the people of the city did not know what they might expect now.

Thaniel led the way into the station, through a deep crack in the brickwork that had grown over with straggling ivy. Inside, the station was a great hollow cave, echoing with the drum and plink and splash and gurgle of the rain. Thin waterfalls puttered through cracks in the ceiling, and gushed from the great, jagged hole at the centre of it all, carpeting the stone floor in a thin layer of water, running around their boots and out to the street or into the indented chasm that sundered the tiles of the hall. It was tomb-dark inside, shapes visible only by the tiny shimmer of light on rippling liquid. The moonless night had sharpened their night-vision considerably on the journey, but it was still impossible to see adequately.

Cathaline lit her lantern and the others followed suit, the damp air filling with the dry scent of burning oil. The glow spread across tumbled pillars, slopes of rubble, and dark doorways. The ticketing foyer was wide and low-roofed. Once it had been a spacious, open hall, but now the fallen stone and shattered tiles made it cluttered and crowded. The bomb had dropped directly on to the roof above, caving it in and exploding, blowing a great dent in the floor and splitting it open to the darkness beneath.

"Over there," said Alaizabel, pointing to where a doorway stood with the word TRAINS picked out in a mock-gold mosaic arch above it.

Cathaline threw an enquiring look at Thaniel, who shook his head, indicating that he felt nothing from his wych-sense. She knew to rely on him; he was ever the more sensitive of the two of them.

They trod carefully across the ruined foyer, skirting the bomb-crater in the centre, stepping over fallen girders and stone supports. None quite trusted where their feet were, as if the floor might fall in beneath them at any moment and pitch them into the dark. But it held, sturdy as ever, and they passed through the archway into a long, stone tunnel that plunged downward, a staircase at their feet.

Alaizabel felt the clawing touch of claustrophobia as they descended, darkness before and behind them and only the shield of their lantern light against utter blindness. With no end in sight and no beginning either, it was easy to imagine them walking for ever downward, the steps endlessly marching up to meet them, the tiles rolling by in identical sequence until their lights ran down and they were claimed. She felt tiny, useless – terribly vulnerable now that she was no longer carrying Thatch with her. The wych-kin would not spare her now.

Thaniel, as if hearing her thoughts, looked back at her over his shoulder and smiled reassuringly. She smiled back.

Finally the stairs ended, and the tunnel levelled out. Faded signs pointed the way to the tracks, two routes running parallel, one east and north to Finsbury Park and one west and south to Hammersmith. No trains ran here now.

"We should take this way," Thaniel said.

A low growl echoed down the tunnel after them, freezing them all where they stood. They looked back as one in the direction from which they had come. In the blackness, three pairs of eyes were watching them, dipping and growing with each soft, padded footstep that approached.

Cathaline levelled her pistol and fired a shot, the noise deafening them temporarily in the close confines of the station. Armand wailed and slapped his ears as if to massage life back into them, or to drive out the loud whine that followed after his hearing had returned.

The eyes had disappeared.

"They will be back," said Cathaline. "They will not stay scared for long."

Alaizabel glared at her reproachfully, wishing that she had warned them before firing. Crott shushed Armand, who slowly quieted. The Beggar Lord was looking weaker now. The grey stain on the skin of his chest was spreading slowly. It remained to be seen if he could hold out long enough to get him help.

Damn what the Devil-boy says, Thaniel thought. *When we get to the airstrip at Finsbury Park, I will see to Crott. I will do the Rite myself if I have to.*

It was bravado; he was not sure whether he knew how to drive out the infection caused by the touch of the ghoul, or whether the trauma to Crott's heart was already too great to save him. But he needed to say something to make him feel strong inside, for they now walked on to the Underground platform, and there was the mouth of the train tunnel, picked out in lantern-light, beckoning them onward.

They accepted the invitation. They were too deeply committed now to even hesitate. They had gone beyond the point of turning back, and they were driven by the desire to get out of the darkness that had swallowed them.

They trod between the rusted tracks, gravel crunching and shifting beneath their boot heels. It was mortally cold here, and their sodden clothes chilled them further until their teeth began to chatter. They tramped into the mouth of the tunnel, walking down the throat of the Underground, and soon their light had passed away and was gone, leaving Caledonian Road alone once more with its ghosts and memories.

Alaizabel's world descended into a frozen misery of plodding, one step and then the next, unable to think of anything but the terrible November temperature and how it was even worse underground. Her experience outside Redwood Acres had left her with a healthy dread of the cold, so she had wrapped up warm as they left Crott's chambers; but the elements had conspired to wet her through and then turn her to ice.

Thaniel walked alongside her. She clung to him, seeking his body warmth, but he did not hold her to him as she wanted. She could feel him shuddering as well, struggling to conceal his own discomfort. And it seemed almost to be getting colder as they walked, their body temperatures falling as if their very blood was becoming cool.

Low growlings and snufflings dogged their footsteps. Their pursuers were not far behind, and even another shot from Cathaline only deterred them for a few minutes. They stayed out of the light, glimpses only of low, sloping things that skirted the edges of their world. They gave out no warning to the senses of either the hunters or the Devil-boy, leading them to presume that it was wolves who hunted them.

"Wolves," Crott said with forced humour. "At last, some God-honest thing that will die when I shoot it."

They came upon Holloway Road station without warning, for the tunnel suddenly fell back and they were faced with the blank, flat eyes of an Underground train. It had died in the station, never to move again. No current flowed through the tracks to power it, and it had long since rusted, its windows broken, a gutted hulk looming up before them.

Thaniel raised his lantern higher, splashing the light across the platform that ran alongside the tracks.

They climbed off the tracks and on to the platform, alongside the silent shape of the train. There was barely enough space between the sides of the tunnel and the front of the train to squeeze through; the bomb-shaken walls had sagged inward with time. Behind them, a wolf bayed a low howl that slid through the tunnels like the mourning of a phantom. Armand looked about nervously, his teeth chattering.

"They are coming," said Cathaline suddenly, and as if in reply, a multitude of answering howls echoed down the tunnel in a jumble.

"There must be dozens of them!" Carver said.

They needed nobody to instruct them in what to do next; there was still something of the primal man in their souls, a prehistoric instinct that quailed in fear at the sound of a wolf pack at hunt. They ran.

The first wolf clambered through the gap and on to the platform before they were halfway to the other end of the station, where a new arch waited to take them further along the Piccadilly line. It ran hungrily from the darkness into the lantern-light, tongue lolling, and though Cathaline's first shot missed, Thaniel's did not. The wolf dropped, shot through the neck.

Three more were coming through even before the reports of their weapons had ceased bouncing around the walls.

"Alaizabel!" Thaniel cried. "Take the others into the tunnel. We can hold them off."

Alaizabel wordlessly obeyed, leading the others in a run, leaving Thaniel, Cathaline and Carver to face the oncoming hordes.

Thaniel hefted his lantern towards the oncoming creatures, shattering it and spreading a slick of burning oil across the platform. Though it was pitched too far to stop the three that were coming at them, the extra light would give them more chance to shoot any further attackers, and the fire would certainly put them off.

Three guns roared, and three wolves dropped dead.

They could see the other wolves gathering on the far side of the blaze, their eyes glinting amber in the light. Cathaline looked back to where the others were clambering down on to the tracks on the other side of the train.

"Shall we make our exit?" she asked.

"I think," said Carver, "that would be wise."

They fled and, as if at a signal, the wolves came for them. They burst through the flames, some with smoking pelts and some as frenzied fireballs, driven by some insane hunger, yelping and howling. Thaniel, Carver and Cathaline turned in horror at the sight, their pistols coming up, and they continued to back away as they aimed at the hellish, fiery things racing towards them.

"Get me up there, for God's sake! I can still shoot a wolf!" Crott demanded as he hurried by Armand into the tunnel, but he was ignored.

A fresh volley of pistol shots sounded through the station, but they could not see up to the platform where their companions were; the train blocked their view.

"Alaizabel has an idea," said the Devil-boy softly, motioning towards where she stood. Their attention fell on her. She appeared to be drawing in the dirt on the flat end of the train, tracing a shape over and over, slow and unhurried.

"What do you think *you're* doing?" Crott asked, but she did not reply and did not need to. For she was making the final pass over her Ward now, lava-like red light glowing in the wake of her finger, defining the curling shape, making it sear the eye and then burst into bright life before suddenly fading.

For a moment, nothing happened. Then a tortured shriek filled the air, making them clamp their hands to their ears.

On the platform, the wolves' assault stuttered as they flinched at the sound. Those who had not jumped the blaze looked about in confusion. Those who had, kept on coming.

For Carver and the others, the situation was desperate. Already, the stretch of platform between the flaming lantern oil and where they were was littered with wolf bodies, and the air was full of the nauseating smell of burning flesh. They had backed up almost to the end of the platform now, but the wolves still howled and hurtled towards them. Carver shot at one of the flaming things, making it stumble but not bringing it down. It took Cathaline's second shot to finally end its life. But behind the flaming creature was a second wolf, one who had jumped the blaze relatively unscathed. Thaniel brought up a pistol but it clicked empty, and suddenly the thing was upon them.

In amid the chaos, the shriek became louder, until it seemed it could not strain any more. At that moment, there was a monolithic wrench, and the train began to grind forward, slowly, centimetre by centimetre, wheels that had long rusted turning after twenty years. The wolves howled, and some of the cleverest ones scampered back into the tunnel from where they had come to prevent themselves becoming trapped. But some were paralysed with indecision, frightened by the terrible noise, and they yelped and ran in circles. One ran too near the fire and its tail caught like a brush, bursting into flame; and in its agony and fear it ran between its fellows, and they shied away from it, fearing the burning thing.

The wolf that Thaniel had failed to shoot pounced, barrelling into Cathaline and knocking her into the hard wall. She shrieked in pain as its claws slashed through her coat, and scrabbled for a knife, but Thaniel was upon it, falling on its back with a knife of his own, driving it into the base of the wolf's neck and severing its spinal cord. It fell limp, dead instantly. Cathaline's lantern had somehow survived the fall, and was rolling noisily on its side. Carver scooped it up and pitched it in one smooth motion, sending it arcing over the fire that Thaniel had made and smashing in the midst of the gathered wolves. The wolf who was on fire became the unwitting match to the oil that sprayed them, and the creatures were engulfed in a river of flame amid a cacophony of dying howls.

There was a deafening crash as the train drove

itself into the tunnel that was a little too small for it, the metal of its sides screeching against the sagging stone of the walls, and then finally it stopped. The wolves' lament faded to a soft crackling as they burned; the wail of the train had ceased, having plugged the tunnel they had come from, and all was silence once more.

"Did it get you?" Thaniel was asking, helping Cathaline up. "Are you hurt?"

She shucked off one arm of her coat, rolled up her sleeve and looked. Deep gouges had been made in her forearm. She flexed her fingers, squeezing a fresh wash of blood from the wounds.

"Tourniquet and a bandage," she said offhandedly. "I'll be all right. Let's get going; I can do it as we travel."

They went on, and their exertion warmed their bodies and damp clothes; but the cold refused to abate. They had fewer lanterns now, and the dark crowded hungrily closer about them. Thaniel helped Cathaline bind her wounds, and they managed to staunch the blood quite effectively with clotting reagents and bandages that she had brought in her pack. Injury was part of a wych-hunter's occupation, and medical supplies were as necessary as guns and charms; they never went without them. Thaniel counted her lucky that it was a wolf and not a Cradlejack that scratched her. Down here, there would be no help if something like that occurred.

They passed through Arsenal without incident, treading carefully along the tracks with wary eyes on the platform to their right. Each of them privately entertained thoughts of clambering up and heading up the stairs to the outside; anything to get out of the terrible blackness that swamped them. Crott was weakening step by step; that much was obvious. But Arsenal station was ruined and impassable, and they had to keep on. Back into the tunnel they went, the final stretch through the foul cold in this dark, damnable place.

"Stop," said Alaizabel suddenly. It could have been a mere minute or half an hour since they had left Arsenal; none of them could tell, and none had the heart to look at their pocketwatches.

They turned to her. She breathed out heavily, and a wispy cloud of vapour outlined her exhalation.

"It is getting colder," she said. "Very fast."

She was right. They all felt it now. The temperature was dropping sharply, plunging towards freezing. Thaniel felt a creeping dread in his breast.

Armand was rubbing his tongue with the back of his hand, as if to rid it of something horrible. Crott noticed him first, and then understood.

"The air tastes salty," he declared.

The Devil-boy came as close to alarm then as anyone had ever seen him. Alaizabel jerked her head around to look at Crott, horrified realization dawning on her face.

"The Draug," the Devil-boy rasped. "The Drowned Folk. They come for us."

Alaizabel quailed, remembering the night when she had come within a hair's breadth of meeting one of the creatures. She had never heard them named before, but she well knew the acrid taste of the sea and freezing temperatures that heralded their arrival.

"Stand together, all of you!" Jack barked, then drew a thick piece of black stone from inside his coat. He walked hurriedly around them, drawing a wide circle by scratching the stone along the floor, running it over tracks and sleepers alike. Even by lantern light, they could not see any sign of the circle he drew; the stone left no mark. But to the Devil-boy's blind eyes, it was as clear as day.

"Cold!" Armand moaned, hugging Crott to him for warmth.

"I think I can make us warmer," Alaizabel suggested. She knew the Ward for heat, though she was not quite sure how to apply it.

"Do not use Wards within this circle," the Devil-boy hissed, still working. "We must conceal ourselves. The circle will make us invisible to them. Warding will draw them like a tide to the moon."

The wet slap of a webbed foot drifted softly through the darkness, coming from the direction they were heading.

"Put out your lanterns," Jack instructed. They hesitated. "Do it, or we shall all die!"

The lanterns went out, and the phantoms of fear crept up behind them to squeeze their throats and hearts. The blackness was utter and complete. There was only the cold, the terrible cold, and the scratching sound of Jack completing his circle, for the Devil-boy was already blind and did not need light. Their clothes, which had warmed a little on their skin, began to dew. Thaniel felt his hair slicken with moisture, chill droplets of salty water. The dark, freezing abyss of the bottomless sea wrapped around them, their breath clouding invisibly about them.

"Make not a sound," the Devil-boy whispered, huddling inside the circle. He heard Crott repeat the instruction to Armand, the simpleton, though Crott's words were so badly slurred as to be barely understandable. In his weakened state, the cold was affecting him far worse than the rest of them, and he was getting hypothermia.

The echo of slapping feet multiplied. Slow, deliberate footsteps, heavy and dolorous. The things seemed to drag themselves, for each laboured step was accompanied by a sound halfway between a scrape and a slither, and the sound bespoke something larger than human. They drew closer and closer towards the huddled and terrified group that stood blind in the centre of the tracks, penned within an invisible circle, their trust placed entirely in a process they did not understand. Only the Devil-boy knew his business; even Cathaline had not heard of this kind of Rite.

Alaizabel hugged herself to Thaniel, and this time, in the dark, he responded, slipping his arms around her and holding her close to his chest, feeling her heart thump against his.

The next sound was so close that she nearly made a small cry of fright, but it died in her throat. She could feel Armand becoming jittery next to her, could almost imagine his lip trembling as he fought to contain a wail of distress.

Then they were all around, their wet scent of rotting fish forcing itself down throats and into nostrils. She could hear the wheezy gurgle of their breath, feel them lumber about, sniffing, questing for their prey. The Draug knew the humans were nearby, yet they could not understand why they could not find them.

Cathaline held herself still as something slid past her, making the fine hairs on her arm prickle beneath the torn sleeve of her coat. She swallowed back terror, the primal fear of the dark that tried to climb the inside of her ribcage and squeeze up her throat and out. She realized then that she had never been in total darkness before. In this world of gaslights and lanterns, who would ever need to be? And even in the countryside, there was always the moon and the ambient night-glow of the world around her, providing enough light so that even the cloudiest midnight was not pitch black.

But here, there was no light. Nothing, not one scrap that the eye could fasten on and utilize. An utter, aching void that threatened to suck their hearts and wills out of their bodies and crush them.

Thaniel stood stonily, fighting to control the trembling that shook his body. The Draug shuffled and gurgled about, terrifyingly close. The wet thump of a tail being dragged over a train track, the bubbling of the wych-kin's breath, the feel of movement as they passed close again and again, searching, searching. They seemed to pass around the circle as if not realizing it was there, yet they were well aware their prey was very close, and they were not soon giving up. The terrible cold emptiness, the lightless salty dark of the deepest seas, and Cathaline felt that the ordeal would never end.

Dark, dark. All is dark.

Alaizabel gave a tiny whimper as a blast of foetid breath blew into her face, a Draug so close that she might have touched it with her nose. The sound, miniscule though it was, fell into silence. The Draug had stopped moving, frozen at the instant the noise escaped her lips. Alaizabel felt her heart sink in terror. They had heard her.

The shuffling now was more deliberate, heavy with purpose. Those who were further away were moving back towards the circle. Thaniel felt something slimy pass by his face, so close that fine tendrils ran across his lips and he almost gagged. The Draug were reaching in for them, into the circle, and it was only a matter of seconds before they were touched and found.

The anguished wail that made them all start was enough to make Thaniel think his time had come, but after a moment, he recognized the dull, nasal tone. It was Armand, and as he realized it he felt himself jostled, and knew that Armand had broken from the circle, yelling and roaring wordlessly, into the blackness. Thaniel held Alaizabel tightly to him as the sounds reached their ears, the suddenly rapid scrape and lunge of the Draug, the howling of Armand, the slither and bump and thud, and Armand's voice gradually fading, dropping down to a sob, then to a gurgle, and finally to nothing.

The quiet that returned was utter. The sounds of the Draug had gone. For what seemed an hour, nobody moved. The atmosphere was no longer salty, and it had warmed considerably.

"Are they gone?" Carver asked at last, his voice barely audible.

The hiss of a match and the swell of light from the Devil-boy's lantern was his answer. In moments, all the remaining lanterns were lit, spreading healing illumination through the terror-slick darkness. Thaniel was shaking; Alaizabel began to shudder also, within the circle of his arms.

Of the Beggar Lord, Crott, and his giant companion, there was not a sign.

Finsbury Park airstrip sat low under the boiling roof of black cloud, a long rectangle of high walls and jagged strips of iron fencing. Lights shone from within, electric bulbs powered by generators over in Hampstead Heath. On the western side, a hollow square of squat, flat buildings was alive with slits of illumination, reflecting shakily on the sodden tarmacadam of the main quad. The eastern side of the enclosure was the airstrip proper, little more than a wide slab of empty space with tall lamp-posts glowing around its edge. Two great airships sat idle there, resting on their gondolas with their balloons like the carapaces of vast, seamed beetles chained to the ground. The rain poured, the sky flashed and roared, stunning the scene in white light, and soldiers ran to and from the quad and across the airstrip, rifles in hand. Over the boom of the thunder the crack of gunfire could be heard. The airstrip sat alone, an island of light amid a barrier of darkened fields, and it was here that the Piccadilly line came to an end.

The Finsbury Park Underground station had fallen into disuse after the Vernichtung and the collapse of Caledonian Road and Arsenal. It was an unfortunate mistake of the city planning authorities that the airstrip should be built around the station building. After the bombing of London and the acquisition of airship technology by the British, the intention was to repair the fallen subway stations, restore the Piccadilly line, and build the newly conceived airstrip over the old Finsbury Park station. The military were to fund the building of the airstrip, while the city councils were to resurrect the fallen stations. Construction of the airstrip had already begun when the wych-kin first began to appear, and the councils suddenly found themselves with far more pressing matters than an old Underground line to contend with. The money was spent on other things, the stations were never repaired, and in the end the airstrip was built at the end of a dead line.

The station itself had been assimilated into the main group of buildings, a heavily guarded iron doorway forming the link between the Underground and the airstrip proper. It stood on the ground level of the administration wing, Wards set on it to deter any wych-kin that might creep up from the darkness, with two jacketed officers on the airstrip side carrying pistols and sabres.

The guards had been briefed about Carver's telegram, but neither of them believed that anyone would make it through several kilometres of Underground tunnels to reach the airstrip. Consequently, when there was a heavy rapping on the door they both exchanged a glance of alarm.

"State your name!" one of them called after a moment.

"It's Detective Carver!" cried an exasperated voice. "Who were you expecting?"

They slid back a viewing-slot in the door, and

hastily unbolted it, saluting as the ragged band stumbled into the room, shivering and exhausted.

"Send for General Montpelier," one of the guards instructed the other. "And take them to some quarters. Get them warm, for God's sake."

They were taken to a briefing room, a sterile grey square with hard wooden benches set against the walls and chalkboards at one end. Small tables were set in rows facing the chalkboards, and high, small windows let in the flashes of light from the storm outside. But most importantly, there was a fire, and during the winter it was kept always burning for the benefit of those pilots and soldiers who had to sit here in the cruel cold to learn about their assignments. They huddled around it, letting its precious heat sink into their chilled bones and turn their wet, icy clothes into damp, lukewarm ones. Once out of the Underground, where the sun never reached, the temperature had become quite bearable again, and soggy clothes were an inevitability in this kind of weather. Thaniel found himself worrying about getting influenza, and laughed at his own ridiculousness. A bout of flu would be a small price to pay if they could only survive this night.

"What happened?" Alaizabel said, after her jaw had stopped shuddering. "To Crott and Armand, I mean? What happened to them?" She directed the question at Jack, who was, ironically, the only one among them who had not been blinded by the darkness.

"They are gone," the Devil-boy said.

"We know *that*," Cathaline snapped.

Jack did not react. "Armand became frightened.

He ran out of the circle, and he took Crott with him. Perhaps he hoped to save them both. Instead, they saved us. The Draug got their victims."

"Two men we knew just died," Cathaline said in amazement. "Do *any* of you realize that? You discuss their deaths like they were strangers."

"Lord Crott is gone now," said the Devil-boy. "None of us but Armand had any special affection for him, and he is gone too. Save any grieving you feel you must do until this is over. It will do us no good here."

There was a silence.

"You knew they were to die," Carver said.

"Yes," Jack replied.

"How many more of us are to go?" he asked.

"That I will not tell you," came the reply. "It would influence the outcome."

The door to the room opened at that moment, and in strode a tall, stout man with a thick white beard and small, piggy blue eyes. He was dressed in an immaculately pressed uniform; a single medal hung at his breast.

"By George!" he bellowed good-naturedly. "Welcome to the lion's den!"

General Montpelier was a foghorn of a man, brash and loud and impossible to ignore. He swept around those assembled, shaking hands and introducing himself, seemingly blithely oblivious to the fact that London was being swamped by wych-kin outside the walls of his airstrip. The General was only truly alive when at war, and he was never in a better mood than when the odds were against him.

"Well, well!" he declared. "Came all the way through the tunnels, did you? I wouldn't have believed it if I couldn't see you with my own eyes. Which of you is Detective Carver?"

Carver replied that it was he.

"Well, Carver, let's not waste time. We're both busy men. Let's talk."

"In your office," said Carver. "If you please. I need your signature on the forms to authorize the use of one of your airships."

"Of course, of course," he said. "We'll be back directly."

The two of them left the room, heading down the corridor to Montpelier's office. On the way, he enthused about how the wych-kin were laying siege to the place, cursed dog-things that just kept on coming no matter how many you shot down.

"I have to say, Carver, I bloody hope that your letter is the real thing. I'd hate to have you come all this way for nothing."

"We need that airship, General. The Palace thinks so too. My letter comes straight from the highest office."

"I should say it would have to!" the General declared. "These things are the pride of the royal fleet! Can't sign them out to just anyone, not even you. Where's old Maycraft, anyway?"

"Oh, he's about," Carver replied.

"Not had this much fun since the Boers," Montpelier declared as they stepped into his office and shut the door.

"I'm afraid it gets a lot less fun from here on in," said Carver, and the tone of his voice made the General turn around. He found himself staring down the barrel of a pistol, held centimetres from his nose.

"What's the bloody meaning of this?" Montpelier cried.

"I'm sorry, General. I'm here under false pretences. There is no letter from the Palace. The Palace have better things to do, and I didn't have time to wait and see if they would give me permission to take an airship. So I brought my own permission."

"You're *stealing* an airship? Don't be a fool, man. You shoot that thing and twenty officers will be in here in a moment."

"What do you care? You'll be dead," Carver replied levelly. "I'm sorry, General, but this is too important to let bureaucracy get in the way. Now I believe you have some papers to sign for me?"

The rain drove itself against the huge grey flanks of the airship, battering the thick fabric before pouring off its sides to fall down to the tarmacadam in curtains. Gregor was there, standing by the door to the great gondola, stamping his boots and rubbing his gloved hands against the cold, his flight coat zipped up to his nose and his flat cap pulled down. He looked small in comparison to the vast craft that he sheltered beneath, a tiny figure against the massive marrow-shaped balloon that sat overhead or the gondola that hung below. And this was only one of the smallest airships in the fleet, and nothing to the sizes that the Prussians were coming up with.

Gregor stuck a cigarette in his hard-lipped mouth and lit it, puffing away as he watched the group hurrying from the western side of the airstrip to get to him. There were distant cracks of gunfire as the soldiers held at bay the dark things that crept across the fields, attracted by the lights.

Interesting, how it had come round to this. Six years ago he had stowed away on a tramp steamer from Siberia, slipping away from a prison colony where he had been sent for desertion from the Russian armed forces. He was not a fighter; he was a coward. Even he admitted that, if only to himself. It was only unfortunate that his nerve had broken in the midst of his term of service.

Some forged papers got him by in London for a time, but for a Russian émigré in England there was only the docks, and he had little talent for fishing. After a year of hauling crates, he heard that the airstrip at Finsbury Park needed airship pilots, and signed up. He had flown the more cumbersome Russian airships for six months back home, and he knew what he was about. The Army were prepared to overlook his heritage in exchange for his skills.

And so Gregor had slipped from one army to another, although he did not altogether mind. The weather was better here, for one. His money was good, his belly was never empty, and he could get American cigarettes whenever he wanted.

He had to admit he was puzzled now, however. A detective called Carver, in the midst of all this calamity, had telegrammed the General saying that he was commandeering an airship, that he had the approval of the Palace and that it was his mission to save all of London.

"I'll be bloody surprised if they turn up at all, let alone bringing a letter with royal authority," Montpelier had declared, but apparently he had been wrong on both counts, for here they were, with documents signed by the General allowing the use of Gregor and his airship for the period of twenty-four hours.

Gregor shrugged to himself. He would rather be in the sky where those filthy wych-kin couldn't get at him than down here on the ground.

The airship lifted itself from the tarmacadam with a deafening drone of engines, hauling its bulk slowly into the turbulent sky. Lightning flickered to the south; the storm, at least, was beginning to peter out. Alaizabel watched through the windows of the gondola as the airstrip receded beneath them, turning as they turned. The ground seemed to be dropping away, as if they were static and the Earth was shrinking.

She raised her eyes to the whirlpool of red that swirled slowly over the Old Quarter. That was their destination, for whatever good it would do them. Could they survive in the heart of the Old Quarter, where no-one had ventured for years, even before the wych-kin invaded the capital? Only airships had flown over it since it became too dangerous to travel into on foot, dropping bombs in a futile effort to keep the demons down. What went on beneath the tangle of streets and ruins there?

The tone of the engines changed as the airship pushed forward, propelling them towards Camberwell, the first district to be infested with wych-kin twenty years ago, and above which the pupil of the evil red eye hung in the clouds.

Alaizabel looked over the streets below. The rain had slackened, and the fog was pushing its way back in, materializing in the deserted lanes and thoroughfares. Gaslights burned atop the black iron lamp-posts, oblivious to the slaughter. The city was a net of stars, a thousand thousand lighted windows spreading out in all directions. It was as if they were flying upside down, with the clear sky beneath them and a roiling sea above.

London is being eaten alive, Alaizabel thought. *Yet it looks so peaceful from up here.*

She knew what the darkness masked. The beauty was false; the lights were all lit because nobody dared turn them off for fear of what might come. In the houses, people were dying. The wych-kin were rampant, and they were too diverse to be kept out. Lock and bolt might keep away some types of wych-kin, but others would come down the chimney, or glide through the ceiling, or materialize from candle smoke. The wych-kin were unstoppable in number, and endless in variation. Tallowcats, cradlejacks, jujus, angel stones, stormwardens, will-o'-the-wisps, dust witches, a million of them and more.

Where do they come from? What do they want?

The questions had been asked too many times to count. The wych-kin never answered.

"Alaizabel," said Thaniel, by her shoulder.

She looked back to see him standing there, wet and bedraggled but still strong, still iron with the fortitude that bore them all up. Returning her gaze to the window, she said, "I am scared, Thaniel."

"That was what I was about to say to you," he replied quietly.

"Really?" she asked, surprised.

"I feel that . . . everything has gone beyond my control," he said quietly. "The way things were . . . I was not happy. But I was safe, and secure. Since you came, everything has changed. I have seen my life crumbling around me, I have abandoned my home, touched madness, I have . . . changed. I feel it. Since you came."

"Do you regret it?" she asked, unconsciously tensing as she waited for his reply.

"Not for a moment," he replied.

She felt a smile of relief touch her lips, and her heart began to beat a little harder.

"I do not know what will happen now," he said. "We are heading into somewhere none of us have ever been. Some of us may not return. I wanted to say, in case I never have the opportunity again . . . what you have given me, Alaizabel, is a gift beyond measure . . . and I. . ."

"Master Fox," she said, turning round from the window to face him, "ssh." And she kissed him then, and he her, long and passionately. The others in the gondola melted away; their presence was unimportant now.

They had been over the lightless and seething Old Quarter for a half-hour. The airship cruised over the killing ground, up above the wych-kin's reach, sliding past the barrier of the Thames and beyond. The rain had choked to fine mist, dewing the windows of the gondola. They looked out across the city, watching the ominous red maelstrom grow and slide towards them. All around was the thick drone of the engines, driving them through the sky.

Only imagination could decide what kinds of things were down there, what stalked in the night amid the shattered, bomb-torn streets. Terraces slumped across each other, their bricks splintered where they met; ancient roofs gaped like mouths with timber-beam teeth; blast patterns of flattened shops described sloping circles of rubble. It was a sea of dereliction, as if several armies of buildings had smashed into each other from different directions and wiped each other out, leaving their dead to soak and bleach and fade in the rain and sun.

But they were slipping beneath the unholy eye now, and the streets below were painted a ghastly vermilion hue. By its light, they could see movement here; things scampering, things drifting and lumbering. The fog was settling back in, but only enough to make it hard to see the shapes of the wych-kin that darted and lunged and thundered and slithered. And there ahead was the centre of the maelstrom, the pivot around which the foul clouds spun.

"Can you see? Can you see what is there?" Cathaline asked, pressing herself against the windows of the gondola.

"By God," Thaniel breathed.

It reared over the surrounding buildings like a claw, a vast Gothic monolith, a cathedral of spite that loomed jagged and malicious and evil. Towers and spires scratched the belly of the sky, leering gargoyles swarming over its surface, frozen in stone. Portions of it seemed to have melted into others, while some sections were sharply defined by rows of twisted blades and balconies. High, arched windows soared above massive round blossoms of dark glass; steeples jumbled with buttresses and bell towers. It was part castle, part church, part temple; a thing beyond the power of all but the world's most insane architects to conceive. Bathing in the red glow of the clouds above, it exhaled infernal wickedness, standing blasphemously proud like a twisted, blood-ied crown.

"The womb of the darkness," Jack intoned from behind them. He had not needed to look. "That is where we must go."

"How did it get there?" Cathaline said. "Why could we not see it before?"

"It has been cloaked from our eyes for many years now," the Devil-boy said. "Wards of a power I have never felt before. But the Wards are down now. The cathedral must be open to receive the Fraternity's gods. The Glau Meska are on their way. Our time is short."

"But . . . how is it *here?*" Cathaline asked, unsat-isfied.

"The same way the wych-kin are here," Jack replied. "Now, make ready. It is almost over; the rest is up to you."

The airship segued closer to the foul edifice, and the companions prepared themselves as best they could, each wondering who was to die within the walls of the Fraternity's demonic cathedral.

The airstrip at Finsbury Park was under siege, and ammunition was running desperately low. The crea-tures kept coming, and no matter how many fell, another three were there to take their place. The once-flat fields were now lumped with corpses, but the wych-kin stepped over their dead without pause, driven by a hunger beyond hunger, drawn by the lights and the lives within the perimeter wall.

Jerob Whately was in command of the defence effort. He had waited in frustration for the order to despatch the bomb-laden airships, to send them for help or to have them use their bombs to defend the base. No such order had come. The two airships had sat idle. He had watched as one was commandeered and taken by a stranger, flying off towards the Old Quarter. He had fought until things had become hopeless, and now he was going to see the General, to demand that they use the last airship to evacuate the base. His men were tired, trapped, and losing. The base would have to be forfeited. If he could not make Montpelier see sense, there might be a mutiny on his hands.

Retreat. Fall back. He thought of how he would phrase his request . . . no, his *demand*, as he knocked on the door to the General's office. There was no reply. He frowned. The General had not been seen for the better part of an hour now. He knocked again. As before, only silence.

He tried the door anyway. It was locked.

"General?" he called, but no reply came to him. He drew his pistol. Now was the time for action, not dallying. Court martial be damned. Stepping back, he fired into the door and blew the lock apart.

The door swung open into a neat office. A thick desk by a shuttered window, books and documents. And there, tied to his chair, trussed up and gagged, was the General, red-faced with anger and making muffled noises through the sock in his mouth.

"Ah," said Jerob, as if that explained it all.

T he cathedral courtyard was empty. The great walls that separated it from the rest of the Old Quarter held back the wych-kin with Wards and charms and forces beyond the senses of humankind. In the broken streets of Camberwell they howled and gibbered, desperate to reach the great airship that lowered itself down to hang five metres above the stone tiles. But the cathedral was cut off from the Old Quarter, quarantined so as not to be infested with the chaotic things that infested London. The people of the Fraternity knew how to deal with wych-kin, but they were still human and still vulnerable. If anything crawled and slid within these walls, it did so at the Fraternity's behest.

The cathedral loomed massively above them, a crimson mountain of curves and pillars and arches. It seemed to hum and pulse, making Thaniel's head and ears throb as he climbed down the rope ladder that hung from the gondola to the floor of the courtyard. Despite the cacophony on the far side of the wall, the sound of the airship's engines and the incessant bass grumble of the cathedral, the courtyard was eerily still and quiet. The rain had not seemed to fall on this place as it had on the rest of London; perhaps because it stood in the eye of the storm.

Thaniel's boots touched the floor and he looked out across the vast emptiness. To his right was the main door of the cathedral, a huge pair of lacquered black doors laden with all manner of shapes and symbols picked out in gold. Nearby, Carver and Cathaline were tethering an anchor rope to the great bar that held shut the courtyard gate. Gregor was to wait for their return. He scarcely had any choice, for untethering the airship required two people: one to hold the airship steady and another to untie the ropes. He could not leave the airship to untie the anchor ropes on his own, for it would float off without him. This was evidently not something he had bargained for, judging by the heated exchanges coming from the cockpit during the descent, but finally, everything went very quiet, and when next they saw him he was white-faced and shaken. Thaniel wondered what Carver had said to him to make him cooperate.

Rain misted down upon them as Alaizabel, the last, came down the ladder.

"It is so empty," she said, echoing his thoughts. "Thaniel, why are there no guards?"

"Because they know you cannot get in," said the Devil-boy at their sides. "The Wards on the entrances are more powerful that even the greatest wych-hunter could overcome. Thatch has laid them herself. Only she can undo them."

Thaniel did not waste his breath on Jack's bait. He knew they would not have been brought here if there was not a way in.

"But perhaps," said Alaizabel, "if there were one who had a modicum of Thatch's wychcraft, she might be able to undo the lock."

The Devil-boy smiled, an expression so rare that it

looked disgusting on him. "She learns," he croaked.

Thaniel looked up at the airship hanging above them. "Can we use the bombs aboard that thing?" he asked, motioning towards the undercarriage where two clumsy-looking finned objects were attached.

"We must be sure," said Jack. "We must have Thatch. Bombing the cathedral might block our way in."

Alaizabel was already approaching the gates, her eyes roaming the surface.

"Do not touch it," warned the Devil-boy. "The Wards could kill you."

"I will not touch it," Alaizabel assured them, and she began to draw her Ward in the air.

Thaniel watched her at work, faint amazement on his face. This new-found ability, a leaving present from Thatch, and she already seemed born to it. To be suddenly bestowed with such a power would unsettle the strongest mind as much as waking up with a new limb, yet Alaizabel had already accepted it. That was *her* power, he decided. She would never be conquered. She had been through more than he would wish on anyone in the previous week, and yet she had rode it out and remained perfectly sane. She adapted to every new situation, fitted the lock to every door.

He thought of the kiss they had shared, and smiled to himself despite his fear, and thought of what might be when all this was over.

Alaizabel made the last pass of the Ward as if she had done it a thousand times. It was a Ward of Negation, used to dispel other Wards. Ordinarily, she would not have had a chance of overcoming Thatch's power; but anyone who placed a Ward could remove it just as easily, and as Alaizabel had inherited her ability from Thatch, the chances were that it would yield to her.

She stepped back, leaving the shape hanging in the air before her.

Nothing. Then: a blinding flash, causing them all to shield their eyes. The Wards on the door blazed bright like gunpowder and then guttered and died, burned out and useless. The gold tracing on the symbols seemed dull and tarnished now, the life within them gone.

Alaizabel looked at Thaniel and gave him a swift smile.

"I'll wager that old wych will have cause to regret ever meeting Miss Alaizabel Cray," said Carver with a grin. "To the purpose, then. Time is short."

The Rite of *pthau'es'maik* took perhaps two days in total. Every member of the Fraternity knew their part backwards. It was required that the ceremony be continuous and uninterrupted for it to be successful, but forty-eight hours was a long time for anyone to maintain concentration. Therefore, the vigil was kept in shifts, four hours at a time, changing not all at once but gradually. Cultists left and were replaced at a steady rate, so that there were never less than twenty performing the ceremony at any one time.

Over a thousand components went into the successful completion of the *pthau'es'maik*. The right prayers had to be said in the right order; the summoning circle had to have each of its one hundred and thirteen Wards individually invoked and treated; the incenses had to be prepared and burned in the correct proportions within the circle; each person performing the ceremony had to ritually purify themselves every time he or she rejoined the group; anointments had to be made ready for when Thatch joined them at the very end of the ceremony to guide the Glau Meska into the world. There were so many ways to get it wrong, and only one to get it right.

And so, on it went, in the great hall of the cathedral, and the ceremony drew ever closer to completion.

"Pyke! Pyke, I say! Where are you, damn your soul!"

Thatch swept through the stone corridors of the cathedral, heading for where Pyke slept, calling all the while. The Doctor had just finished presiding over a particularly exhausting section of the *pthau'es'-maik*, one which was too delicate to entrust to anyone else. He had hoped for rest.

"Well, ma'am. What can ah do for you?" drawled Curien Blake, who stood outside the door to the room where Pyke slept.

"Out of my way, you insufferable colonial twig! Be off, I say! Pyke!"

The tall American regarded the woman who stood before him. Such a waste, he thought. That beautiful eighteen year old, a fine English rose if ever there was one, and they stuffed her full of thorns. Thatch had the face and body of that young lady, but she still looked old. Her healthy bones still hunched stiffly; her fine, smooth fingers still clawed with arthritis; and her voice was a sharp crow. Such a waste.

"He's sleepin', Miss Thatch," Blake said. "He said he was not to be disturbed." Unlike the Fraternity members, Blake offered Thatch no more respect than anyone else. While they bowed and scurried to her every whim, he treated her as nothing special. It infuriated her.

"Are you his servant now, eh? Speak up, I say! A servant?"

"As long as this servant keeps gettin' paid like Doctor Pyke pays, he does what the man asks."

"*Pyke!*" she hollered, and now the door opened and it was the Doctor himself, dressed in a nightshirt and pushing his glasses on to his nose.

"Oh! Miss Thatch. What a——"

"*Someone's opened the cathedral door!*" she howled at him. "I can feel it. My Wards are all broken. Someone's come inside, you fool!"

It took a moment for this to sink in, and then the Doctor was fully alert and awake. "Mister Blake!" he snapped. "Find the intruders and deal with them."

"Pleasure," he said, and stalked away.

"I'll be dressed directly," he said to Thatch. "I confess, I did not expect anyone to get this close to us, but there are ways and means of dealing with such things."

It was like walking through the arteries of some great and sleeping beast.

The interior of the cathedral was of gold and black stone and red lacquer; gold and black and red, red and black and gold and no shade or variation in-between. Ornamented arches, votive altars, small alcoves of red with burning black candles inside. The colours were so rich and so unwavering that they forcefully overtook the eyes, oppressing those who walked in their light. Colours so plush, yet aggressive and dark and overwhelming.

"I hate this place," Alaizabel whispered.

"It has a certain appeal," Cathaline replied, who often wore red and black herself and who blended in nicely.

"Careful," said Carver. "They may know we are here." His pistol was held at the ready, like those of the hunters.

"They know," said the Devil-boy.

"You know, I imagine, of the type of wych-kin that has no form of its own," said Pyke, striding down the darkened corridor. "They possess already living creatures. Cradlejacks, dog-rats and so forth."

"Fool! I know everything there is to know about wych-kin!" Thatch snapped back at him.

"Of course you do," Pyke replied. "My deepest apologies. I mean to say, that we have been summoning these wych-kin for some time now."

"A simple task. Yes, simple," Thatch said. She could hear a snarling now, and she turned and fixed Pyke with a beady eye. "What was that, eh?"

"That was what I was talking about," said the Doctor. "These wych-kin need a host to live, rather like you do. One of our oldest members is a breeder of particularly vicious guard dogs. We put wych-kin inside them. The results were rather spectacular, as far as our experiments went."

"Hmm. Be swift, I must begin my part in the ceremony soon," she replied sharply.

Pyke halted in front of a locked and barred door. A pair of thickset men stood there, identified as animal handlers by their attire. The snarling came from within, deep and guttural. The Doctor handed Thatch a thin bracelet of smooth metal, with a single Ward in raised filigree crafted on to it.

"Please put this on. We all have one. It will stop the dogs from attacking you."

Thatch did so, and one of the handlers unlocked the door and pushed it open. The reaction was immediate. The growls erupted into frenzied barks, and the sound of chains clashing taut mixed with the sound of heavy bodies hitting thick bars as the creatures lunged at their cages. The room was pitch dark, but in the light from the doorway, Thatch could see two rows of cages and the silhouettes of the things inside.

"Delightful, aren't they?" Pyke said, and the two handlers stepped inside to open the cages and let free the wych-dogs.

T hey heard the dogs coming long before they saw them, and they knew these were no ordinary dogs.

"There's dozens of them!" Cathaline guessed. Carver was checking the chamber of his pistol. Thaniel's wych-sense was growing in volume inside his head as the creatures approached.

They stood in a tall chamber, with high, red-lacquer ribs reaching up to the sloped ceiling above them. Wooden benches and thick tables were arranged in rows, giving the place the impression of some kind of dining hall. There were two pointed archways – one that they had entered from and one directly opposite – and two further small doors set in the other walls.

The sounds were coming from the large archway ahead of them, and coming fast.

"Turn over the tables!" Carver shouted. "Make barricades!"

They did so, hefting two of the great tables up against the archway where the dogs would come from. After that, they tipped the rest of the tables and benches, turning the hall into a broken maze of obstacles. It was all accomplished within a minute and they retreated, to wait. They had laid out three rough rows of the heavy tables, so they could fall back from each one to new cover if they were overwhelmed. Gaps had been left in the tables behind them, allowing them to dart through and then slide the tables together to form a strong barrier. Now they took position behind the foremost one, their eyes fixed on the gaping archway through which the baying of the hounds was approaching.

Thaniel handed Alaizabel a short, narrow-bladed sword that had hung at his belt. "In case they get too close," he said. Alaizabel took it and said nothing.

The first dogs reached them then, two of the creatures springing over the blockade in the archway and landing four-square on the flagstones. Cathaline swore under her breath at the sight of them. There was no question that they were wych-kin. They had the vague shape of dogs, but they seemed swollen and twisted from the inside. Barrel-chested, legs knotted with muscles so thick as to be grotesque, their teeth had overgrown their gums and splintered in their mouths, making their drool pink with blood. Their eyes were blank and dark, set within prominent ridges of bone that shadowed them. Their fur was a bristly black, but they were bathed in the red light that filled the room from outside, making them seem hellish in aspect.

Thaniel was the first to fire, and the others followed a moment later. The first two dogs were shot to pieces by the initial salvo, but there were already more pouncing and scrabbling over the blockade, howling at the scent. Thaniel levelled and took the head off one of them as it tried to pull itself up and over the tables by its forepaws; Carver and Cathaline both discharged their weapons into the flank of another. Two more fell that way, picked off as they tried to clamber over the barricade, and then four of the wych-dogs took the blockade at once, and the tables tipped forward and collapsed under their great weight. The creatures burst in, pistols roared, and two of them fell dead. But the dogs would not be stopped, and they had numbers now. Racing across the room, they threw themselves at the overturned tables behind which the intruders hid. One of them scrambled over the top, only to find a pistol barrel in its mouth and its brains liberated from its skull. Still, the tide could not be turned back, and another wych-dog appeared from nowhere, squeezing through a gap between the tables and rushing at Alaizabel; but she lifted her blade two-handed like a dagger, and thrust it into the creature's side. It yowled in agony, skidding past her, and a moment later Carver was there to finish it off with a bullet. He pulled the blade from the dead thing's ribs and threw it back to Alaizabel, not able to spare another instant as the dogs were pouring into the room now. He shot at another dog that had got stuck wriggling through the tables, missed and hit wood, and Cathaline cried out as a thick, blunt splinter hit her just above the eye. Thaniel killed the dog with his sabre before it could free itself.

"Fall back!" Cathaline cried, and they did so, ducking through the gaps between the next row of tables and sliding them shut to block out the enemy.

Thaniel was frantically reloading as the second wave struck. Cathaline wiped the trickle of blood from her forehead and took aim again. The damned things were relentless, coming from all sides now.

The brighter ones had learned not to try and climb the tables or scramble through, but to run around the edges of the room and attack from the sides, slipping in behind the barricades. Thaniel looked round and saw one such dog wrestling with the Devil-boy, scratching at him with vicious claws as he fought to keep its snapping teeth away from his face. The Devil-boy produced a dart, feathered with exotic colours, and stabbed it into the creature on top of him. As it struck, the dog shrieked and exploded into ochre flame. The creatures paused, taken aback by the sight of their kin writhing in agony as the Devil-boy threw it off. And then something was arcing through the air, thrown by Cathaline, rattling to a halt. . .

The air was torn with an ear-shattering explosion and a flash of light bright enough to dazzle. One of Cathaline's flash bombs, with a little extra added for noise.

Gunfire erupted again, but this time it was from behind them. It took a few seconds for Thaniel to realize that it was not Cathaline or Carver, but some-one else, shooting at *them!* He whirled round to see four men, two dressed incongruously in dinner jack-ets, one in a Stetson and riding leathers, and the last in a crimson robe with his cowl gathered around his shoulders. They were standing in the archway from which the intruders had entered the room, the over-turned tables blocking a clear firing line. They were sandwiched; the wych-dogs on one side, the Fraternity on the other.

"Stay together!" Cathaline shouted, but her voice was drowned out by another flash bomb, this time aimed at the cultists.

"You must see this to the end, you and Thaniel," hissed the Devil-boy suddenly, appearing at Alaizabel's elbow.

"What? Where are *you* going?" she cried.

"My time is now. I will not be——"

He was cut short as Curien Blake levelled and fired, and Alaizabel shrieked and shuddered as blood sprayed the wooden surface of the table and lashed up her dress and across her face and hair. The Devil-boy slumped forward into her, and she shrieked again as she pushed him off, staggering backward. She felt herself being pulled up to her feet. It was Thaniel, firing over her shoulder at a wych-dog that leaped to intercept.

"Now!" Curien Blake called over the racket, and he and his two remaining companions sprang around the sides of their table and rushed towards the defenders. Egmont, the man in the crimson robes, lay dead nearby, having taken one of Cathaline's bullets in his heart. Darston, one of those who wore a dinner suit – for he had not yet taken his part in the *pthau'es'-maik* – was dropped before he could reach the spot where Cathaline, Carver, Thaniel and Alaizabel sheltered. But Blake had timed his attack to coincide with the moment when the few remaining wych-dogs had launched their final assault, and so Carver and Thaniel had been occupied with keeping them back; there was only Cathaline's gun to oppose them, and as she turned it towards Blake, he shot her in the hand.

She screamed against the pain, recoiling as Blake and his surviving companion, Hodge, vaulted the tables and brought their guns up. Carver spun, but Blake's gun roared and he was thrown backwards over a table where he slumped, still. The click of the hammers on their pistols signalled an end to the conflict; Hodge's gun was pressed to Thaniel's head, and Blake's was pointed at Cathaline where she knelt on the floor, clutching the red mess of her hand. Alaizabel froze where she was.

"Sure hate to shoot a lady, ma'am, but you don't leave a man much choice," he drawled.

"*Bastard,*" Cathaline hissed through gritted teeth, trying to flex her fingers and only managing to make them twitch. There was a hole through her palm, ragged with bleeding flesh so dark that it seemed black in the red light.

"Mercy, and ah thought English women were all manners," he said with a grin. There was a snarl, and Blake whipped out a second pistol with his free hand and shot the last wych-dog as it clambered over the barrier of tables. "Devilish hard to control, they are. Can't have 'em chewin' on mah captives."

"I know you," said Thaniel, and Blake turned to face him, tipping his hat.

"Curien Blake, best wych-hunter in the whole damn States. And I know *you*, sir. Thaniel Fox, if ah ain't mistaken. Son of the best wych-hunter in all of England, so ah'm told."

"Mr Blake, we should deal with them now," Hodge said.

"Now you hush up, Hodge," said the American. "Ah got business to attend to here. Nobody's goin' nowhere; Pyke's precious ceremony is safe. Ah want to have some fun."

Hodge subsided doubtfully, keeping his weapon trained on Thaniel.

"Now, sir," Blake said to Thaniel. "I wonder if you'd do me a great honour."

"I doubt that," said Thaniel. "Since you seem to have aligned yourself against me."

"Well, ah go where the money's greatest, that's true," said Blake, in his infuriating drawl. "But ah can't pass up an opportunity like this. The greatest in the States, against the greatest in the Kingdom. Ah'd always wanted to take on your father, boy. But folks say the son's got the same mettle. You and me, Thaniel Fox. Let's see who walks away."

"You're asking him for a *duel?*" Cathaline exclaimed in disbelief.

"Well, either that or ah shoot you both right now," Blake replied. "And that pretty lil' thing over there." He motioned at where Hodge had gathered Alaizabel to them, holding her by the arm while he kept his gun on Thaniel.

Hodge now: "Mr Blake, I really must protest."

"Ah said *shut up*, limey!" shouted the American. "Where ah come from, a man does what a man has to do, you got that? It's the law of William Kidd; you ain't the best until you've beaten the best. Well *ah'm* the best, and ah'm here to prove it right now! Do we got a deal, Mister Thaniel Fox?"

"Not guns," said Thaniel. "Blades."

"Blades it is," grinned Blake. "Ah knew you'd say that. Ain't nobody stupid enough to go up against a Kentucky man on the draw. Let's clear us some space."

Hodge switched his gun to Cathaline while Blake patted down Thaniel and disarmed him of everything but his chosen knife, a long-bladed dagger with an ornamental crossguard, inscribed with Wards and runes. Blake and Thaniel pulled the tables out of the way of the centre of the room, cleared the bodies of the wych-dogs and the Devil-boy, making a small, blood-stained arena for themselves. Hodge took Cathaline and Alaizabel over to the side of the room, out of the way, and sweated uneasily while he watched the manic Yankee about his work.

"Ah hope you'll forgive this indulgence," Blake said, drawing his blade. "Wanting to fight with you 'n' all. Just have to know; are you your father's son or ain'cha?"

"We shall see," Thaniel said.

Then his blade was drawn, and the two faced each other, settling their weight so that it was evenly spread, ready to fight. They circled for a time, making tiny feints, testing their enemy's reflexes. Blake was fast, no doubt about that; probably faster than Thaniel, but Thaniel knew a trick or two, and he had something of an idea forming behind that impassive visage.

"Ah'm curious," said Blake, who evidently loved the sound of his own voice. "Ah'd heard stories about your father, that he killed his first ever wych-kin with one o' them Warded knives, and he preferred 'em over guns ever since. That true?"

"He killed it with *this* knife," said Thaniel, holding up his blade. "He gave it to me when I was eight. It has never let me down yet."

Blake was impressed. "Well don't that just take the biscuit?"

He sent a quick slash towards Thaniel's cheek, parried away with a sharp ring of steel. Thaniel counter-thrust, jabbing up towards the American's chin, but Blake turned it away and shoved his boot into Thaniel's chest. Thaniel was faster than that, though; he rode the force of the push and slashed across Blake's shin, and regained his balance as Blake retreated.

"Hmm," Blake said, their eyes locked once more. "The good God bless Yankee leather, ah say." The cut had only scratched him, for most of what Thaniel had sliced was Blake's boot.

Cathaline wanted to shout encouragement, but she kept her mouth shut and watched. She was conscious of Hodge standing next to her, his gun at her head; she was conscious also that his aim was drifting as he paid less and less attention to his prisoner and more to the fight. Still, it would have to drift a lot more before she dared try anything. So she watched Thaniel, and willed him to win. Alaizabel, on the other side of Hodge, was absorbed in the fight, her face a picture of terror.

Thaniel attacked now, a high thrust to mid-slash and then one across the eyes. Blake tapped them all away, then returned in kind, a three-strike combination that Thaniel handled easily. They were testing each other, probing for weaknesses. Neither of them were fighting to their full potential yet, and Thaniel wanted to delay that moment as long as possible; for if Blake came at him with everything he had, he doubted he could hold out for long. It would only take a slip to let Blake win; but he could not allow that to happen. He had come to a decision, and he knew what he had to do. But it all relied on perfect timing.

And with that thought, he lunged and swiped. Blake was taken aback by the sudden savagery, and his parry was sloppy; he got scored across the back of his hand for his trouble. He cursed, pulling back, but the cut had not been deep enough to sever any nerves and his hand was still in working order. Thaniel pressed the advantage, the short blades blurring between them, chiming and clashing as they riposted and dodged and lunged.

"You ain't bad, Mister Thaniel Fox," said Blake. "Ain't bad at all. Ah'm enjoying mahself now."

"How nice for you," said Thaniel, and struck again, this time knocking Blake's blade aside and punching him square in the nose. Blake swore and staggered back, his hand flying to his face.

"Broke my damn nose!" he cried. Thaniel was breaking through his defences by sheer recklessness. A knife fighter was supposed to be cagey and defensive, striking only when the opportunity was there. To do otherwise was to lose fingers. But every so often Thaniel threw an attack for which Blake wasn't prepared, one that was simply inviting a knife to the throat, and purely because of its audacity it overwhelmed the American. He was fighting like a man who didn't care for his life.

Not any more, though. Next time, Blake would be ready. He had Thaniel's measure now. One more mistake, and he was in.

Thaniel glanced over at Cathaline, and something in his gaze made her tense; she saw the resolve therein. He was about to do something, but what? Hodge was hardly even pointing the gun at her any more, but she would still be killed if she moved. She was fast, but not *that* fast.

"That was a dirty trick, boy," Blake said, not quite so cheery now. His nose was squashed and his eyes were bruising in a dark domino-mask. Blake raised his knife, and his expression of anger was made evil by the foul red light that smothered the room through the tall windows. He lunged at Thaniel. "Ah'm through playing now."

"So am I," said Thaniel, and with a swift movement, he dodged aside and pushed Blake past him like a bullfighter, spun and flung his knife into Hodge's forehead. Blake's blade scored his side, but the American was too surprised by Thaniel's move to lend it much force and it tore from his grip. Cathaline twisted, pulling the gun from Hodge's hands even as he stood with an expression of dumb amazement on his face and the hilt of Thaniel's knife between his eyes. Blake regained his balance in a second and pulled his pistol from its holster, bringing it to bear on Cathaline.

Too slow. Left-handed, Cathaline levelled and fired, and Blake's shot went high as he was thrown backwards and fell to the ground, dead.

Cathaline stood for a moment, her brain catching up to her reactions. Alaizabel was open-mouthed. Thaniel stood there, his hand held to his side.

Then: realization.

"Thaniel!" Alaizabel cried, rushing over to where the wych-hunter stood. He grinned, and she hugged herself to him. He sucked in his breath in pain, and she drew back, sudden concern on her face.

"You're hurt," she said, moving his coat aside so that she could examine the wound he had been dealt.

"Do not trouble yourself," he said. "Just a scratch."

Cathaline stepped up behind Alaizabel. "Well, Thaniel Fox," she said with a grin, surveying the scene around them. "I suppose you are your father's son after all." She stopped suddenly, her grin fading.

"What is it?" Thaniel asked.

"Over there," she said. "Something moved." And she was there in a moment, dodging between the tables to the source of the disturbance.

"Ah," said Carver, smiling through lips flecked with blood from where he lay among the clutter. "Miss Bennett. I do apologize. It seems I got myself shot."

here were running footsteps, voices approaching them.

They were in a narrow stone corridor, one of the many that ran between the great chambers of the cathedral, and they were lost. Devil-boy Jack had told them that the ceremony had to be in a hall, one large enough to accommodate many people. They would not have thought it hard to find, except that the insides of this awful place seemed to twist around on themselves, a nightmare maze of red and gold and black, and now they had no idea where they were.

Alaizabel shoved open a blank oak door that led off the corridor and hurried them inside, closing it behind them. It was some kind of book repository, a small room piled with old tomes kept in no particular order and with no apparent care. The footsteps came closer, louder, and then passed by and receded.

"The whole place must be after us now," Cathaline said.

Thaniel was reloading his pistol distractedly. "Just let me get within sight of Thatch and I will put a bullet in her brain," he muttered to himself.

"You do not know what she looks like," Alaizabel pointed out.

"*You* do," he retorted.

"I think I will recognize her," she replied, not half so sure as Thaniel seemed to be.

"We must be close," Thaniel said. "The ceremony must be nearby."

"It is a big cathedral," Alaizabel said.

"It is a big ceremony," he answered.

They had left Carver behind, bandaged and treated as best they could. He would live, as far as Cathaline could guess, but he was in no state to move. They hid him as best they could in a room off to the side of the hall where they had fought the wych-dogs, promising to be back for him. He told them to go, and quickly. There were more important things than his life at stake.

They opened the door and continued down the passageway, listening. Their way ahead appeared clear; it was evident that the Fraternity's forces were depleted by the need to attend the ceremony.

The sudden force of Thaniel's wych-sense battering at his mind took him completely by surprise, and drove him to one knee in mid-stride. He could hear Alaizabel saying something, but her voice was thin and tinny and hard to hear. She was leaning over him, fearful concern written on her doll-features. Cathaline was similarly affected nearby.

By God, what was it?

Terrible visions flashed before his eyes, swept him up and consumed him. Darkness, terrible cold darkness, the salty depths of the deepest oceans where no light warmed the rocks and the weight of the black water would crush a man like a grape. And he saw then the result of the Fraternity's meddling, what would happen if the ceremony came to pass. Oceans would rise, and their beds would split, disgorging the foulness long buried there; London would be drowned by the sea, and the things that came with the water from the abysses of the Atlantic and the Arctic Circle; wych-kin would run amok, screaming and howling, across what land remained. In his mind, vast loping things a kilometre high or more lumbered half-seen through billows of fog; things that should not exist rose from the ocean and sent tidal waves to destroy man's cities; babies would be born with gills, their little digits webbed and atrocious.

The land would be swallowed by the sea, and when it retreated, all would be in ruins. And then the new breed would come, the creatures from the deep, the servants of the dark gods known by humans as the Glau Meska. They would erect great temples, and cities built of bone and sinew, and their foulness would spread like a cancer until finally, a hundred years from now, Mother Earth would be theirs.

The vision ceased abruptly, leaving Thaniel panting and sweating and clutching his arms tight to his body. His wych-sense had ceased pounding him, but it still throbbed. He spent a few moments just breathing, regaining control.

"Thaniel, are you all right? What is it?"

"The ceremony proper has begun," he said, suddenly certain of his own words. "Thatch has started the process of guiding the Glau Meska to us. Can you not *feel* them coming?"

"I . . . I feel nothing," said Alaizabel, uncertainly.

"I do," Cathaline said. "And it is coming from *that* way." She pointed up the corridor.

The sensation they felt had a definite epicentre.

The gateway, where Thatch stood and called like a beacon to the Glau Meska. Thaniel could feel the dread gaze of those immense entities, creatures beyond the span of human imagination. And at that moment, he desired above all else to close that gate, to blind those eyes so that his soul did not have to crawl under their stare.

Footsteps again, but Thaniel and Cathaline did not even try to hide. They strode on up the corridor, through the jarringly rich interior of the cathedral, and when the two cowled and robed cultists ran around the door, they were shot dead before they had a chance to raise their weapons.

Thaniel stepped over their bodies without another thought. He had never killed a man before, except once, a long time ago, when the man was possessed by wych-kin. He felt no remorse now. The Fraternity helped bring the wych-kin. They had murdered hundreds, perhaps thousands more on the streets of London. And now they sought to bring an evil into the world that could swallow it whole.

Against all that, their lives paled into nothing, and for the first time Thaniel truly understood how his father must have felt, all those years ago, when the only thing he had truly loved had been savaged and slaughtered in a graveyard. He understood now how Jedriah could close himself up. Because he had felt a pain like Thaniel felt now, and after that, all else was merely a shadow of a care.

Thaniel's route took them up a set of stairs, then deeper into the heart of the cathedral. On the way, three more Fraternity cultists opposed them, and he shot them all with such calm that he might have been shooting at tin cans on a wall. The journey was short, for they had been close to the ceremony hall when the vision struck. Finally, Thaniel halted them at the base of another set of stone stairs, these ones narrow and unobtrusive. He held his finger over his lips, then peered around the corner, looking up. Cathaline watched him pull back swiftly; then a moment later, he darted out with his gun raised and fired thrice. There was a slump, and he stepped back to allow the Fraternity guard to slide and roll limply down to the bottom.

"They cannot oppose us," he said. "There are not enough of them, and they need their members for their ceremony."

"Thaniel," said Cathaline, laying a hand on his arm. "Be careful."

He gazed at her, stone-faced.

"I will not fail," he said, and with that he ascended the stairs, and they came with him. At the top was a door of lacquered black wood, heavy with carvings and symbols.

He pushed his way in, and the sound swelled. A chanting, a deep monotone full of harsh, guttural consonants and throaty vowels. It was the ceremony hall, all right. A high, short balcony, gilded with gold; an ornate banister standing between deep-red curtains that were bunched on either side. It was wide enough to be intended as a viewing gallery, but there were no benches here; instead, it was a platform where people could stand to watch the proceedings below. No light was lit, and the corners where the curtains gathered were black with shadow; but the glow of the hall below spread up and over the black stone tiles, the vile red luminescence from outside staining the candlelight with blood.

The hall was as vast as Jack had promised. Thin windows, fifteen metres high and only half a metre across, raked down the wall like claw-scratches, descending from a massive, diamond-shaped piece of stained glass at the same height as the balcony where Thaniel, Alaizabel and Cathaline now stood. Below them, a huge summoning-circle of gold had been made, set in black obsidian and surrounded by gold alloy braziers that glittered and flamed. A fire-trench ran from the summoning-circle and down the central aisle, lined with Fraternity cultists in their crimson robes and their mirrored masks. On one side of the room, several wooden podiums stood with ancient books resting on the backs of carven demons and gargoyles; one cultist was reading aloud now, above the chant of the others. Another side was devoted to an altar of stone, with blood-gullies carved into it and running in a circle around it. Even in the already red light, it was obvious that those gullies had not long ago run with gore.

And there, in the summoning-circle, was a young girl who was hunched like an old woman, her claw-hands outstretched and raised, her head hanging down and her eyes closed as if in sleep or deepest concentration.

"It is her," Cathaline said.

"So it is," replied a voice from the shadows, and the cool barrel of a gun pressed itself to the nape of Alaizabel's neck.

Gregor peered nervously through the windows of the cockpit and prayed that they would come back. He had been sitting there, terrified, for almost an hour, holding the airship aloft at anchor. The rain had stopped, and the lightning flashed only intermittently now. He could see over the cathedral's outer wall, to where awful things howled and scratched and fought to get in. The wych-kin desired whatever power was building inside, drawn to it as iron filings to a magnet. The wall held them out, yet at any moment he expected something to come for him, something to crawl up the primary line that tethered him to the great bar across the front gate. Something evil.

He never wanted this. He most certainly had not intended to do more than drop Carver and his companions down to the cathedral and then escape.

Where will you go? he thought to himself in Russian. *The airstrip is overrun by now, the soldiers dead or evacuating. You cannot get out of London, just as the Army cannot get in. You will get lost, and find yourself heading back towards the centre. If you're lucky.*

He was trapped. He was unable to free himself without assistance from the ropes that secured the airship, for it would float away as he unknotted the final one. Surrounded by death and with nowhere to go. Where he was was the safest place he could think of in the hell beneath him, yet he was helpless.

Blessed Mother, I want to leave, Gregor thought.

But where were the others? *Probably dead,* he thought. Well, he did not mean to join them.

Enough. He could bear it no longer. He engaged the engines and began to rise. He had got no more than five metres when the airship shuddered, and he was wrenched forward on to the controls. The anchor ropes that were attached to the great bar across the cathedral's gate went taut and held.

He thought of the wych-kin massed outside and

pushed the airship still harder, praying that the ropes would break before the engines overheated.

Inspector Maycraft was losing his nerve. Why, he could not have said. He had attended dozens of Fraternity gatherings; he had seen Thatch called and put into the body of Alaizabel Cray; he had been present as they summoned Rawhead to carry out the Green Tack murders; he had been there when poor Chastity Blaine – she who now stood in the summoning-circle of the ceremony room – was poisoned and Thatch was transferred from Alaizabel into her. He knew the power of the Fraternity and what they could do. He knew that they had been heading towards this moment for nearly thirty years now, when their gods would be brought into the world, born screaming into cataclysm. So why, now that the moment was at hand, did he fear it? Was it possible that he liked the world the way it was? Was it possible that he harboured a little doubt about Pyke's promises that the Fraternity would be spared the destruction to come? Did he really believe that entities so massive that they defied human sight would care about the insects that brought them?

Were they making a huge mistake?

No matter. It was too late to change it now. Yet he feared that he might do something irrational if he stayed in the ceremony hall, so he had taken up his pistol and headed out into the cathedral. The walls of the cathedral were thick, and the black stone muted sounds somehow, but it was still possible to hear distant gunfire as he made his way through the corridors. The wych-hunters were inside, that much he knew. The dogs had been released, and those of the Fraternity who were not part of the ceremony had taken up arms in defence; but the cathedral was huge and its ways were winding, and it was impossible to tell from which direction the shots came.

Damn it all, nobody had prepared for this! Nobody was supposed to even know the cathedral was there, let alone *get* to it. There was no way on Earth anyone could have got to them overground. The airships were a consideration, of course; the Wards had always kept them away before, disguising the cathedral from their sight and subtly suggesting that they drop their payloads elsewhere when they came to the Old Quarter on their bombing runs. But careful use of their contacts in the military meant that the airships would never get the authorization to fly.

All of his fellow cultists had been occupied with what was happening inside the cathedral. None had thought to look out to the sheltered courtyard. At a casual glance, all seemed normal; and there were few windows that let on to the front gate anyway, and those were narrow and fogged with stained glass. But it was only Maycraft who had wondered how the wych-hunters *got* here, and looked out, and seen the great tether attached to the bar on the front gate. And then he had looked up, and seen it, the faint drone of the engine masked by the hum of the cathedral and the racket of the rabid wych-kin outside.

An airship! A blasted airship!

Now he stepped through the dining hall where the heart of the fighting had been, pushing his way through tables and running his eyes distastefully over the warped and twisted corpses of the wych-dogs that lay about. He paused when he came to the body of the Devil-boy, and then laughed aloud when he saw

Blake nearby. So, he finally got the end he deserved. Bloody good job, as well. The man was an animal.

He found his way out to the great doors, the only entrance to the cathedral. Those which were supposed to be locked and Warded with guards so strong that not even Pyke could break them. They stood ajar now.

His pistol held to his shoulder, he crept towards the thin ray of red light that slit the tall black doors in two, and looked outside.

Gregor peered out of the gondola's passenger door and down at the courtyard below. In the glaring red light from the vile swirl of clouds above, he could see that the airship's primary anchor was still in place, wrapped around the bar of the outer gate. He swore in Russian. The ropes were not going to tear, nor the bar. He knew what waited beyond that gate, but he did not care. Anyone inside the cathedral could fend for themselves; he was getting away fast.

"Pah!" he said, slamming the gondola door. "I am done with you all!"

He stalked back to the cockpit and sat down in his chair. The airship did not have enough engine power to break away; that much he knew. The engines were weak, only designed to push along the great balloon that hung above it.

Well, if he wanted the anchor ropes gone, there was one easy way to do it. He would be glad to be finished with the whole lot. Before he could think better of it, he flipped a pair of switches on the dash, and the airship jolted as the pair of bombs hanging beneath it came loose and dropped.

*

Maycraft was just wondering what he was going to do about the airship hanging above him when he saw the dull bulb-shapes detach from its underside. Of the four seconds they took to reach the ground, Maycraft spent two wondering what they were, one in horrified realization and the last with his entire life literally flashing before his eyes. He disappeared in a blast of white heat, annihilated in the heart of the explosion. The front door and gate of the cathedral were blown to matchwood, the courtyard erupting in a volley of rubble. The near section of the cathedral wall buckled and then collapsed under the weight of the stone that it held up, slumping into a heap with a terrible roar.

Above it all, the airship jolted free and began to rise, trailing the tattered remains of its anchor rope. Gregor whooped in exultation as he climbed away from the foul cathedral, turning his airship towards the north and heading away with as much speed as he could muster.

He did not hear the howls of glee as the wych-kin came, pouring in through the broken gate, clambering over the rubble and seeping into the cathedral like a poison. They sought the gateway, blindly groping for the power they felt. In their hundreds they came, loping and jumping and gibbering and sliding, shadows and monstrosities and ghosts. In their hundreds, to the unholy cathedral, to feast on what walked within.

The moment was all scuffle and noise and flash, and then Thaniel hit the floor, a bullet in his gut.

The ringing echo of the shot made those in the ceremony hall jump, but they were well disciplined and knew the consequences of interrupting a Rite as powerful as this one. They had heard the distant gunshots as the wych-hunters had fought their way in, and so they were not wholly unprepared, but some glanced around to see if any of them had fallen. The chant stuttered, but picked up again. The moment of danger passed. Thatch stood immobile; the one reading from the dark texts read on. Even if they were shot one by one, they had to finish the Rite. To break at this late stage would snap their minds like brittle ice on a puddle.

They ignored Alaizabel's shriek as they had ignored the voices coming from the balcony for a few minutes now, as they had ignored the great rumble that had just shook and staggered them, nearly overturning one of the braziers. An explosion nearby. Beneath their masks, they sweated cold. If that brazier had fallen, it would all be over. Even something that small could upset the *pthau'es'maik.*

Doctor Mammon Pyke trained his weapon on Cathaline's forehead.

"My dear Miss Bennett, I did warn him not to try anything."

"You *shot* him!" Alaizabel cried.

"Yes, it appears I did," the Doctor said dryly. "You really must learn that I don't bluff."

The explosion at the gates had made the room rattle enough to make Pyke stumble. Thaniel had leaped for the advantage, but it had been too slim for even him. Pyke had brought up his American seven-shot revolver and fired it in haste, laying him low. The bullet rested in the wall now, a dark centre in a blood-spattered web of cracks.

Alaizabel was on her knees next to the boy, trying hopelessly to protect or help him. Cathaline stood nearby, tensed, her gaze flicking from Thaniel to Pyke, as if gauging the chance of revenge against the wiry man.

Thaniel groaned and began to get to his feet.

"No, Thaniel, you must not," Alaizabel urged, but when it became apparent that he was not staying down, she lent him her arm and helped him. Blood flecked his lips as he faced the Doctor and spoke.

"One lesson I will not soon forget, Doctor," he wheezed, grimacing. The tear in his clothes was barely visible, but the seeping red to the left of his belly was very obvious.

"My, you do have spirit," the Doctor said. "It appears by that explosion that someone is causing mischief in my cathedral. You are only alive now in case, by some mischance, they should make it this far. A hostage is a terribly useful thing."

"Stay still," Alaizabel hissed, pulling off his coat

and tearing back his shirt. If the stubborn fool had to be on his feet, she was damned if she would let him bleed to death. A glance behind him revealed that the bullet had gone right through, which was good. All she could do was staunch the flow until they could get him help.

"You were lucky," Cathaline said to Pyke. "You did not know we were here. We could have walked into the hall and Thatch would be dead now."

Pyke laughed, a sound like leaves crunching underfoot. "Miss Bennett, you have walked through four of my Wards without noticing it. I knew exactly where you where. The area around the hall is littered with little alarms, you see."

"Cathaline, give me your belt," Alaizabel ordered. Cathaline did as she was told. Her trousers were tight enough on her hips to not need the leather strap that held them up. Still, if she had been wearing a dress like women were supposed to. . .

"Pyke," Thaniel said, then gritted his teeth as a bolt of pain slammed up his side from his wound. He took a breath, steadying himself. "Pyke, you have to stop this."

"Stop what? Stop the *ceremony?* Dear boy, you have no idea how long I have worked to make this happen. Whyever should I stop it?"

"You will all die. The Fraternity will be destroyed along with everything else."

"Possibly," Pyke conceded, blinking his heavy-lidded eyes and craning his vulture head forward. "I doubt it, though. And what rewards will be ours if we do survive."

"What?" Thaniel cried. "What will you get? You are already rich, powerful . . . you have already got more influence than Parliament! Why risk it? You are already the kings and queens of the world!"

Pyke smiled. "You flatter me. Very kind, Thaniel, but ask yourself this: who *wants* this world? The wych-kin are the new order. They are taking us over, wiping us out, piece by piece. I would rather have it over with and be on their side than die meekly like the rest of you."

"Fight them, then!"

He laughed then, deep and cruel. "By all that's holy, boy. Haven't any of you figured it out yet? *You can't beat them!*"

"Why?" asked Thaniel defiantly, spitting blood. "Why not?"

"Because we created them!" he cried. "We create them every day! More and more, darker and nastier, wych-kin upon wych-kin until there's no-one left. And then they'll disappear, too." He gazed at Thaniel levelly. "Thaniel Fox, the wych-kin are not born of wyches like Thatch. They are *us!*"

Nobody spoke on the balcony. The only sound was the chanting and a faint noise in the very background, a rustling, rattling noise that none of them noticed.

"You're lying," Cathaline said.

"No, Miss Bennett!" Pyke cried, astounded, his gaunt frame animate as he spoke. "It's so obvious! Didn't you ever wonder why some wych-kin came in the shape of old legends, that had been written before the wych-kin even appeared? We take our own worst nightmares, and we turn them into wych-kin. We take all our sordid guilt, all our hate, all our shame, everything that we dislike about ourselves, and we fashion ghosts to haunt us and monsters to plague us. And we *don't even know we are doing it!*"

He stalked over to the other side of the balcony, in full flow now. "Do you know that a human only ever uses ten per cent of its brain in its lifetime, Thaniel? I do! I've spent a lot of time examining brains and minds, and what makes them tick. Don't you wonder what we do with the *other* nine-tenths? Don't you wonder what might happen if we began to use a little of that extra? By God, nobody had even *heard* of a wych-sense thirty years ago. Asylum admissions have quadrupled since the Vernichtung, and you'd be amazed how many of them hear voices, or claim to be in touch with the other side, and sometimes, just *sometimes*, you can believe them."

"The Vernichtung," Thaniel said, too lost in the knowledge that Pyke was providing to even think about where he was, or the hole in his gut. "That was when it began. What happened? What did the Prussians bomb that let it all out?"

"Us," Pyke replied. He frowned suddenly; it seemed as if he could hear a noise, somewhere distant. It was faintly disturbing, but he could not place why. "They bombed *us*," he said, recovering himself. "That was when we stopped believing. That was when we truly entered the Age of Reason."

Alaizabel had torn the sleeve off her dress and wadded it into a compress, as Thaniel seemed not to notice that he was bleeding badly. She could see that he was not just trying to play for time or to distract Pyke, but rather he was genuinely captivated by what the elder man was saying. Cathaline was still poised, waiting for a split-second of an opportunity, but Pyke was too canny to let his guard down.

"The Age of Reason?" she asked. "What has *that* got to do with anything?"

Alaizabel gave the compress to Thaniel, telling him to hold it in place at his back while she prepared another one for the entry wound. He coughed flecks of blood and did so.

"Ah, Miss Bennett. The Age of Reason is why we're all here, you know. Since the dawn of time, man has believed in something. Cavemen feared the fires from the sky, the Red Indians had their animal spirits, the Greeks and Romans had their gods, Aztecs had their idols, we had our churches. . . Don't you understand? *We always had someone to blame!* When a tidal wave destroyed a village, it was because the gods were angry, not because we had not built it far enough from the coast. When a baby died of fever, it was because the village was sinful, not because it had inadequate water-filtration systems. When we committed a terrible sin, when we were heavy with shame and guilt, we could atone. We could be forgiven. It didn't matter what we believed in, just that we *believed.*

"Once the Vernichtung came, once we had dropped bombs from the sky . . . why, that was the end. The triumph of science. No longer did we need to fear a god smiting us from the heavens. Man has taken on God's role. Now *we* have the power to level cities, to take a thousand lives at a stroke. The good Charles Darwin *explained life*, you see! Science takes great steps every day, and every step is one away from the old ways. Science has removed the need to believe in anything, because we can explain it all now. What's left? Who is there to take away our guilt and pain and anguish? *Who can we blame but ourselves?*"

"The wych-kin," Thaniel whispered, mesmerized.

"When there's no more belief, the wych-kin come." He winced suddenly as Alaizabel wrapped Cathaline's belt around him and pulled it tight over the compresses, securing them in place.

The Doctor nodded. "Mankind is not yet mature enough to take responsibility for its mistakes," Pyke said. "We have to believe in something beyond ourselves. As we took great strides in science, as we explained everything, we were left with nothing. A drudgery of factories and orphans and soot and smog. If that is all there is to existence, is it truly worth bothering to exist? Is it worth dragging yourself through all the pain, just to see that the end does not justify the effort of getting to it? The wych-kin live in cities the world over, Thaniel, because that's where the hopeless gather to make their fortunes and fail.

"Somehow, though we could not admit it to ourselves, we were panicking. In the deep parts where science cannot reach, we were afraid of the emptiness we were making for ourselves, the self-destruction we started. So we made the wych-kin, woke some ancient part of our minds that we did not know we had, and fashioned creatures out of our own nightmares to terrorize us. Because all the hate and guilt and shame has to go *somewhere*, Thaniel, or it would eat us alive. Keep it in, and we'd all be like Stitch-face.

"You see," Pyke concluded, "we in the Fraternity . . . we're not destroying humanity. Humanity is destroying itself. We are giving it something to believe in again. Our gift to the world: new and hungry gods, something beyond science, beyond maths and the five senses. The Glau Meska, my boy. Oh, they'll wake Darwin up, all right."

The noise was too loud to ignore now, a seething, hissing, shrieking sound that sawed at the ears as it rampaged closer. Pyke, who had been caught up in his speech, had not paid any attention to it; but now the expression of satisfaction slid from his face, and uncertainty replaced it.

"What is that?" Alaizabel asked, looking up.

"I think," said Thaniel with a red-edged grin, "your precious wych-kin want to meet you, Doctor Pyke."

The Doctor's eyes widened in horror as Thaniel said what he had not dared think. That sound, that sound.

Wych-kin.

"*You let them in!*" he screamed, and a moment later he was pointing his revolver square at Thaniel's head. "You've killed us all!"

And he pulled the trigger.

The wych-kin burst into the hall beneath them in a horde, shrieking and gibbering, and the screams of the cultists mixed with the insane cries of the creatures. Cathaline smacked the gun from Pyke's hand before she had time to realize that the gun had jammed. Thaniel lunged at him, but Pyke was away, nimble for his age, and he was out of the door before anyone could stop him, disappearing down the stairs.

Thaniel scooped up the gun, spun the chamber with his palm and aimed, and suddenly the words of the Devil-boy came into his head, spoken in the lair of the Hallow Ghoul.

I speak of the force that created the physics of the universe, the force that makes time flow forwards and not allow everything to happen at once, the force that sets the patterns to which the planets turn. Its weapons are coincidence, unlikelihood, happenstance.

Beneath him, all was chaos. The cultists were being torn to pieces, but Thatch remained untouched in the centre, protected within the summoning-circle, her arms still outstretched and her head hung.

He fired.

Thatch jolted, the old wych inside the young girl, and her eyes flew open, piercing up into Thaniel even across the great, crimson-lit hall. Between her breasts, a patch of blood was soaking through the white dress that she wore. Her arms sagged as if under a great weight. The face of Chastity Blaine wore an expression of surprise, but the eyes within it cursed him unto eternity. And then she toppled backward, falling out of the summoning-circle, and was devoured.

The sky was torn with a terrible boom of thunder, a sound so huge that it seemed to flatten all before it, and an unearthly howl brought Thaniel to his knees. A great wind, smelling of salt and the sea, tore through the cathedral, a thwarted fury shrieking in frustration; and the great and terrible eyes of the Glau Meska turned away from the world of humanity, their dread gaze passing and dimming as the gateway that might have let them in was suddenly slammed shut. Alaizabel held on to Thaniel, and the three of them huddled as small as they could against the hurricane that blasted around them, tiny figures on the balcony above the howling hordes.

The wind dropped. A beat of silence.

Then the shock wave ripped out from the cathedral, a vast quake of earth and air, and the enormous red swirl in the clouds spun free like a snapped chain on a bicycle, the hole in its centre blasted wide. The sky was tattered, ripped apart as if by harpies, and in moments what had been a thick blanket of darkness had been shredded into ribbons, drifting aimlessly away.

The ground bucked and heaved across London, buildings groaning as they slumped and collapsed, windows cracking and smashing and falling in thick shards to the ground. People screamed, monuments toppled, stone crashed down. Tower Bridge bowed and slid into the Thames. Fires began from candles and hearths. The Old Quarter took the brunt, its buildings pulverized and already blazing in many places.

There was a terrible screaming again, this time a multitude of voices. Alaizabel squeezed her eyes shut and held on to to Thaniel, who did not even feel the wound in his side in his terror.

And then it was over. There was quiet. The rustle of the curtains on the balcony, the chime of something metal rolling on the floor . . . that was all.

Alaizabel opened her eyes. Sunlight shone through the smashed windows of the cathedral, beaming through the knife-slit arches. No longer was there the foul red glow, but the clean ambience of morning. She stood up slowly, bringing Thaniel with her, his arm held to his side. The remains of the cultists and Thatch lay unrecognizable in the hall below them, but of the wych-kin, there was nothing. The clouds that had blocked out the sun and allowed them to travel by day had betrayed them and left, caught them in daylight. They were gone.

Cathaline stood with them, her eyes on the warm shafts of illumination that splayed across the scene.

"I think it is over," she said, then looked at Thaniel.

There was a troubled look in his eyes. "I think it has just begun," he replied.

etective Carver sat on a bench in Hyde Park and looked up at the night. London was enjoying a rare clear sky, and the brightest stars overcame the glow of the city's gaslights to shine down on him. He was seated alone beneath a lamppost, his breath steaming the January air, and London was still all ashiver with the tingle of Christmas and New Year's Day. The disaster that had befallen them had not curbed their taste for festivity; in fact, this Christmas they celebrated like never before, even amid the rubble of broken and charred buildings. There were no grand decorations, no parades, but each man and woman knew that they had been granted a second chance, that they had inched by death and survived, and they raised what glasses they had and toasted to new beginnings and new lives.

New beginnings indeed, Carver thought. The aftermath of what became known as the Darkening had been harsh and cruel, but like the Great Fire of London before it, it had cleansed things that needed cleansing. The night after Thaniel had slain Thatch, the Old Quarter had burned to the ground, and only the great river Thames held back the blaze from the north side. Carver remembered how the flames had leaped high into the night, a raging wall that seethed and gnashed and rumbled, knowing that it could not reach over the water to what lay beyond. The fires in the north had been quelled fast, and had not caught. Finally, the rains came, and the great blaze died.

The city was picking itself back up again. Thaniel and Alaizabel had gone now; he knew not where. Thaniel had spoken of studying, attempting to compile a tome that would explain the wych-kin, to search for a way of destroying them. He saw it as his duty to use what Pyke had told him, to spread the word and arm wych-hunters against their foes. He swore to hunt no longer, but he had resolved to study wychlore now. Wherever he and Alaizabel were now, they went there together and in the full flush of love. What she would do, he could not imagine. She had something of a fortune and an estate, a legacy from her parents, but Alaizabel was never one Carver could easily understand. She would wend her way as she fancied.

Carver still saw Cathaline from time to time. She was safe and well, and though her hand was a little stiff on cold nights like this one, she continued to hunt. He felt that he owed her, for it was she who spotted him after he had been shot by Blake, and she who had bandaged him and hid him while they finished the job in the cathedral. He had felt the shudder of the bomb, heard the howls of the wych-kin as they invaded, but after that he had fainted and knew no more until Cathaline and the others had returned to take him away from that foul place. A poor show, to miss the finale, but he counted himself lucky to be breathing at all, and was happy.

Carver stood and rolled his shoulders in their sockets, then adjusted his thick greatcoat. He picked up his top hat and began to walk, strolling in a leisurely fashion towards Park Lane.

How complex was the pattern they walked, the web of coincidences that stretched over years and centuries to bring them to one conclusion or another, never ending, allowing only a victory here or a defeat there and each one connected to the next. Everything served a purpose. Even Stitch-face served a purpose, for without Stitch-face, he and Maycraft would never have been brought together; he would never have discovered the hand of the Fraternity, and they would not have been able to stop it. In the same way, Alaizabel. How had she escaped from the Fraternity that first time, when Thaniel had discovered her? Even she did not know.

We are guided by hands vaster than any of us can see, he thought.

But there was one loose end, one point of frustration that jarred. Doctor Mammon Pyke, head of the Fraternity, lived still in his country retreat. None knew of his involvement in the Darkening; none ever would. But he had escaped the cathedral like the rest of them. He hid behind his wall of respectability, and he worked as ever at Redford Acres, treating the patients there. And Carver couldn't touch him.

Tonight, Pyke was going to a party. A society gathering of medical minds. Carver knew this for he kept his eye close on the good Doctor. Still, nothing had borne fruit. Pyke kept himself clean now, as pure as the snow on the Downs. The law had no power over him.

Feeling dejected, Carver walked away along Park Lane. There was little traffic now, only a lone carriage rattling along the cobbles. The driver rode with his collar up high against the chill and his top hat pulled down so that his face was in shadow. With his riding-crop, he tapped the horses on their backs: the black stallion, the white mare. As he passed, he doffed his hat politely to Carver, and Carver did the same.

Carver walked home, and Stitch-face drove on, heading for an appointment with one Doctor Mammon Pyke, with whom he had something of a score to settle.